# AMRIT

# AMRITA

Usha Rajagopalan

Rupa . Co

Published 2004 by
Rupa . Co
7/16, Ansari Road, Daryaganj,
New Delhi 110 002

*Sales Centres:*
Allahabad Bangalore Chandigarh Chennai
Hyderabad Jaipur Kathmandu Kolkata
Mumbai Pune



Typeset in 11 pts. AGaramond by A & D Co.
Printed in India by Saurabh Printers Pvt Ltd.
A-16 Sector 4, Noida 201301

*Dedicated to*
*Dr. A. S. Aiyer, my grandfather*
*and*
*Prof. A. S. Balakrishnan, my uncle,*
*for kindling my interest in literature.*

## *Acknowledgements*

*Amrita* was born out of a fleeting visual on the television. To coax that nebulous idea to assume a form and life has been a long haul, exciting, exasperating but a deeply satisfying, learning experience. The children at the special schools I visited, their parents and trainers taught me more than what this book contains.

I drafted the first version of the novel during the three-month tenure as Andrew Fellow in Fiction at the University of British Columbia, Canada. I am indebted to the Andrew Family, the UBC, the Department of Creative Writing and to Dr. Errol Durbach; to Margaret and Anna Murray for sharing their house with me and to Dr. Shadi and Dr. Shobha Khanna for 'adopting' me as their own.

Writing that first draft was the easiest state in the evolution of *Amrita*. Subsequent rewriting and revising took the bulk of the next three years. My thanks to Hanno Pinder, Linda Svendsen, Avinash Paranjape, R. C. Natarajan, Samir Barua, R. C. Sekhar and Bhavani Sekhar and Rema Unnikrishnan for their encouragement, for believing that I could do even better in the 'next version'.

Even before I wrote the first draft of *Amrita*, a chance perusal of the 2 November 1998 issue of *India Today* gave me the graphic for the jacket of my yet-to-be written, even christened, novel. My thanks to Sri A. Ramachandran for helping me convert my wish to reality.

My editors at Rupa & Co. were perhaps even more enthusiastic about *Amrita* than me! A special thanks to all of them.

To Raja, my husband, for teaching me to use the scissors liberally while editing the manuscript. To my parents and my children Aparna and Gopu who have had to bear the ups and downs in my writing career.

Archana Jaivittal's assistance has been the most precious. She did the illustrations in this novel. My thanks to her and her parents. If everybody were as caring and sensitive as the Jaivittals are towards their daughter, there would be no need for *Amrita*.

***

# PART ONE

## 1

"Gauri?" he asked, opening the door.

I let go of my little suitcase and looked up at Raghu. The April heat together with the heaviness in the pit of my stomach made sweat erupt on my face. I wiped my upper lip with the side of my forefinger and forced a smile.

"Yes, I'm Gauri."

"Your mother had called just now to find out if you'd reached. Come on in. Call her first, then everything else," he stood aside for me to enter the house and gestured to the telephone in a corner of the room.

"First time you were travelling on your own?" he asked when I joined him after a quick one-sided talk to reassure amma.

"Long distance, yes."

"No wonder Nandini sounded worried!"

It wasn't only my travelling that worried amma. She was concerned about what I would do to Raghu, her old college mate. She had not met him after I was born. In fact, he hadn't even known about my existence till I made her call him to ask if I could visit them. The reason she gave? That I wanted to meet my brother Sunder who'd been staying with them for the last two months.

"How is she coping? he asked. "After your father's death?"

"Okay," I shrugged. "After all, Kittu had been ailing for a while."

"You called him by his name?" he paused and continued. "Well, Nandini's a strong woman. She'll pull through. That's how she was when we were in college. Delicate looking but with an inner core of steel. Is she still the same?" he asked.

Before I could reply a small mousy woman peeped through the half-open door.

"Gauri, meet my wife. Kamala, this is Sundar's sister," he said. "She's so attached to him," he told her, "she's come to meet him. Gauri, I can understand your feeling. When did your father die? Two months now?"

"Yes..." I began when a heavy hand on my shoulder rocked me on my feet.

"Hey you! When did you come? I thought I was free from you at last and here you are!"

That was Sundar, my dear brother. If it hadn't been for him,

Kittu would have lived for a few more years perhaps. Amma and I had tried to hide Sundar's misdeeds from Kittu but sometimes we had been helpless. Like the time one of his girlfriends came home with her two hulking brothers accusing Sundar of misbehaving with her. It was just as well that he had warned us the previous day about her and amma had sent him away from home to Raghu's. Raghu, her old college friend.

"What's up? Mom all right?" asked Sundar.

"She's fine. Not missing you one bit. Good ridd..."

"Don't start now," he warned. Like a flower, his fingers slowly curled on either side. He's never hurt me physically. I know too much about him to be afraid of him.

I turned to our hosts. Mrs. Raghavan was looking uncertainly from me to Sundar. Raghu was rubbing his chin and sizing us up.

"I'm sorry. This is how we talk to each other. We'll behave. Right, Sundar?" I asked.

He nodded but he wasn't happy to see me.

"Good. Come, sit down, Gauri. Tell us more about yourself ..." Raghu began.

"Uncle, perhaps she should freshen up. She's travelled two days by train," said Sundar.

"Yes, you're right," said Raghu. "Gauri, you must be tired. Take her upstairs, Sundar, to the girl's room. I hope it's clean... Kamala?"

"That's okay. If necessary, we'll clean it up ourselves," said Sundar picking up my suitcase and walking towards the staircase with quick long steps leaving me no option but to scuttle after him.

Was Mrs. Raghavan dumb? She didn't speak a single word...

We reached a small landing with three doors. The open one on the right led to a terrace. The one to my left was closed while the third, straight ahead, was partly open. I caught a quick glimpse of Sundar's clothes scattered everywhere and hid a smile. The number of times amma has shouted at him about the state of his room!

"Here's where you stay," he said, making no attempt to open the door. His bluster downstairs had evaporated and now he shuffled and tugged his ear lobe. I reached past him, pushed open the door and entered the room, observing him covertly. He followed, looking around as if he was seeing everything for the first time. The two cots, a cupboard built into the wall, a small table and chair, dressing table, clearly a new acquisition despite its thick layer of dust and a closed door that perhaps led to the bathroom.

Well, this wasn't the Taj Hotel and I wasn't planning to live here. Just occupy it for a week while I drive Sundar away and confront my host. Raghu was not only my mother's friend but also my biological father. Only he didn't know it. Yet.

"What do you think?" my brother asked, still looking ready to run away.

"Looks okay to me," I shrugged. I was getting used to surprises. The house was drab, as far as I could see, indifferently maintained but the garden was beautiful and neat. A troubled stillness pervaded the house, quite like Mrs. Raghavan. Her husband was like the garden, neat, smart, youthful in appearance though I knew that he was well into his fifties.

"Good!" Sundar replied. "I'll see you downstairs."

He turned to leave.

"What's the hurry?" I asked. "Tell me something about the Raghavans. I don't know anything about them and you have been staying here for quite a while."

"Not too long," he said. "First for about two months and then dad died. I had to return. Now for two months. I may return with you. After all, Raghu Uncle hasn't been able to get me a good job. I don't want to hang around here any longer."

"We'll see. What kind of people are they?"

"Nothing special. Ordinary. Like everyone. Now you tell me why you've come here. Can't you leave me alone? Ever?" he asked.

"Cool it, man! I wanted a break from work and I missed you so I came. That's all."

Sundar's lips curled. "Expect me to believe that? After fighting with me all the time at home? Ha!"

"Okay, okay. Tell me about the girls," I asked to divert him.

"Amrita. Amrita and Maya. Raghu Uncle's daughters" he

paused and burst out abruptly. "I really hope you'll be comfortable here."

"Why shouldn't I be? What's wrong with this room?" I asked.

"Well … Amrita died a couple of months ago."

"That's all right. I don't believe in ghosts."

"This is what I hate about you," my brother exploded. "You never take anything I say seriously."

"What do you want me to do? Cry for someone I don't know, who died god-knows-when?"

"You don't understand. Amrita died on the same night Maya got married. A horrible death. No one knows how it happened. She was not like you and me. You know, not quite all right up here," he tapped his head. "She was like a child. And for such a thing to happen to…."

"Sundar … Gauri … your coffee's getting cold," Raghu called.

"In a minute…" Sundar shouted back. "Look, don't mention anything about Amrita. Pretend you don't know about her, 'right?" he whispered hurriedly with one eye on the door as if he feared that Raghu or his wife may enter any time. I threw my knapsack on one of the cots and ran down the stairs behind him quite forgetting that I hadn't freshened up and was as travel-stained as I had been when I entered the house.

Sundar and I sat with Raghu at the dining table. His wife shuttled between the kitchen and the table, filling our plates and cups, embarrassing me with the attention.

"Won't you join us?" I asked.

"She's making herself useful. Let her be," Raghu replied.

"Oh, but I don't think we'll need anything more. Even if we do, we can always get it from the kitchen. Come, do sit down," I patted the seat next to me.

She hesitated, then took the chair opposite her husband. I turned to make small talk with her but her eyes were fixed on the table top in front of her. Every time Raghu started to speak she tensed visibly as if wondering what he would say. There was nothing startling in what Raghu said though he did have lots to talk about! He spoke about his job, his colleagues, cities he had visited in India and abroad, different cuisine in different places, architecture, art, literature and music. Everything, in short. Everything except what mattered to me – his friendship with my mother. She could have been a total stranger to him. Of course, he may have been constrained by his wife's presence. Mrs. Raghavan controlled her tongue but with her husband talking about trivialities she withdrew into herself, occasionally letting her eyes flit between my brother and me. Sundar hogged while I picked at the food. Without absorbing his words I looked at Raghu.

He was almost a male version of amma as far as looks were concerned. Almost, because his forehead was grooved deeply and the sides of his mouth drooped a little. Raghu wasn't carrying his age quite as well as amma did. My mother was still the slim statuesque beauty with faint streaks of silver at the temples. Her eyes crinkled at the corners when she laughed, which was often, but Raghu looked as if he was too busy or too important to smile.

Amma's beauty, even now, is not of the voluptuous kind but the understated one that grows on the admirer. She never wears grand saris, make-up or jewellery, standard trappings of those with inferior looks. She's no goddess though, just a mortal desiring human pleasures. Maybe Kittu was, perhaps, inadequate? Come to think of it … he had been too frail, too limp, too effete compared to my friends' fathers. Indeed, as Kittu had been fond of saying, he was more mouse than man.

For all his ailments I'd never thought I'd lose Kittu. But he left and here was another man taking his place. Or … was he? That was what I had to find out. What did they have in common? Only their love for amma and the 'u' in their names. If Krishnan had been called Kittu, Raghavan was Raghu. Kittu's was the riches to rags story, while Raghu worked his way up from nothing to everything. What did amma say about him? Yes, that Raghu had been ambitious and intelligent. She had always known that he would do very well in life, not like Kittu. But Kittu was the one who won her hand. Won or grabbed?

"I saw your mother at a wedding," Kittu told me once. "Lovelier than the bride. So gentle, so ethereal, elegant, exquisite, breathtaking. I couldn't take my eyes off her. I'm sure no one else could either. I found out who this fairy was, where she lived, who were her parents, everything. I then told my brothers that I wanted to marry this girl, Nandini. Only Nandini. No other. Even Romeo didn't fall for Juliet like I did for your mother."

And what did amma say? Of course, years later, after Kittu died and his body was consigned to flames.

"Raghu and I were in the same college. We would have got married if Kittu hadn't seen me somewhere and got his people to visit us. I didn't even remember noticing him! They came home one day in their fancy car, wearing heavy silk saris, carrying silver plates and asked for my hand for their youngest son. While the neighbours gaped, my parents decided my future. They didn't bother to ask me what I wanted nor did they get any information about the groom, nothing. I didn't even get an opportunity to tell Raghu what was happening. One day I was a college student, next day a married woman."

That didn't stop her from thinking about him though. Kittu's personality made matters worse. He got the prized catch but didn't know how to keep her happy. He was inept in all matters concerning finance. His brothers fleeced him of his share of the family property and left him bits and pieces that they didn't want, like the sprawling ancestral house we live in. Any repair work on it was like trying to clothe an elephant.

"What's funny?" asked Raghu suddenly, shooting my elephant to bits.

Disconcerted, I looked around. Mrs. Raghavan was still doing a Sphinx, while Sundar was running a finger over his plate and licking it.

"Nothing. Why?" I asked.

"You were smiling and I wasn't being jocular," said Raghu.

"Oh, that! I was imagining how my brother would react when I tell him why I'm here."

Sundar stopped licking, thank God, and looked at me.

"Eh?" he asked.

"Actually I've come to give some good news to you in person, Sundar."

"Well?"

"You are going to Saudi Arabia, dear brother."

"What do you mean?"

"Exactly what I said. My friend is hiring people for a restaurant and has agreed to take you on. Just as well that he can't see you now looking so dazed and dumb!"

"That's wonderful news!" said Raghu with a wide smile.

His wife did not comment, but her eyes had stopped flitting and were now focused on me.

"I suppose you are interested?" I asked.

"Of course! Of course! Tell me about it," said Sundar.

"My friend Jagan telephoned me last week to say that he was in town to recruit people for his brother's restaurant in Saudi. I told him about you and he said he could take you as well. You'll have to meet him as soon as possible before he fills up all the vacancies."

"Then why the hell did you wait all this time?" he complained, getting up and pushing his chair back so hard that it fell with a thud. "You only had to telephone and I'd have rushed back! You know I've been waiting for just such an opportunity."

"This is gratitude for you," I said, satisfied with his reaction. "I get you a job, beg and plead with my boss to grant me leave. I take the trouble to travel two days by train to give you the good news in person and what do I get in return? Criticism."

"You should have telephoned," he insisted. "There's no time to waste. Let's leave today. I'll find out if we can get tickets. Otherwise we'll go in the general compartment. Or else we could take a bus."

"Calm down, Sundar," said Raghu, laughing. "She's just arrived. Don't rush her."

"Then let her stay here. I'll go alone. I can't afford to miss this chance. Who knows, I may not get another."

Bingo! Sending Sundar away was a piece of cake. The next task of tackling Raghu was not going to be so easy. I'd have to stifle my conscience first and break the promise I'd made to amma. She hadn't told Raghu about me and didn't want me to tell him either. I was equally determined that he must face the consequence of his action.

"What purpose will it serve?" amma had asked. "You'll only disturb his peace, his family's happiness. I don't know anything about them except that he doesn't get along with his wife."

"Then let me find out what sort of people they are. If I think that they can take the truth from me, I'll tell them. Otherwise I'll keep quiet," I'd promised her and come to Ahmedabad.

I helped my brother pack his things while Mrs. Raghavan kept peeping into the room as if, like Sundar, she couldn't believe what was happening. A couple of hours later Raghu and I returned from the bus stand after seeing him off. Sundar got the last seat at the back of the bus. He was going to feel battered after his long ride but he couldn't be choosy.

"I know it sounds very impolite but how long will you be here, Gauri?" asked Raghu. "Only till next Friday? That's too bad. I'm leaving early tomorrow morning for Delhi. I'll be back only on Thursday night. That doesn't give me much time to talk to you."

Damn! Just when I thought I had him all to myself!

"Auntie will give you company..." he said, not sounding very convincing.

She was so quiet, what will we talk about? I was tempted to pack up and follow Sundar.

Raghu continued before I could say anything. "Since I'll return before you leave, maybe I can accompany you till Mumbai. I have some work there as well. What do you say?"

Well, if I couldn't get the whole loaf, at least I'd get the crumbs, even though it will take a week for him to return and throw them to me.

***

By the time I woke up the next morning Raghu had left. While having my breakfast I wondered what to do. I'd never been one for sightseeing but I couldn't possibly stay indoors with a morose woman for company. The *idli* melted in my mouth. I didn't feel like complimenting the cook. However, Mrs. Raghavan sat down in the chair opposite mine.

"Gauri, I wanted to thank you."

I gaped at her.

"I'd been wondering how to get Sundar to leave and you did it," she said, smiling at me but looking sadder than ever.

"Let me explain. My second daughter Maya got married in January this year. Soon after the ceremony, when we'd just returned from the *choultry*, she came up to me and started saying something about your brother. The house was full of guests, the boy's people, getting ready to leave that night. I didn't have the time to listen to her nor, I must admit, the patience. And now when I want to question her about it she doesn't want to talk. I can only guess that something had happened between them either that day or earlier, when Sundar was staying with us before your father died. It's no longer important. After all, she's married a good man. But, if Sundar's presence will keep her away then I don't want him here. I couldn't tell this to my husband without knowing the details. You've solved the problem so quickly I don't know how to thank you."

The words cascading like a torrent from the reticent looking woman made me speechless. She wasn't done yet.

"I'd been breaking my head imagining what Maya could possibly have wanted to tell me that day. The irony of this is that she didn't have a kind word for me all these years. She behaved as if I was her enemy. Can a mother ever hurt her child? In trying to avoid me, she cut herself off from the whole world. She kept within the house not seeing or talking to anyone. She and her sister, each a shadow of the other. They wouldn't let another person come between them, not even me, their mother. Are you close to your mother? You tell her everything? Does she confide in you?" she asked, finally giving me a chance to say something.

"Yes, especially after my father's death," I said carefully. When amma told me that the man whose death I mourned was not my father at all. Kittu had been amma's husband all right but the man responsible for my birth was her flame from college, Raghu.

"Lucky woman," said Raghu's wife. "That she can talk to you so openly. Maya has taken after her father, keeping things close to her heart. It's not good. Everybody needs someone to talk to, somebody with whom they can share their grief as well as their happiness."

Amma hadn't wanted to confide in me at all. It was a momentary indiscretion, a wretched slip of the tongue that killed my complacency, my identity.

***

On the 13th day, when the number of visitors dwindled, I took refuge in Kittu's room pretending to go through his effects. Most of the time though, I was trying to convince myself that he hadn't left me after all.

The door opened suddenly. I swivelled round, bristling at the intrusion. It was amma.

"You are here," she stated and went to the cupboard behind me.

I sat stiffly, looking at the tears that fell on my hands. Amma was opening and closing the cupboards one after another. I had to compose myself quickly. Sure enough, she came up to the desk and stood behind me. Her restless fingers beat a tattoo on the back of the chair and rustled my hair.

"Gauri, I think it's time you went back to your office," she said at last. "It's not good to take such long leave."

"I'll go in another day or two. They'll understand," I sounded husky enough for her to come around, bend down and look at me.

"*Tchah*! Just look at you … puffy face, red eyes, black circles…. Go and wash your face."

I continued to sit on Kittu's chair. She overlooked my obstinacy and kept talking.

"Did Sundar say anything about his stay at Raghu's? He only told me that Raghu is trying to get a groom for his daughter."

She flipped through Kittu's papers, broke the point of a pencil, opened the little drawers and dropped the few clips and pins he had stored so carefully in them.

"Did you have anything special to tell me?" I asked, controlling my anger. I didn't want anyone to tamper with his things, not even amma.

"When should we send Sundar back to Raghu?" she asked.

"Why should he go back?" I looked up at her. "He didn't get a job there either."

"We can't blame Raghu for this. He did fix him up somewhere but Sundar was too quick to resign."

"Then what's the point in sending him there again?"

"If I know Raghu, he won't give up till he has Sundar well entrenched…"

I had to smile. Sundar stick to some place?

"I also think it'll be good to maintain contact with Raghu. He's an influential man and may help us out with Kittu's papers…."

"Please! Kittu didn't have so many assets that we should seek anybody's help. His will is very clear. Everything's in your name to be divided equally between Sundar and me after your lifetime. Why make an outsider privy to our family affairs?"

"Well, he's been very helpful to us. He's looked after Sundar well for these past two months..."

"For heaven's sake, amma, Sundar is not a baby to be 'looked after'. He's 26!"

"Even then. Who would have taken on such a responsibility?"

"Maybe he had a vested interest. You just said that Mr. Raghavan's trying to get his daughter married. Maybe he wanted to make Sundar his son-in-law..."

"Don't be silly. Even if Raghu wanted this alliance I can't let it happen."

"Why not? Perhaps marriage will make Sundar more responsible. Mr. Raghavan has two daughters. Sundar can decide which one he likes more. After all, he's stayed with them."

"Enough of this nonsense. I'm sorry I raised the topic at all." She turned to leave.

"Wait," I went behind her. "It might just work. A strong woman might make him mend his ways. At least get him enga..."

The flash in amma's eyes stopped me midway. I'd never seen her so angry before!

"Don't even think about it. I don't want to hear another word about this."

"But you want Sundar to go back..."

"Did I say to marry Raghu's daughter? How can he when he's like a brother to them? Raghu and I . . ."

I was fascinated by the speed with which the angry pink patches on her cheeks drained and her words didn't make much sense. Not at first.

"What?" I asked automatically.

She slumped into the chair I had just vacated. There was no sound in the room except the whirr of the ceiling fan that suddenly seemed loud. That was when she told me, hesitantly at first and then with greater confidence about how Raghu entered her life in college and how Kittu came and snatched her from him.

"The worst days of my life were soon after I married Kittu. I knew he was madly in love with me but what did he have to make me attracted to him? Nothing. My parents thought he was rich but his family had left him next to nothing. Instead of trying to get some job he spent all his time in the library with his poetry and drama. I felt crushed with our plight, my helplessness, the turn my life had taken because of my parents' insistence I marry Kittu, everything. And then Raghu came home. I didn't want him to find out the truth so I pretended that I was very happy with my husband. He broke down and talked about what a rough deal he was having. He was doing very well financially but his personal life was in shambles since he had nothing in common with his wife. He didn't want to leave her either so he was caught in a stifling relationship. That meeting was cathartic for both of us. It was certainly a new beginning for me. Till then I'd been making myself even more miserable by imagining what a difference it'd have made to my life if only I'd married Raghu. After this visit somehow I was able to forget ... no, not quite forget, but think less about him and reconcile myself to living with Kittu. Yes," she nodded thoughtfully, "I was at peace with myself."

What about my peace of mind? I took out my anger on that poor scapegoat, Sundar, that good for nothing wastrel who gets into trouble and doesn't know how to get out of it. I'm younger to him by six years and I'm the one who hauls him out of the hot water. He resents this of course and we argue. God, do we argue. Our quarrels made amma send Sundar back to Ahmedabad. The first time was when his girlfriend threatened to lynch him. Now she used Raghu's daughter's wedding as her trump card.

"It's too soon after your father's death," she told him. "It won't be proper for me to attend. Gauri won't get leave from office. At least you should go and represent us. After all, you know Maya. We haven't even seen her. Go, Sundar. Go and stay there for a while. Raghu's promised to get you a better job than the last one."

I knew why she was so insistent. I might get angry with Sundar but I would never blurt the truth about Raghu to him.

Getting Sundar the job was my way of saying sorry to him. With his departure I had a clear field to tackle Raghu but, well, he had left too. What am I going to do till Raghu returned? Mrs. Raghavan was still sitting in front of me. It looked as if her outburst had exhausted her and she was as lost in her thoughts as I had been. I looked at her with greater interest.

Mrs. Raghavan was short and dark with midlife spread around her waist. Her crumpled cotton sari aggravated the general sense of disarray, as did the little wisps of greying hair that had broken loose from her tight knot. With her shoulders drooping, she gave the impression of wanting to curl up somewhere out of sight. That was what I'd thought of her the previous evening too. At first she'd seemed tensed but when the talk became general she shrank into herself. Raghu knew it perhaps and talked so much to cover up for her. What was bugging her? Amrita's death? Or was she suspicious about her husband and my mother?

***

# 2

Mrs. Raghavan sat twisting a corner of her sari tightly and winding it around her forefinger. She tightened it slowly making me wince with every turn. It would cut off the blood supply. Didn't it hurt?

"Auntie," I leaned forward and patted her knee. "I can see you're disturbed. What's the problem? Can I help?"

She stopped torturing herself and looked at me. "Did Sundar tell you about Amrita?"

Oh, Oh.

"Did he? Anything?" she asked.

"Well… nothing much except that she died recently and that she wasn't quite …hmmm… normal."

She sighed. "That's all he could say about her. He was an

outsider after all but I still remember her as a baby. Such a sweet little thing she was. A miniature version of her father. There was no trace of me in her. How much worse would it have been if she'd looked like me?"

She shook her head to answer her own question.

"I'd no problem in looking after my daughter but, on Raghu's insistence, I hired a middle-aged Gujarati woman, Revabehn, to help me with the household chores. Just as well, since he was on tour most of the time and the garrulous woman kept me from feeling lonely."

"One day I asked Raghu to accompany me to the hospital for Amrita's vaccination shots," said Kamala auntie.

"Why? You've never asked me to go with you before," Raghu had replied.

"Last time one of the nurses at the hospital commented to others about a dark woman having such a fair baby. I want her to see you and understand why Amrita is so fair and pretty."

"Don't be stupid. You're managing her very well on your own. Take Revabehn if you don't want to go alone."

"I want you to come along," Kamala insisted.

The waiting room was crowded as usual. That day she could share her thoughts with Raghu.

"See that child?" she whispered to him. "He must be as old as Ammu but he's so puny. Don't turn around but behind you a woman in a pink sari is having such a tough time controlling her brat."

"Ammu's such a darling," she said, holding the baby against her left shoulder. "Even though she's in a strange place and there are so many people around she is not scared, like that little boy. God, how he's screaming. You can see the vein throbbing in his neck. No wonder the mother's so thin…"

Her commentary went on till it was their turn to enter the doctor's room.

"We've come for the vaccination, doctor," Kamala sat on a stool with the baby on her lap.

Amrita lay quietly, letting the doctor press the stethoscope against her chest and on her back, pry open her curling fingers, inspect the back of her neck and pinch the flesh on her arm.

"Let's finish the vaccination first," said Dr. Bhatt, pressing Amrita's cheeks firmly till the mouth formed a little 'o' and squeezed in the polio drops. Kamala held the baby up while the doctor plunged the needle into a firm cheek-like rump. Amrita stiffened but did not protest. The sudden tension in the baby's body made Kamala wince and turn her head away.

"Hold this cotton in place for a little while. She might cry later, in the evening perhaps. No need to worry if she has a slight temperature. It is quite normal."

The doctor began to write in the medical record. Kamala made a move to get up but Dr. Bhatt gestured to her to sit down.

"One moment please. Dr. Avinash…" she called out to the junior doctor who had just entered the room.

"What do you think?" she asked, gesturing towards Kamala and the baby.

The young man was equally deft in examining Amrita, who was such a co-operative patient.

"No doubt at all," he said, reading the senior doctor's comments.

Raghu and Kamala looked at one another. Doubt about what? What was wrong with their child?

Kamala was still rubbing the baby's bottom but her hand moved mechanically. She could sense her husband's tension as he stood behind her. She strained to listen to the doctors' muted discussion which was lost in the sounds coming through the open door leading to the waiting room.

"Well," Dr. Bhatt said, turning to Kamala and Raghu. "Your baby has a problem … no, nothing physical. She's a fine healthy baby but her mental development is not quite…."

"What do you mean?" Kamala felt her lips grow stiff as she stared at the doctor.

"We will know the extent of retardation later, after conducting the necessary tests but, she will not be like the other children. In fact, you might have realised the difference yourselves between…"

"What difference? She *is* like other children. She's a happy child, never troubles me…" Kamala interrupted the doctor.

"What about her milestones?"

"She's just an infant, only five months old," Raghu protested.

"You're most welcome to get a second opinion though I'm quite sure about it. She's typical, a classic textbook case. Your baby is not normal. I'm terribly sorry. Don't blame each other for her condition. It is a genetic disorder and no one is responsible for it."

Raghu and Kamala looked at each other in disbelief. Dr. Avinash walked away quietly while the lady doctor reached for a paperweight and spun it on the table, causing the white flecks inside to scatter and swirl like a snowstorm. No one spoke. Even the noise from the adjacent room seemed to have ceased. Kamala was gripped by a sense of unreality. She knew the doctor was talking since her lips were opening and closing like a fish, but the words made no sense to her at all. She forced herself to listen.

"… to another paediatrician, anyone you want. It is very hard to accept such a diagnosis."

"I know my baby is all right. She is just like other children. You are wrong. You've made a mistake. My Ammu is all right," Kamala's voice fell to a whisper as she clenched the squirming baby tightly to her chest.

A woman peeped into the room and the nurse quickly shut the door.

"We will do that. I'm sure we'll find there is nothing wrong with her," Raghu said, more calmly than his wife.

Kamala and Raghu were quiet for most of the drive back home. He sat tensed over the steering wheel trying to avoid the potholes, the pedestrians, the cyclists and the buses picking up passengers wherever they were flagged down.

She did not see any of them. She was scrutinising the baby's face as she lay fast asleep on her lap. Amrita made little suckling movements and turned her face towards Kamala. What did the doctor see in her that was not normal? She gently opened the tiny fingers as they clutched her sari and ran her thumb over the palm.

Kamala hadn't really paid such close attention to any child. In fact, she had not even inspected Amrita so minutely, leave alone notice any defect in her. That was what her mother had done as soon as she entered the room where Kamala was lying with her newborn baby. She had examined the little toes and fingers, lightly scratched the pink soles, peered into the eyes, passed a hand over the head and replaced the baby on the bed.

"What is it, amma? What were you looking for?" asked Kamala.

"Nothing. I was ensuring that the little one is all right," her mother replied.

"Oh, you are such a pessimist," Kamala said, lifting up the baby and hugging her possessively.

"I just wanted to be sure, that's all."

"What would we have done if there was something wrong? Exchange her for another? Not many were born today, the nurse told me, so we don't have much choice. In any case, I won't part with my little princess for the most handsome baby in the world!"

Kamala had rubbed her nose lightly on top of Amrita's head. She couldn't believe that this perfect little piece of humanity was her creation, hers and Raghu's. Her parents had laughed. How would they feel when they learnt that Ammu was not so perfect after all?

*What an ill omen! If only I hadn't said such a thing.... How could I have been so foolish? But what is wrong with her?*

Kamala recalled the doctor's physical examination and looked at the baby closely.

*The palm ... so soft, so tender. What did the doctor want? Calloussed fingers? The face. How could anyone just look at a baby and say there's something wrong? Ammu's eyes only seem chinky because of the harsh sun.*

Kamala held the baby in the crook of her hand away from the shaft of sunlight falling on her lap. She ran her forefinger down the short length of the nose.

*It is slightly flat, I agree. So is the back of your head. Those shouldn't matter. A little rubbing down your nose will make it longer. I remember amma saying that the baby's head is so soft that it gets rounded even while lying on the bed and turning from side to side. Really! How could the doctor say such a thing without conducting some test first?*

She turned to Raghu, who was still intent on the road.

"I'm sure the doctor is wrong. My baby is just like any of those other children we saw at the clinic. Better than them in fact. They were howling so much! You heard what the woman sitting next to me said? The one whose husband was walking in the verandah with their son? She was amazed that Ammu should be so quiet. 'You are lucky,' she said, 'Your baby is not giving you any trouble at all! Not like my *baba*. He's scared to see so many people together. I took him for a wedding last month and the same thing happened. He wouldn't let me sit for a minute.' And that girl in green *salwar kameez* … she even took Ammu from me for a while, remember? 'China doll,' she called her. No, the doctor is wrong, I am sure. We shouldn't have gone to her. Let's consult someone else."

Raghu glanced quickly at Kamala. "She's supposed to be very good. My colleagues had recommended her very highly. Anyway, we'll talk about this when we are home."

He had had a couple of minor accidents in the past while driving and Kamala didn't want to distract him into another. She kept quiet but couldn't control her thoughts.

*Who is the best doctor in town? Or should I take her home? Appa will know someone good. If it had been so obvious to this Bhatt woman, why didn't anyone else notice it? The woman is a quack, a fraud.*

Kamala shook her head vehemently and turned to her husband again.

"Do you know of any other doctor?" she asked. "Your friends might know of someone else?"

"Hmm…"

"Shall I ask my father to come? He will know what to do.

Amma's health is not good or else I would have asked her too."

"Don't get into a panic. Relax."

"Relax? How can you ask me to relax? Aren't you shocked by what the doctor said?"

"I am, I am."

Kamala clutched the window frame as he wrenched the steering wheel sharply to avoid a cyclist who veered nonchalantly and rode away.

"I told you not to raise the topic now," he glared at her.

Kamala clenched her hands. She wanted to fly home in a flash. She wanted Raghu to talk, to assure her that there was nothing wrong with their baby. She wanted Ammu to grow up immediately so that the doctor could see how normal she was. She wanted to locate all the babies born on the same day as Ammu, line them up and compare them feature by feature with her daughter. She wanted to shield Ammu from all the doctors in the world. She wanted Ammu to be the first in her school, college, get the best paying job. She wanted Raghu to stop the car right there in the middle of the road, take her in his arms and tell her that the doctor was wrong, that Ammu was as normal as any other child.

She did not feel the car grind up the steep road. She did not see the snarl of traffic outside the window. She did not hear the medley of impatient horns, the abuses, the vendors' shouts, nothing. She did not feel the weight on her left arm and shoulder as Amrita slept. She was conscious only of the thunder in her mind as thoughts clashed with one another.

Revabehn was waiting for them.

"I'll take the baby. How soundly she's sleeping, the poor thing..." said the maid.

"Poor thing? What do you mean 'poor thing'?" Kamala asked her sharply, getting out of the car.

"Oh nothing. She...."

Raghu laid a restraining hand on Kamala's arm. "It is all right Revabehn. Take the baby inside. Kamala is very tired."

"Revabehn, please make us some *chai*. I am feeling tired. We had to wait for such a long time at the clinic," Kamala said, forcing a smile.

"You should've gone to the doctor round the corner. He gives injections for every illness."

"Oh, there was nothing wrong with Ammu. We only had to get her vaccinated," said Raghu.

"Did it pain you a lot, my little *bulbul*? Where did that wicked doctor give the injection? In your arm or leg? What a cruel doctor! Don't be afraid. I'll do '*choo mantar*' and make the pain disappear...." Revabehn carried the sleeping baby inside the house while Kamala and Raghu followed her.

"Now tell me...." Kamala began.

"Sh... I don't want Revabehn to hear our conversation. Wait till she's gone."

Kamala was horrified. "But she'll leave only in the evening!"

"Then send her away earlier."

"Maybe I can ask her to come back after some time, when you have gone to work."

Raghu tied a *dhoti* round his waist and removed his trousers deftly. "I'm taking the day off."

"Are you okay?" Kamala touched his forehead.

He brushed her hand aside. "Nothing's wrong. Just tired, that's all."

"It is the tension. I feel exhausted too – as if I have run a hundred miles! Revabehn… is the *chai* ready? *Sa'ab* is waiting," she called.

Even as she shouted, the maid entered with a cup in each hand.

"What happened to the tray? I've told you…"

"That's all right," Raghu took a cup from the maid. "Revabehn, I have taken leave today. If you have any urgent work at home you can go."

"You mean I can take *chutti* today?"

"Well, yes. I hope you have finished all the chores?" asked Kamala.

"That I have, long ago. I did want to visit my brother. Maybe I can…"

"Good, do that. You deserve a break too."

Revabehn looked at Kamala and Raghu, smiled knowingly at them and left the room.

"Did you see that?" Kamala was shocked. "The audacity of that woman!"

"Well, you wanted to talk and I didn't want her to listen. The purpose is served. How does it matter what she thinks?"

Revabehn had added too much sugar in the tea as usual and Kamala found it cloying. The idea of having something sweet so soon after hearing such news about her daughter's condition appalled her. She kept the cup down and turned to her husband.

"What is the meaning of genetic disorder?"

"Well … that there is something wrong in the genes."

"Genes?"

"You know, genes… that's what we all have… some characteristic that runs in the family…"

"There is nothing wrong with my family. We're all normal."

"Are you hinting there's something wrong with mine?"

"No, no, I didn't mean anything like that. Maybe there is some cousin or aunt on my side who … anyway, the doctor didn't specify what's wrong with Ammu."

"That's what she meant by genetic disorder. Ammu … our little baby won't be …like other children," Raghu sank his face into his hands.

"You mean… she will be…? She is…? You are wrong, the doctor is wrong. The other doctor is just a boy, what will he know? You are all jealous of me, that I have such a lovely baby.

She's not like anyone else in the whole world. She's special, very precious to me. You know that and you're trying to hurt me…" Kamala had got up from her chair and was screaming at Raghu.

He looked up wearily at her, "Don't shout. The neighbours may hear you. The walls are so thin. Sit down. Maybe the doctor was wrong after all. We'll go to someone else for a second opinion…"

Kamala did not hear him.

"But what if she is right?" she continued talking loudly to herself. "What if there is something wrong with Ammu? Why? What harm did we do to deserve such a fate? What did the little one do? Who will marry her? What will become of her? Oh God, why are you doing this to us? Didn't you get anyone else? What sin have I committed that you are punishing me like this? Are you jealous of our happiness?"

She crumpled to the ground.

"Don't cry. This is not because of anything you or I did. It just happens…" said Raghu, lifting her up.

"But why us?"

"Isn't that what everyone will say?"

"I don't care about others. My daughter. Why my daughter?" She beat her hands on his chest and cried. Raghu patted her back. There was a faint noise from the bedroom.

"Kamala, control yourself. She's awake. Ammu must be hungry, go and see."

She wiped her face with the end of her sari *pallu* and went to fetch her daughter.

"Don't you think we should go to the doctor once again and find out what to do next?" asked Raghu.

"No! I don't want to have anything to do with that woman! She doesn't know what she's talking about. We'll go to another doctor," Kamala insisted, as she nursed the baby.

Just taking a decision, even if it was only to postpone the inevitable seemed to lighten their mood though not for long. That night was one of the worst Kamala auntie had ever experienced.

***

# 3

Kamala auntie would not concede that Amrita was different from other children.

"If I had known that I would fail so miserably to train my daughter, I wouldn't even have started it. Raghu did tell me not to waste my time on her," she told me as we sat at the dining table. Now that she had begun telling me about her eldest daughter perhaps she'd tell me about Maya too and, of course, Raghu. That was part of my agenda, finding out as much as I can about Raghu and his family.

"What do you know about training such children?" he had asked Kamala auntie. "You are not qualified for it. Why do you want to experiment? If you insist on going ahead with this crazy idea, do it alone, don't ask me for any help. I'm not going to waste time on something that may not even succeed. Let's get a trained *ayah* to look after her and get on with our own lives."

Kamala auntie had got books instead. With all the earnestness of a student, she had compared her daughter with the case studies, took down notes and drawn a plan of action to rehabilitate her child.

"We will forget about appa," she told her baby daughter. "We don't really need his help, do we? No. We'll work quietly and surprise him one day. He'll say, 'My precious darling! How did you learn so much? And the doctors thought you were retarded...'"

"I don't like this word 'retarded'. You are only different from others. That doesn't mean you are hopeless, to be written off. Your brain is like soft dough that's all. I'll mould you into a good shape," she said, chucking under the baby's chin and getting a toothless smile in response.

"I'm also going to talk a lot to you. This is what the books suggest, 'Talk, describe, explain even if the baby doesn't understand.' So I'll tell you what I'm doing with you and why, okay? We'll first concentrate on building up your muscles. You are a floppy baby because your muscles lack strength. This is why you can't hold your head up for long."

She laid Ammu on a rug in the balcony. Sunlight filigreed through the leaves of the neem tree outside the house and fell on the baby in shifting patterns.

"Massaging is good for the body. If it hadn't been for Lakshmikutty I wouldn't have recovered so quickly after giving birth to you. How many women complain of backache and stiffness but look at me, like a supple bamboo shoot thanks to Lakshmi's magic hands and herbs."

Even thinking of that blissful hour while Lakshmi kneaded strength into her body still recovering from her recent parturition made Kamala yawn widely. She would lie on a reed mat while Lakshmi rubbed medicinal oil on her as if pushing it in through the pores of the skin. The bath that followed was no less relaxing, in water that had been boiled with special roots and leaves and cooled to tepidity. Kamala shook her head to rouse herself from the languor that overtook her suddenly and looked at the baby with watery eyes.

"Oh, I could go off to sleep just thinking of her massage!" she remarked. "You should have seen Lakshmi! Short, dark and fat yet so brisk and energetic. Always dressed in a spotless off-white *dhoti*, blouse and a length of white cloth tucked in at the waist and thrown over her ample bosom," Kamala told her daughter. "Whatever the weather our Lakshmikutty wouldn't venture out without her umbrella. Her hair showed no sign of greying even though she was in her mid-fifties. How I used to envy her long hair! She knew that and took care not to let it down in case I cast an evil eye on it. She knotted it at the nape and kept her head slightly forward to maintain her balance. It made her look meek but there was nothing submissive about her, let me tell you. The way she used to boss over me … shooting words like pellets from a gun! But she was a real professional and very, very good at her work."

On the first day Lakshmi had told Kamala's mother, "Give me an old sari. I don't want oil stains on my new *dhoti*. I have to share it with my husband. The *zari* is real, not like the yellow thread you get these days."

Then she had turned to Kamala.

"So, you have had a baby. Good. Girl or boy? Girl? Not so good. You'll need a dowry to get rid of her. I have two sons. They brought money home with their wives. Don't feel bad. You are young. You may still be blessed with a son. Don't give a long gap between the two. Tell your husband that. It is good to bring up the kids together. Good for them and for the parents. You won't have to worry about them in your old age. Also tell your husband only two, no more, boy or girl. A woman's body needs rest. She is not a machine. If you take proper care of yourself, your man will not stray from you. Otherwise some other woman will snap him up and you'll be nowhere. Don't smile, girl. Lakshmikutty is not made of hollow words and he knows that, my husband. I have him here…" she had thrust her right fist at Kamala and clicked two fingers crisply.

"If I do this he will come running. He knows he cannot play games with his Lakshmi. He also knows that the moment I catch him with another woman, he's finished. So is she, the harlot. I am a tough woman, let them not have any doubt about that. He may be a forgetful Dushyant but I am no forgiving Shakuntala," Lakshmi looked grim, as though she was confronting the culprits.

Before Kamala could burst into laughter, her mother had said, "Lakshmi, it's getting late. You'd better get started soon. I don't want the baby to wake up and cry for her feed while you're still working on the mother."

"This is the way Lakshmi massaged me. She took the oil in her hand ... we don't have medicinal oil but Johnson's is good enough. It has such a nice smell. I want you to become like the Johnson baby, chubby and happy. Lakshmi would pour the oil in the palm of her hand, rub both hands together like this and then..."

Kamala massaged the oil in smooth circular movements like Lakshmi had done. However, instead of the base of her palm she used the hollow on the infant's skin.

"Lakshmi was a small woman but she had a lot of strength. You, my little baby cannot bear too much force so we'll do it gently. Like this ... like this..."

Round and round her hand flew like a kite cut loose from its string. Under the even pressure of her hand Ammu's fair skin turned a light pink and then cleared. Her eyes were closed but the baby was not sleeping, only enjoying the massage as much as her mother had done.

Kamala was cautious while oiling the head, her fingers barely skimming over the gently throbbing fontanelle though she cupped the back of the head and ran her hand from side to side. She warmed the oil with the heat of her palms and massaged up and down the short neck, across the rounded chest, the fat thighs, dimpled knees and down to the toes, so close together that not even her little finger would get through. Soon the baby began to slip and slide on the mat and Kamala had to hold her in place with one hand while massaging with the other.

"There you are! Now we'll do some exercises," she said at last, catching the slippery little feet firmly in her hands and stretching the legs. She then slowly pushed them up till the knees touched the belly. She pulled them out once again and gently crossed them, right over the left; left leg over the right. It was then the turn of the hands. Ammu monkey-gripped Kamala's thumbs as her mother brought the hands over the little chest, raised them, brought them down and held them to the sides.

"Like an army man doing his exercise ... except that you are on the floor. You have so much to learn, my little one. How to turn over, crawl, stand without support and how to walk. Then you'll run, jump and skip.... Let's begin. This is how you turn over."

Kamala rocked the baby from side to side like a seesaw, singing all the while.

"Like a ship a-sailing, a-sailing in the sea.
See the ship a-rolling, rolling o'er the sea.
The sailors are all falling, tumpittee, tumpittee dee
Ammu's come to help them, him and him and he.
See the ship...."

"What are you doing?" asked Raghu, standing at the doorway.

"Oh, I'm teaching her how to turn over. She's already eight

months, high time she turned onto her stomach."

"She'll catch a cold before she does that. You'd better give her a bath now. Is lunch ready? I'm getting late. Today's Sunday but I have to meet a couple of clients."

"Everything's on the table. Help yourself … if you don't mind," she added and turned to the baby once more, "Now, let's give you a bath."

That took long too since Kamala was still talking to her, sprinkling water on her and massaging the flat head and nose. By the time she brought the baby out of the bathroom wrapped in a thick Turkish towel, Ammu was very sleepy. She nodded through the elaborate process of getting dried, powdered and dressed. She didn't want her feed but Kamala would not let her sleep on an empty stomach. She tickled her soles, scratched her ears and blew on her legs forcing Ammu to suckle. Kamala didn't mind the time it took to nurse Ammu, just as she did not grudge spending several hours every day, teaching her daughter what a normal child would have done routinely in the process of growing up.

It was only when she sat down to eat did she notice that once again Raghu had left home without having his lunch. It used to worry her at first but soon it was her daughter who was causing her greater concern. When Ammu should have been standing without support and trying to take a few steps she was still crawling on all fours, unsteadily and laboriously following her mother around the house like a puppy. Kamala tried to be positive about the delay.

"The point is that she is crawling. She'll walk. Maybe not on her birthday but soon enough and then we'll have a tough time running after her. That may be when she starts talking too - like a bird. Right now I'm concentrating on her movements. Talking can wait. I know exactly what she wants even without her telling me anything."

"You don't know what I want, do you?" Raghu asked her once.

"What do you mean?"

"I want my wife! I've forgotten what it is to hold you ... to..."

"Shh... that's enough. Revabehn is around, remember?" she warned.

Revabehn was now working for Kamala the whole day. She had to cook, water the plants in the balcony and do all the other chores that Kamala once did, in addition to her own old routine of sweeping, mopping, doing the dishes and washing clothes. The maid was happy with the additional pay but Raghu complained about Kamala's new absorption.

"Don't you think you're spending too much time with Ammu? Look at you! You don't bother about anything any more."

"How can I think of myself? My priority is my daughter..."

"She is my daughter too, am I neglecting my work?"

"That's the difference between you and me! As a man, as a father, you can get away with less involvement in your family but a woman can't. Our priorities are different too. Children come first for us."

"Rubbish! I'm as concerned about Ammu but I haven't given up my routine because of her. I do my work like before, I go to the club, meet my friends..."

"But my 'routine' is Ammu. She is everything to me," Kamala hugged her daughter.

"You used to say I was everything to you ... and not so long ago," he said wryly.

Kamala melted a little. "You are talking like a petulant child. Come on, you're a big boy. You don't need amma any more. In any case, whenever you want me I'll be there for you."

"Really? Then how about going out for dinner tonight? Let's ask Revabehn to stay back and look after Ammu. We'll go to the club. You haven't been there even once. It would divert you. They show good movies..."

"What on earth are you talking about? You know very well that I don't give her to Revabehn and you are asking me to go out with you, leaving Ammu with her for a few hours?"

"Then let's take her with us."

"Take Ammu? God knows what infection she'll catch in a crowded place. We can't run such risks, can we?"

Raghu did not reply but his silences no longer disturbed Kamala. She continued to tell him about Amrita's progress, even if he was not always attentive.

"I tried to show her how to stand. I held her hands and . . . are you sleeping?"

"Eh? . . . No, I am drowsy though," he replied.

"How can you think of sleep when I am talking to you about our daughter?"

"That's what you always do," he muttered.

"What did you say?"

"Nothing. Are you through? I have an important meeting tomorrow. I want to sleep."

"Sleep! That's all you can think about. You're simply not bothered about our daughter."

"You are looking after her well enough."

"That's not the point! You hardly spend any time with her. At this rate she won't even recognise you. She clings to me because I am with her always. She is. . . ."

"Okay, okay. We will talk about this tomorrow. I'm really feeling very sleepy." Raghu lay back on the bed, closed his eyes and laid an arm across them but Kamala hadn't finished her account.

"I wonder how she'll react to my parents."

That got Raghu's attention.

"Your parents? They are coming here? When?" he asked.

"Oh, great! I told you only this morning that they want to attend Ammu's birthday. Of course, they said they would confirm their visit later. My mother has not been keeping too well but she doesn't want to miss her granddaughter's first birthday. What about your mother? Did you talk to her?"

"I'll telephone her one of these days, though it is not worth travelling such a distance for a mere birthday. Are you planning to have a party or what? I thought you've become a total recluse?"

"I feel guilty even to think of doing something else and not spending that time with my daughter. Now I realise that it's not healthy for her to be so attached to me. She must learn to mingle with others. She'll like to see other children, I'm sure."

As Ammu's birthday approached, Kamala became irritable, made endless plans and worried into the night.

"Look," Raghu told her when he could no longer stand it. "If you are going to get so worked up, let's call it off. After all, your parents have also cancelled their visit. We can give some excuse to our neighbours."

"No, I want to go ahead with the party. It will be a test for Ammu. When she is old enough to travel we can take her to my parents and also visit your mother. What I am concerned about is that for a month now I've been teaching Ammu to stand and she still can't balance herself. What will everyone think? There's only a week left for her birthday."

"What's there to think? If she can't balance herself, she can't. That's it. Let her crawl around the guests," he snapped.

"I knew you would say something like this! You simply don't understand my problem. You are the most self-centred man I have ever seen."

"Who's talking! For so many months now you have not bothered about me at all. It is Ammu, Ammu all the time … don't I count any more?"

"Once again the same old complaint? Shame on you for being jealous of your own daughter and that too one who is not like other children. You are not able to accept the truth about Amrita. You don't want me to spend so much time with her. You are looking for excuses to blame me for everything. Go on, say it. Say I am responsible for her condition!"

The more Kamala argued the more Raghu withdrew from her and Amrita. She knew this but couldn't stop herself from hurting him. It was as if she wanted to test the limit of his patience. Raghu, however, did not retaliate till the day of the party.

***

"We lived in Srinagar colony those days," Kamala auntie said. "With eight houses to a block there were five such blocks built around a central park-cum-children's playground. This was also the venue of all society functions. A couple of neem trees and a scattering of benches below them gave the clearing an identification, a name as 'park'. But the swing, the seesaw and the slide also made it the 'children's playground'. Many arguments and disagreements in the colony arose because of this duality. The children did not stop with using only the facilities in the playground but soon graduated to playing cricket, making it hazardous for others in the park. Rubber balls whizzed threateningly, players kicked up dust while running between the wickets and arguments raged about the umpire's decisions, making it all very distracting for the elderly who occupied the benches and others who made the park their meeting place to share a little gossip. The elders and the children carried the disagreement throughout the year, culminating in the annual general meeting of the colony welfare committee. The standard item on the agenda was the need to bifurcate the 'two public facilities' but no decision could ever be reached and it was carried over to the next annual meeting and another august body. It was on this ground that I planned to hold the birthday party. I didn't realise my stupidity even when Raghu shouted at me."

"Have you gone mad, Kamala? Do you realise how many people live here?" he asked.

"Of course, I do. So many of them have invited us for something or the other. We have to return the invitation some time and this is a good opportunity."

Raghu prevailed upon her to invite only the younger children and a few mothers whose babies were too small to come on their own. That still made a sizeable number but ensured that the party could be held indoors.

It was a hot day and the electricity board had been playing hooky since morning. Fortunately, on Raghu's advice, Kamala had placed an order with the local caterer for the snacks and soft drinks instead of trying to make everything at home. This eased her tension somewhat and also gave her time to decorate the house.

Raghu had been impressed with the profusion of streamers, balloons and paper decorations that greeted him when he returned from work.

"How I wish my parents and your mother had come. They would have been so happy to see Ammu."

Kamala waited for Raghu's response but he was still admiring her handiwork.

"Hmm... yes. Is Ammu awake? I don't see her around," he said finally.

"I sent her to the park with Revabehn. She's been a little cranky since I couldn't spend much time with her today. Here she is! She's still crying, Revabehn?"

"Yes, she wants you," replied the maid, handing the child over to Kamala.

"This is of your own making," said Raghu. "You never let her out of your sight."

"I'm scared. I don't want her to get hurt."

"You will have to wean her sometime. She's one..."

"Don't! It is not auspicious to reveal the age on one's birthday!"

"Nonsense!"

Nevertheless, Kamala took the precaution of taking a five-rupee note and circling it around Ammu's head to ward off ill luck.

"She looks like a little doll, doesn't she?" she asked Revabehn.

Kamala had dressed her daughter in a new dark pink frock that enhanced Amrita's fair colour. Two pink bows on either side held back the thick mass of black curls from falling into her eyes. She wore matching pink shoes and shiny silver anklets over the socks. The tiný bells on them would have jingled if she had run around, at least walked. She did neither but sat in her baby chair looking like a dainty doll while the guests crowded around her with their gifts.

"Give them to me, she's just a small baby," Kamala explained, quickly wiping the dribble from Ammu's chin.

"Games, aunty?" one child asked.

"Oh no, it didn't occur to me at all. Next time perhaps, when Ammu is older, then she will also play with you."

"Does she talk?" asked a boy of about 11 or 12 years.

"Of course, only a few words though. She's a little shy but she likes children. Haven't you seen her in the park?"

"Yes, stupid! She's the one…" whispered his friend in his ear while Kamala tried to ignore it.

"May I carry her?" asked a girl.

"Sure … if you won't drop her. What's your name?"

Kamala lifted Ammu from the chair and gave her to Chandra.

"I like carrying babies but not my brother. He is two years old and doesn't stay in one place."

Kamala smiled at Chandra tentatively, not sure if the thin girl would have the strength to carry Amrita. Ammu looked from

Kamala's face to Chandra's. Her lips quivered and tears flowed down her cheeks but the little piteous sounds she made were lost in the loud talk and laughter of other children. A bunch of four or five balloons came loose and floated down to the delight of the boys who fell on them with a whoop.

"Give them to me, I shall put them up," Raghu shouted and ran to them but by then they had sent bits of rubber flying everywhere.

"Raghu, leave them. Here, distribute these caps and masks," Kamala thrust a cardboard box in his hand. The children immediately crowded around him shouting their preferences.

Kamala's enthusiasm for the party was flagging quickly. Like her daughter she was distracted by the enthusiasm of the children who seemed to be everywhere at the same time. Ammu clung to her and refused to let anyone carry her.

"Come on folks, let's cut the cake..." shouted Raghu and got immediate attention. Everybody crowded around the table.

"Ooh, look at that! A rabbit cake..."

"What a cake!"

"My mother had baked a clock cake for my birthday. Bigger than this, much bigger."

"This is not a whole rabbit, only the face!"

"Shouldn't a rabbit have long ears? I saw my friend's father hold a rabbit by its ears, their pet rabbit. It drinks Coca Cola through a straw!"

"It can't. Only people can."

"It can! I saw it."

"Prove it."

"How can I unless you come with me to their house?"

"Boys, no fighting please. When Ammu blows out the candle, everybody will sing, 'happy birthday to you...' okay?" Raghu ordered, fetching a chair to stand on.

"Yes, uncle," chorused the children.

"Kamala, you hold the baby while I take the photo. Get her to blow out the candle when I tell you, okay?" he shouted over the children's heads.

Kamala seated Ammu on the table. She had been training her to do it for a couple of weeks and hoped Ammu would remember her lesson.

"Now!" shouted Raghu.

"Ammu, blow at the candle... I showed you, remember? Like this..."

The little girl looked around at everyone staring at her and her lips began to quiver. Some of the children were leaning forward with their cheeks puffed and lips rounded, ready to do the task if need be.

Kamala turned her daughter's face towards her and repeated the instructions. Ammu's eyes filled steadily. Shaking her head with little quick movements, she buried her face against her mother and tried to climb into her arms.

The children fell back from the table in anticlimactic exasperation.

"No use auntie, you blow it out yourself," advised one.

"It is only one candle, Ammu, you can do it," said Chandra.

"I blew out all eight on my birthday. Poof… finished!"

"I had nine candles. No problem at all," added another.

"She can't handle even one. Such a baby."

"She is a baby. She is only one year old today," Chandra gave the speaker next to her a dirty look which made Kamala smile at her though she did wish the girl hadn't mentioned Ammu's age.

"Hey, what's happening? The flash is ready. Get her to blow!" ordered Raghu still perched on his chair.

"Don't wait any longer. Do it yourself," said one of the women.

Kamala held her daughter to her chest and blew out the candle while the children sang. She was seething inside, at herself, at Ammu and at her guests for their impatience. With a little persuasion she could have got Ammu to do it herself.

She forced the baby into Raghu's reluctant arms and started serving the eats with Revabehn and Chandra assisting her. The girl surprised Kamala with her maturity and thoughtfulness.

"How old are you, Chandra?"

"Fourteen."

"You help your mother always like this? She's so lucky. I don't think I have met her. Of course, I've been too busy with Ammu to socialise with everybody. That's why I wanted to hold this party."

Mrs. Kumar overheard her. "No one will misunderstand you for being so aloof. You must have your hands full with the child."

"Revabehn is a big help."

"Even then it must be tough. It will become worse when she grows up," added another woman.

Kamala looked closely at her. This was Mrs. Sharma who always walked with her baby in the pram, never in her arms.

"What do you mean?" she asked.

"Oh, it is not easy bringing up a child like her…"

"Poor thing," added Mrs. Kumar, feeding her toddler.

Kamala tried to control herself and spoke as calmly as she could. "She has not given me any trouble so far and I don't see how it will change when she grows."

"If you can train her maybe it will not be too difficult but in the long run…" Mrs. Sharma stopped her child from turning the plate over.

Kamala walked away from them abruptly. She picked up a large bowl piled with *puri* and went around putting two or three into the children's plates, even of those who were clearly dazed by the little mountain of food confronting them. Her mouth ached with having to smile and her throat hurt with all the words she tried to keep within herself.

'Take a deep breath. Don't lose your temper now,' she repeated to herself.

She heard snatches of conversation wherever she went, happy young voices discussing their feats during games, at school and elsewhere. For the first time she wondered if her daughter would ever talk like these children. Suddenly she wanted to cry. She grabbed a glass of water and drank it in one go, spilling it down the front of her silk sari. She looked around for Ammu and saw her on Revabehn's lap high up on the staircase away from the children milling all over the room. The party lasted as long as the food did. Then the children trooped out and the women followed with their babies.

Mrs. Sharma and her friend hung back.

"Kamala, don't misunderstand us, we didn't mean to hurt you," said Mrs. Sharma and Mrs. Kumar nodded vigorously.

"It is all right. I don't want to talk about it. Thank you for coming. Good-night," Kamala closed the door firmly behind them as Raghu looked at her aghast.

"Kamala, what happened? Why were you so brusque with them?"

"You don't know those … those bitches! They come to my house and insult me to my face!"

"What did they say?"

"I don't want to repeat it. I'm so angry. I wish I had never held this party. Nothing like this would have happened then," she ran to the bedroom.

Raghu raised his eyebrows questioningly at Revabehn but the maid didn't know what it was about either. He left her to clean the room and followed his wife inside.

***

# 4

"What's the matter?" asked Raghu.

Kamala sank her face deeper into the pillow and refused to answer. Ammu crawled to her and tried to climb on her back. Raghu put her on the ground.

"Come on Kamala, you are crying on a day like this? You are exhausted… right? No? Okay, tell me what those women said that has upset you so much."

She lifted her head. "Those blasted women! What do they think of themselves?"

"You are letting some strangers spoil your mood. Whatever they said can't be all that important. Forget them. Get up. If we don't clear the front room we'll be faced with the trash tomorrow morning. I don't want to see paper plates and cups strewn all over the place as soon as I wake up so let's do it now," he got up to leave but she pulled him down by his hand.

"They were commenting on Ammu, on how difficult it must be to look after her … as if I asked them for help. They also said that when she grows up it'll be even more difficult to handle her."

"I told you to ignore them," he replied.

"What kind of an answer is this? I want to teach them a lesson for thinking that their child is perfect and mine is not and you're telling me to keep quiet."

"Don't get into any trouble, let things be."

"I won't. They can't insult my daughter and get away with it."

"Kamala, be reasonable. They didn't say anything wrong…"

She pounced on him.

"What do you mean 'they didn't say anything wrong'? Everything is wrong in what they said. Why are you taking their side?"

"There's no question of sides here. Ammu is my daughter but those women were not entirely off the mark either."

"So, you also think that she's a difficult child? How can you say such a thing? I look after her myself totally so that you're not troubled in any way. If at all anybody should complain, it's me and I'm not saying a word against my baby."

"Whether you like it or not, the fact remains that we will not have a very easy time with her. After all, we do know that she's not normal. How are we…okay, you. How are you going to handle her? What will happen when we grow old? Who will look after her? That's what those women meant…"

"When did you become an advocate of those bitches? Do you realise that it is your own daughter you're talking about? You think I don't worry about these things? That's the reason I work so hard on her, trying to make her as independent as possible, even when you complain that I don't spend enough time with you…."

"Ammu is our problem but we should have a life of our own. I've already told you this before. If we bury ourselves completely in her then there is no life for us, no hope, no future."

"*Wah*, great words! They only prove what I've always suspected – that you are a selfish man. You wouldn't care what happens to my daughter or to me as long as you are happy, as long as you are not disturbed in any way. And what will make you happy? Going to the club, meeting your friends, showing off…"

"Watch it, Kamala."

"Don't threaten me. What will you do if I tell you some more truths? That you married me to forget your past? You thought I didn't know that? My brother hinted to me before our wedding that you were marrying me on the rebound. Some woman ditched you and you found me, another victim. Who knows how many more were there like her? Come to think of it, the way you are supporting those women, the way you stay away from Amrita and me, these are not natural. It is these doings of yours that has got us into this situation, saddled us with such a child. There's no need to look stunned. I've been ignoring it all these days but now that we have opened the can of worms, tell me the truth. What was she to you, that lucky woman who escaped your clutches?"

"What's the matter with you? You are getting worked up for no reason at all. You are just imagining things. There's no one in my life except you…"

"Oh yes? Then this wouldn't have happened."

"Absurd … not that I'm saying I did anything wrong," he added quickly.

"That's what you'll say now anyway. The least you can do is to tell me the name of the woman who had the sense to have her fun with you and toss you aside like banana skin when she was through. I will know whom to curse for my fall."

"I'm telling you there was no one. You're just looking for trouble. Why else would you twist my words from somewhere to somewhere else? If this is how you're going to talk then I don't want to listen to you any more."

He left the room slamming the door behind him, almost knocking Revabehn down.

"Two people can play this game. I don't want to have anything to do with you either. Having given birth to this girl I will look after her till the end. You can do whatever you want, I don't care!" she called behind him.

Raghu had not only walked out of the room but out of the house as well.

"*Sa'ab* went off in such a temper!" Revabehn pounced on Kamala. "Why did you make him so angry? It is not good."

Kamala forced herself to be calm and began to pick up the cups and plates. The old woman resumed her work still muttering under her breath.

"God knows where *Sa'ab* has gone. I hope he doesn't do anything drastic."

"What can he do? He won't do anything rash," replied Kamala, more to reassure herself than the maid.

"I wish you hadn't said anything. I didn't feel so bad even when you told me what's wrong with *bitiya* as I am feeling now. …"

"You don't know how it has been troubling me all these days, Revabehn. I couldn't keep quiet any longer. Why should I suffer for his wrongdoing?" Kamala asked, drying the glasses. She didn't want to confide in the maid but it was a relief to be able to talk to someone freely since Raghu had always dismissed her fears and anxieties as foolish.

"I agree with *Sa'ab* on one thing – *bitiya* is not a punishment."

Kamala turned to the maid, anger flaring in her eyes once again.

"So, like him, you think I'm exaggerating? By ignoring her

condition it'll go away? I've read too much about it to know better. The only thing I can do is to make her as independent as possible. This is what I've been trying to do with her all these days except that I don't seem to be making any progress at all. I'm scared, Revabehn, very scared."

"Then pray for strength to bear your troubles. Now sit down and relax. I will finish the rest of the work and leave. It is already late and the children will wonder what happened to me," she began to sweep the room vigorously, her wide skirt flouncing in her hurry to leave.

Kamala shut the door behind the maid and waited for Raghu to return. Amrita woke up and cried. She brought her to the drawing room and rocked the baby to sleep on her lap.

It was way past mid-night and her eyes drooped. She was not used to late nights. The baby was heavy on her lap. She wanted to put her back on the bed but felt too sleepy to get up. She had been busy throughout the day but more than that, it was her quarrel with Raghu that had left her drained. However exhausted in mind and body, she wasn't going to bed without ensuring that he was back home. This was the first time he had gone off in a huff so late at night and she had no idea what he would do, where he would go.

"Where can he be?"

Her voice breaking the quietness of the room disturbed Amrita, who was still sleeping on her lap. Kamala got up, put her on the bed and went back to her chair.

"Could I have imagined it? No, my brother won't lie to me even if others did. He was moving around with someone in college. That was so long ago, she must have forgotten him by now. I shouldn't have raised the topic today when both of us were tired. I had been looking forward to Ammu's first birthday so much! It was my fault. I could have simply ignored those women and not mentioned anything to Raghu. How can their words hurt us or worsen our plight? Words shouldn't have such power. Now my accusations have driven him out of the house. Where's he now? When will he return? Whom can I telephone? I don't want to involve anyone else in this and have the whole thing come out and multiply. You can't gag people's mouths. As it is I wonder what those two women will say to others. Tchah, I've made matters worse for myself. If only he would come home now.... I must apologise to him."

Despite her intention to stay awake till he returned, Kamala dozed off as she sat in the chair. A muffled sound outside the front door stirred her. She stretched her legs stiffly, wondering why her bed was uncomfortable. Awareness slowly dawned on her. Raghu! She looked at the clock. It was 2.25 a.m. She heard a noise outside, as if someone was scraping the metal disc around the keyhole. She tiptoed to the door and kept her ear against it.

A slurred "Damn" was followed by the sound of a key bunch falling on the cemented ground. Kamala opened the door cautiously, not more than a mere slit and peeped. Raghu stood outside swaying unsteadily, the naked low watt bulb on one end of the corridor casting deep shadows on his face.

"Oh my God, what happened?" She threw the door open and Raghu fell inside.

A strong stench assailed her and Kamala covered her nose and mouth. She steeled herself and helped him to his feet but he was in no condition to stand on his own. Holding the wall for support with one hand, the other firmly around him, she staggered inside. He was a tall, well-built man and she was no match for him physically. A few steps later, her legs wobbled and her body protested at the weight that it had to bear. She loosened her grip and let him slide to the ground.

"I can't move an inch more with you," she said, standing over him, arms akimbo and chest heaving with exertion. "You'll have to sleep it off here, on the floor. You deserve it for causing me so much trouble. What did you hope to achieve by this? Forget us, your problems? Or forget your girl friends?"

He lay on his back snoring with whistles and grunts, completely unaware of her anger. She left him where he was and went to bed.

Only a few hours remained for daybreak. The thick curtains blocked the coral red of the early morning sun. She felt Raghu's length along her back and instinctively turned to him, forgetting the tension and bitterness that had held them apart. With his arms wrapped around her, she felt safe and secure. She wondered sleepily why she had not sought his refuge before. She ran her hand down his bare back and let the coarse hair on his body tickle her palm. There was such pleasure in feeling him with her hands, with her tongue, with all of her. It had been a long time since she had done any of these.

Ever since they found out about Amrita's condition she had been so scared of conceiving again that she had used some pretext or the other to dissuade Raghu. She had watched him meekly accept her reluctance sometimes or, more often, seen him storm out of the room and sleep elsewhere. This was the first time she had surrendered to him totally and she was also the first to realise what had happened.

She sat up on the bed, shocked into awareness. The curtains kept out most of the sunlight but the room was no longer dark as before. Raghu was fast asleep.

"What have we done? After those arguments and discussions! How could we have forgotten all that? I don't even know when he came to the bed. What if the worst happens? I can't have another child with the same problem. And look at this man, sleeping so innocently!"

She shook him vigorously till he opened his eyes.

"How could we do this?" she asked.

"Eh?" his eyes were bloodshot and dazed.

"Wake up!"

"Okay … okay… What's the matter?"

"Didn't we decide not to have another baby?"

"So early in the morning ... you woke me up to say this?" he slurred and slumped on the bed again.

"No, you won't!" She snatched Ammu's feeding bottle, poured water into her hand and sprinkled it on Raghu's face.

He sat up again, shaking his head.

"Stop it! Don't irritate..."

"Then listen to me. Do you realise what we've done?"

Raghu stared blankly at her and then smiled groggily, "No wonder I feel so sleepy. I read somewhere that it's the best medicine for insomnia." He laid back and closed his eyes once more.

"If you don't get up this instant I'll empty the bottle over your head!"

He opened his eyes slightly and looked at her through his long lashes.

"Didn't we decide not to have another baby?" she asked him again.

"So? Doing it once doesn't mean hitting the bull's eye. It happens only in movies. The villain rapes the heroine and ... bang!"

"Stop talking like an idiot. I'm trying to be serious."

"What do you want me to do? Nothing may have happened after all. I'm just a human not a stud-horse. Okay, okay! Wait and see what happens. Why worry about it now itself? Admit you enjoyed it as much as I did even though I was not quite awake. My head is still buzzing. I do wish you'd leave me alone for some time. God, what a time to talk about such things when I can barely keep my eyes open," he turned away from her.

"What about going to work? Do you realise that it is..." She looked at the clock, "Oh no, it is past 8.30! How could I sleep for so long? Ammu?" she turned anxiously to the crib. Amrita was wide-awake and smiling. Kamala felt her bottom.

"Chee, you dirty girl! Why didn't you wake me?" she began to clean the baby while Raghu gratefully went back to sleep.

During the next few weeks Kamala rushed to the toilet at every instant of doubt. She kept her fears to herself since she didn't want another showdown with Raghu, but that didn't stop her from feeling tensed and irritable. She couldn't concentrate on her household chores. She didn't feel like playing with her daughter. She only wanted to sit in seclusion and not see anyone, least of all her husband.

*Nothing has happened. Nothing can happen,* she told herself a hundred times but till she saw the first spot, the merest stain, she couldn't relax. She looked at the calendar, counted the days on her fingers and tried to remember earlier occasions when she had been late.

*I have always been more regular than a clock. If only it would start on time I'd be so relieved! Ganesha, I'll break ten coconuts at your altar if only you listen to my prayer. Everybody comes to you when they are starting a new enterprise but I want you to end this misery and uncertainty.*

Her due date seemed to approach very slowly. It came and went without anything happening.

*Tension can delay it. I should unwind. How?*

Her agitation grew. She began to think that her stomach was showing, that she felt a slight movement within her, that her appetite had increased and that she found food nauseating. She finally told her fears to Raghu, who dismissed them with a sweep of his hand.

"Imagination, nothing else. Or it could be gas. Don't eat potatoes for a couple of days and you'll be all right."

Nothing helped. She was now scared to count or look at the calendar. The days that had crawled earlier now seemed to race. One day she worked up courage and calculated, double checking her count. She had crossed 45 days! That morning she went to the doctor who confirmed her suspicion. She had conceived.

"I don't want this baby or any other. I'm through. It's enough that we have Amrita. No more. I'm going in for abortion," she declared to Raghu.

"Fine, if that's what you want but wait for another few days. We have to give Ammu the booster shot now that she has crossed one year. Get it done after that. We can ask Dr. Bhatt to suggest someone reliable."

"I was going to tell you to have another child," said the doctor. "This is what we tell all such parents. It will be good, both for you and for the older child to have a sibling. There is no reason to fear that the next child will also have the same defect. You can get an amniocentesis done and find out if the foetus has any abnormality. If everything is all right, you should go ahead and have the baby."

"I'm scared, doctor," said Kamala. "What if the test is not reliable? What if the baby turns out like the elder one?"

"Nothing is in our hands. It could be a perfect pregnancy, even then something could go terribly wrong during the delivery or even after the birth of the child. I can only tell you that an amniocentesis will not cause any problem, either to you or to the baby. You can get it done here, in our hospital. I can refer you to a specialist, Dr. Vijaya. She will attend to you personally. What do you say?"

Kamala looked at her husband. She was not keen on going through the pregnancy but she also felt that another child, a normal one, might bring her closer to Raghu. He might begin to spend more time at home rather than at the club, as he had been doing of late. Maybe a son might…she checked herself.

"We have to think over this, doctor. We'll come back to you in a day or two. We had been very sure that we didn't want another baby but now you've put us in a quandary."

Raghu left the decision to her.

*After getting me into trouble in the first place, he's backing out. Perhaps the doctor is right. Another child might bridge the gap the first one caused between us. As for looking after two children … would that really be so difficult? So many women have half a dozen or more. My own mother brought up three though one died later. I did have lots of fun with my brothers.*

She had grown up playing cricket, football and cycling with her brothers and their friends, all boys. By the time she realised that she was physically different from them she had lost interest in their games. From being a tomboy and everybody's despair she became her mother's closest friend and greatest comfort, especially when her younger brother died in an accident a few years later.

*The second child might be our support when we are old and I won't have to worry about Ammu*, she thought.

Maya was born in due course, a healthy, normal baby so different from her sister and so like her mother in appearance.

"You are dark but you'll get a handsome husband like I did," she whispered into the baby's ear. "What name shall we give you? Krishna, since you're so dark or Shyama? Krishna sounds like a boy and Shyama is difficult on the tongue. You will have a light, gentle name that slips off the tongue easily. Hmmm...? Maya! Yes, we'll call you Maya. It's another name for Lakshmi, the goddess of prosperity. You'll bring happiness to our home. I know you will!"

She infused Raghu with similar enthusiasm and they decided to make a fresh start. They would move to another house, away from troublemakers like Mrs. Sharma. The new house would be an independent one, more spacious than their rented flat and they would be the owner not the tenant.

Raghu used his wide contacts and located a suitable house,

the one that they continue to occupy, and named it after both their daughters, 'Mayamrita'.

"This is the right kind of environment for our children," said Kamala. "Lots of space for the girls to move around and, best of all, no nosy neighbour to find out what is wrong with our daughter. Revabehn is also happy since this house is closer to where she stays."

Her relief that at least her second child was normal buoyed her and gave her the patience to bring up two young children, each with such different needs. Maya started walking when she was barely eight months old and her elder sister Amrita had just about managed to stand steadily for a few minutes at a stretch. In no time, Maya began to use all the space outside and inside the house. She ran the whole day, away from Revabehn, into her mother in the kitchen, in the way of the swing when Raghu relaxed or tried to. Short of tying her up, Kamala did not know how to restrain her daughter. She had to for Maya was always hurting herself. Before she turned one, she had bruises and scars all over her little body, that upset her mother no end.

Kamala found it difficult to keep an eye on the younger girl and maintain her rehabilitation efforts with the elder. In fact, compared to her sister's intelligence and exuberance, Amrita seemed even more helpless, making Kamala feel guilty. Severe nausea and exhaustion during her second pregnancy had forced her to hand over the care of Amrita to Revabehn. And now, she was constantly behind Maya, to ensure that the child did not get hurt. She felt torn between her daughters. Should she concentrate on her normal child, ensure that she was kept engaged and safe or spend time with the older girl, who needed long hours of patient teaching for the simplest task?

"Hire another maid. It will be expensive but if that will make you happier and give you a little time..." said Raghu.

"Maybe I can ask Revabehn if one of her daughters will look after Maya. Where does she stock all this energy in her little body? She doesn't eat on her own, I have to run after her for every morsel. As for getting her to drink milk..."

"Maybe you should drink that milk. You need the strength more than she does."

"Motherhood is not easy. In my next birth I want to be born a male, an Indian male, pampered, indifferent..."

"Hey, there's no need to insult me. Don't I do my share of baby-sitting Maya? Of course, I can only do it in the evenings when I return. I can't help it if I have to go on tour sometimes."

"Not sometimes, all the time."

"Shall I resign from my job and stay at home? You won't have to hire another maid, I'll be around 24 hours."

Revabehn brought her daughter, Shanti to babysit Maya. She looked much younger than her 13 years and Kamala hesitated to hire her.

"The girl's very sharp. She'll ensure that Maya doesn't get into any trouble. I'll also be around to keep an eye on both,"

Revabehn said and got her daughter the job.

Now there were two girls running all over the house instead of one. Amrita did not like the noise they made and stayed out of their way. She watched the girls from her corner as if they would bump into her any moment but they never noticed her. She could be a fixture in the room for all they cared. Maya was too busy getting into trouble and Shanti, trying to prevent her.

The biggest advantage in having Shanti around was that she fed the younger girl. Kamala was not very happy about entrusting this task to the servant but the girl seemed to do it better than her. She told Maya stories and popped in a mouthful at every opportunity. Kamala suspected that some of it probably went into the servant girl but how much can she eat, she reasoned and left them alone. Just as she left her husband alone. If Kamala had ignored Raghu after Amrita's birth she now ensured that he could come nowhere near her. She slept with a daughter on either side while he had the bedroom to himself.

"I've had enough of taking risks. In any case, I am so exhausted with all this work I cannot think of anything else. Is it my fault that I'm so busy?" she asked her husband one night, as he stood at the doorway of the children's room. "Even with Revabehn and her daughter to help I don't get to comb my hair some days. I'm not complaining, mind you. Children must be active. I want Amrita to be like her sister but it will not be possible without my help and where is the time to help her? It is by the grace of God that the younger one is normal. Just imagine what would have happened if she had turned out like her sister?"

Maya made the days seem longer. She created such a racket that Amrita clung to her mother and wouldn't go to Revabehn even for a minute. Kamala's arms ached with carrying the girl. Amrita was nearly four years old and made up in size what she lacked in intelligence.

"Shanti, play with the elder one," she said.

The girl paused in the middle of their game and replied, "*Na, behnji.* She is very quiet but I can't carry her. She is too fat. Maya is more fun. I am teaching her how to climb steps."

Kamala could see that. The two girls had been climbing up and down the whole morning without showing any sign of boredom or exhaustion.

"Be careful, Shanti," she said. "I don't want her to try it on her own. If you encourage her to climb, she will do it when there is nobody to supervise her."

"She's smart. She holds on to the wall. I have taught her to keep both feet on a step before going to the next one. Don't worry, nothing will happen."

Kamala watched them for a while, satisfied herself that Shanti was taking good care of the toddler and went to Amrita. She was not happy about her daughter's appearance. Her face was too flushed and she was restless though she did not seem to have a temperature. Kamala waited for Raghu to come home and take over but he telephoned from his office.

"Kamala, I'm leaving early tomorrow morning for Madras and Calcutta. I'll be late in the evening so I won't be able to pack. Do you mind doing it? Thanks and bye."

By the time he returned home that night she was exhausted and irritable.

"Are you married to your office or to me? It is bad enough that you spend so much time there and then you go on tours, leaving me to manage these two all by myself. When do I get a break?"

"What do you want me to do? You don't want me to look after Amrita. You think I can't handle Maya. You don't want to go out with me nor will you let me go to the club to unwind. One drink does not make a person a drunkard but you act as if you must keep an eye on me all the time, as if I'm Maya," he complained in return.

"If Maya is troublesome I can carry her on my hip and still do my work but if you are up to any mischief, I am the one to get into trouble. No thanks. You will behave yourself while you're home. I don't care what you do when you're out of town."

*Let him flirt or dream about any girl, how does it matter? I suppose he must have his share of fun. Why shouldn't a woman have an equal right in such matters? Is a woman not expected to have sexual desires? Not that I am interested. With these two around it is not even possible to think of such a thing!*

"What are you thinking about? More sticks to beat me with? Keep them to yourself. I have to finish these papers tonight. I'll leave them here. Give them to the peon tomorrow morning. They are very important."

"Why do you keep everything till the last minute? You could have done this earlier and not thrust that responsibility as well on me. You are no better than a child sometimes."

Raghu left on a tour for fifteen days, the longest he had ever been away. Amrita had another of her bronchial attacks, which made her flushed and breathless. Kamala had been up the whole night tending to her and she fell into an exhausted sleep early in the morning. Maya woke up, crawled over her mother and got off the cot. She poked a finger into Amrita's tummy and went slowly towards the steps.

She must have gone for not more than a couple of minutes when Kamala woke up and looked around for her. Even as she wondered where the girl had vanished to, she heard a tumbling noise as Maya rolled down the steps.

***

# 5

Maya was declared out of danger after two days in the Intensive Care Unit that nearly killed Kamala with worry. She couldn't bear to see the tiny figure in the crib, head swathed in bandage, eyes closed, tubes inserted into her arms and nose. The only time Maya lay down was when sleep overtook her and then she thrashed around or sat up prattling. Her stillness now made Kamala's stomach churn with fear. She could do nothing but stand outside the closed doors of the ICU and look hopefully at the nurses who came out for a sign that her daughter was well. She did not dare to think of how Amrita was coping with her absence.

*Revabehn is with her. She will be all right. My place is beside the younger one. I can't help it. If only Raghu were here…*

Yet, she feared his return.

*What will he say? Will he get angry with me for not taking better care of her? But what can I do? Which one do I attend to? They are both my girls, equally precious.*

Raghu said nothing. He neither chastised nor consoled her as they took turns at the hospital till they could bring Maya home with a small bandage over the stitches on her forehead. Kamala's worst fear that the injury might affect her daughter mentally fled as soon as Maya regained consciousness, when she opened her eyes, smiled at her parents and wanted to get out of the bed, all in the same instant.

"Shanti doesn't seem reliable. Take care of the little brat yourself. It's only a matter of a few years. She will quieten when she grows up. Revabehn can manage Amrita. Let's not run the risk of having something disastrous happen to Maya too," was all that Raghu said when they returned home.

Maya found it difficult to hoodwink her mother like she had done with Shanti but that didn't stop her from trying. She waited for Kamala to turn her back and swung into action, dropping bottles, removing utensils from the kitchen shelves or playing with the gas regulator. She did not protest if she was thrown out of the kitchen for she found the rest of the house equally promising. There were power points at the right height in all the rooms, taps in the bathroom waiting to be opened, the W.C. with its little inviting pool, cockroaches and insects in the darkest corners and cupboards full of clothes that she could pull out and scatter. Opportunities were endless, or so it seemed with Maya around.

Mornings were the best when Raghu was getting ready to leave for work and Kamala was bustling around him. The next peak time was soon after lunch when Kamala's reflexes slowed and often she did not notice Maya slip out of the bed. A sudden noise would startle her and bring her rushing to the spot. Those were the times when Kamala was grateful for Amrita's docility and diffidence. It was so easy to forget her. In fact, if it hadn't been for Revabehn, Kamala might not have remembered the older girl at all.

The maid fussed over Amrita from the time she came to work till she left. She seated the girl behind her and washed clothes or scoured vessels. Sucking a thumb and holding on to the old woman's skirt with the other hand, the little girl followed her from room to room as she swept and mopped the floor.

Kamala might not notice Amrita but Maya did, like a bull to the colour red. Her very presence seemed to provoke the girl and she charged at her, pulling Amrita's hair or biting her.

"Don't hurt your sister, Maya. You'll have to look after her some day," Kamala remonstrated, pulling one away from the other. "Ammu, don't cry. Your sister didn't mean to hurt you. She won't do it again, will you, Maya?"

"Words never cured anybody," Revabehn snorted. "Why don't you use a stick? She's much stronger than you think. A few sharp whacks will cure wilful children like her. A chit of a girl, scaring the life out of her sister! What will happen when they grow up?"

"I just cannot punish anyone. Argue, try to make them understand, yes. But I could never raise my hand even when my brothers irritated me nor now, to make my daughter understand the difference between right and wrong," Kamala protested weakly.

"If she had been my child, I would have cured her in no time," Revabehn continued her condemnation.

"She will calm down when she's older but Ammu should also show some spunk. She can't let her younger sister trample all over her like this. Why don't you teach her to toughen up?"

"Can you make a kitten face a tiger? If at all anyone has to change, it has to be your spitfire. My baby won't."

Far from reducing, Maya's inexplicable ferocity grew, sending her sister deeper into her shell. Finally, Kamala enrolled Amrita in a school hoping that the teachers and the other children may work the wonder that neither she nor Revabehn could effect. It didn't. Amrita became even more fearful and timid. Loud noises startled her and proximity with so many children increased her susceptibility to cold and throat infections. To make matters worse, her teachers constantly complained about her inadequacies and backwardness. Kamala often went to the school and tried to convince them otherwise but not a single teacher saw the child as she herself did – docile, introverted but affectionate.

"We cannot handle such a child. She clearly needs special attention and that is not possible in a class of 50 or 55," said one teacher.

"Please give her a little more time. She may settle down soon," Kamala pleaded and won a temporary reprieve. She had to think of an alternative arrangement and couldn't come up with any.

"Why seek my advice now?" asked Raghu. "Did you ask me before getting her admission? You know very well that Amrita can't cope with the rigour of a regular school. For heaven's sake, don't be in a hurry to send Maya away as well and then come cribbing to me."

"Another two months and then I'll see. Maybe she would have adjusted by then."

"Fine, but don't complain to me again. I have nothing to do with this."

Kamala couldn't pinpoint exactly when Raghu detached himself from the family affairs. The rope had slackened as gently and unobtrusively as the children grew. Somewhere along the line she stopped telling him what happened at home in his absence and he did not try to find out.

*His duty is to give my girls and me food and shelter. At least he's doing this. Any other man may have deserted us altogether,* she thought in her more charitable moments. Sometimes though, she confronted him.

"It doesn't matter that you don't have any time for me but

that little girl, Ammu ... she should know her father. Why don't you take over her training while I play with Maya?" she asked one day.

"Why the sudden shift in your argument? You wouldn't involve me in whatever you did with her as a kid. 'I am following the books,' you used to say those days and keep me out. After reading so much if you couldn't help her how can I? Moreover, where do I have the time, tell me," he argued, silencing her.

He couldn't do the same with Maya though. She waited for him to return from office, demanded he take her to the playground and play with her like other fathers did with their children.

"Come appa, I've been waiting for you. Revabehn shouts at me and amma's always busy," she insisted.

"Teach your sister how to play."

"No use, appa. She doesn't know anything other than crying 'boo ... hoo...' all the time!"

When Raghu could no longer handle Maya, he got her admitted in the same school as Amrita. Now Kamala had to worry about both her children and Amrita collected complaints as easily as a well gathers moss on its wall. One day the headmistress summoned Kamala and issued an ultimatum.

"Either you withdraw the child or we'll expel her. Put her in a special school. That'll be the best for her. She's out of place here. The children tease her and they all get distracted. I don't want parents to complain about her influence on their children. The younger one is all right, very naughty but she should not be much of a problem… I hope."

Kamala no longer wanted to plead for time. She couldn't bear the daily drama that marked Amrita leaving for school. Raghu would wait with Maya in the car while she tried to persuade Amrita to join them, the sound of his impatient horn aggravating the girl's resistance. Some days he got so incensed by the delay that either he left without her or else he rushed inside, grabbed her and threw her into the car. Her wails grew fainter with distance but Kamala would be so shaken that she had to lie down till her heartbeat became normal. Now, with Amrita at home she had one worry less.

Maya was troublesome in her own way. She did not like the confinement but revelled in the company of so many children who were only too willing to play with her. She led them from prank to prank and faithfully told her mother what punishment she had received from her teachers.

"I pinched Ram. He was pulling my hair so I gave him one nice pinch. He cried. The teacher made me stand in a corner."

"I didn't feel sleepy today afternoon. Asha Madam told me to sit on her table as I was disturbing the other children."

"Why can't I stay at home like Amrita? I don't want to learn writing. Singing is all right. I can shout and nobody will notice."

"It will be very boring for you at home. You don't want to play with your sister. What else will you do?" asked Kamala, helping Maya put on her uniform.

"Okay, I'll play with her. You can teach me too like you teach her sometimes."

"Those lessons are boring. I can't teach you songs or tell you stories like your teachers do."

"But they tell the same stories everyday. 'Once upon a time...'" she mimicked making her mother laugh.

"I thought you liked school. You can wear a nice frock like this one, take tiffin in a box..."

"I don't want to wear frocks any more. I'm going to become a boy. Get me shorts and cut my hair or I won't go to school."

Before Kamala could say anything, her husband intervened, "Stop this nonsense. Time you became less playful. In any case, girls must have long hair."

"But Ram pulls my hair!"

"Don't start wailing now. Tell your teacher and she will punish him. Hurry up, it's getting late. I've to drop you and then go to office," he ordered.

Ram soon grew tired of pulling her hair but he didn't stop troubling Maya, nor did she give up retaliating.

"Maya, Maya...why don't you understand?" Kamala tried to control her exasperation. "What will happen if the headmistress expels you from school too?"

"Was Amrita expelled?"

"N...o... not expelled. The teachers felt they couldn't handle her. You know she's different from you. She needs to go to another school, a place for children like her."

"Then Ram was right. She is mad, isn't she?"

Kamala slapped the girl's cheek sharply.

"Don't use that word again. She's only different from you. That is not the same thing."

Maya stood dazed for a moment then she turned and ran upstairs. Kamala was shocked too. Shocked that she had struck her daughter! With heavy steps she climbed up to the girls' room. Maya was lying on the bed, face buried in her crossed arms. Her narrow back heaved in sorrow and anger but that didn't stop her from brushing away her mother's hand.

"I didn't mean to hurt you. I'm sorry. You're still too young to understand why I got angry with you..."

"I'll tell appa what you did," she threatened in a muffled voice.

"Tell him, tell the whole world. I'm tired of it all!"

Kamala sat on the ground, rested her head on the edge of the bed and wept.

Maya looked dazed at her mother and then got down to the floor herself to hug her mother.

"Oh, I won't tell appa. You can beat me some more if you want. I won't tell anyone but please don't cry," she pleaded over and over, with trembling lips till her mother's tears subsided.

"I'm all right," Kamala said, wiping her eyes and smiling at her daughter. "Sit down."

Maya perched gingerly on the bed as if she was not convinced by her mother's assurance.

"It was my fault. I've been upset about your sister having to drop out of school and then to hear that you were causing trouble too ... I couldn't bear it."

"I won't do it any more. I'll keep quiet even if Ram teases me."

"Good girl. Just ignore people like him."

"But tell me, why is she different? Why is she not like me?"

"She was born that way. I'm trying to make her like you but it's not easy. It will take a very long time. She's not as smart as you are."

"Why don't you send her to some other school? At least then you can spend some time with me. You are always with her, even when I come back from school. You won't play with me..."

"I'm too old for your hide and seek or..." Kamala could not think of any game. In her childhood she had played so much but those days seemed to have gone way beyond retrieval.

"See! This is what I said. You like Amrita so you spend all the time with her. You don't even want to send her to a school. You don't like me, that's why..."

"It is not that. You are a smart girl, you can take care of yourself but Ammu needs someone."

"Then let Revabehn take her. I don't want such a sister. You get me a brother instead. I don't like having sisters. My best friends, Hema and Ramya have brothers. In fact, Ramya has two and I don't have any, only this stupid Amrita."

Kamala forced herself to stay calm.

"I'll tell you what we can do, we can all play together. You, Ammu and I, what do you say?"

Maya shook her head impatiently. "I don't want to play with her. I told you she doesn't know anything. Either you play with me, only you and me, or I'll play alone. That's what I always do anyway."

Her face brightened. "Maybe I can practise with my catapult..."

She ran out before Kamala could say anything.

Kamala did not know which phase of childhood was easier to manage – Maya as a restless, naughty child or now, a strong-willed girl.

*If she doesn't change soon ... Oh, I don't want to think of what will happen to my baby. If only Ammu would improve just a little!*

Amrita was still sitting in her corner looking at her. She was wary whenever her sister was around. And now, even though Maya had left she didn't feel confident enough to go to her mother.

"Come here, Ammu..." Kamala continued to sit on the ground near the bed and Amrita came slowly towards her with a hesitant smile.

Kamala wiped the thin line of spittle on her daughter's chin that never seemed to dry and brushed her hair out of her eyes.

"Thanks to all this drama I haven't been able to spend time with you and just look at you. Tangled hair, dirty face… *chee*! Maybe I should ask Revabehn to be with you full time. I thought she needn't spend such long hours here now that you and Maya are no longer babies. I was wrong."

Revabehn, however, had taken on work in other houses and couldn't leave them, neither could she come to look after Amrita in the evenings to enable Kamala to be with her younger daughter.

Maya gradually grew indifferent to her mother's tears. She changed in other ways as well. She argued at every step and did the opposite of whatever Kamala asked her to do. Only her father's presence could quieten her, but Raghu was hardly ever home.

***

"Gauri, were you this troublesome as a child?" Kamala auntie asked. "Of course, you didn't have an Amrita to boss over."

"Oh, more than me it was Sundar who gave my parents a tough time. Till Kittu became too ill to be disturbed, amma always complained to him about Sundar's antics. Kittu could never bring himself to beat anyone. A lecture was his maximum punishment," I laughed.

"You called your father by his name?" Kamala auntie was shocked. "If my children had dared to do such a thing Raghu would have skinned them alive."

"Thank God Kittu was different," I said. "When I was young I used to imitate amma all the time so I also began to call my father 'Kittu'. Sundar would call 'appa' or 'dad' to his face and 'old man' behind his back. I'm sure Kittu wouldn't have minded that. He was such a darling. Very lenient with everybody, more so with amma. If you had complained to him about Maya he would have said, 'She's just a child. She'll outgrow it.'"

Kamala auntie sighed. "That's what I told myself all the time but she didn't show any sign of changing her ways. I would have complained to her father but things weren't too good between Raghu and me. I didn't want him to think I couldn't handle Maya. I did try to explain things and make her understand. Why, once when her school closed for summer I had such a terrible time trying to keep her indoors. She wanted to throw stones at mango clusters instead."

"'You'll become darker,' I told her. 'Too much exposure to the sun causes ...'"

"If I don't go now others will, then I won't get a single mango," Maya had insisted.

"Be sensible, girl. It is much too hot. No one will venture out in this heat, believe me. Go at about 6 o'clock. It won't be cooler then but at least it'll be better than now. There will be enough light for you to see the mangoes. I don't understand this craze for throwing stones. You're going to hit somebody on the head and they will come charging here."

"They won't. First, my aim is very good and second, no one will know I have thrown it. I will hide. No one will see me."

"They are not fools. Moreover, you have to study. Your marks are very low, really borderline. One or two marks the other way and you would have failed, you know?"

"Rubbish! The teachers won't dare to fail me."

"What will you do if they did?"

"Do? I will throw stones at them."

"Great, you are born to be a bully or a party worker, wanting to pounce at the slightest provocation."

"Who's a party worker?"

"A member of a political party. The smallest excuse and they start throwing stones, burning buses, calling a *bandh*, stopping trains…"

"Wow! That's what I'll be, a party worker." Maya's eyes gleamed.

"Let's think about that later. First things first. Are you going to do your maths or no?"

"No!" She glared back at her mother.

Kamala clenched her ha ds tightly behind her back but spoke calmly enough. "Listen to me, Maya. Be a good girl. I'll make a nice lemon sherbet. With ice cubes in it. Go upstairs. Play with your sister … at least for a little while. You can do your maths later."

"I won't do anything later and I won't play with that mad girl. I'm going out."

Even as she turned to leave, Kamala's composure gave way to anger. She caught her daughter by the shoulders, whirled her around and slapped her cheeks.

"Don't talk back to me. And don't talk about your sister like that!"

Maya pushed her hand away and turned to the door but Kamala was too quick for her. She caught the girl by her shoulders once again, forced her towards the steps and made her walk upstairs as if leading a prisoner to the cell. She threw open the door and shoved Maya inside.

"I don't want to hear a single word from you. You will sit quietly and finish all your work. I'll come in exactly half an hour to see how much you have done."

Kamala banged the door behind her and went downstairs.

Her hands quaked at the fury of her anger and her legs were wobbly as if they were stuffed with cotton. She took a bottle of water from the fridge and drank straight from it. The water blocked her throat and she spluttered, spraying tiny droplets into the air. It helped her a little though and she sat heavily on the swing, making it protest with a loud and prolonged creak.

"This is too much. He's the one who uses the swing always, like some great maharaja. Can't he do this simple task? He might be a bachelor for all the care he takes of us, his family. What does he think of himself? Am I a slave to slog the whole day? All he does is to eat and sleep in ... "Kamala's Boarding and Lodging". What do I get in return? A big ZERO. And that girl, Maya! She's got his temper and arrogance. What will happen when she grows up? If she doesn't change her ways, she's finished. I am an idiot to put up with this nonsense."

She stood on the swing and angrily squished oil on the topmost joint. The viscid machine oil spurted out, slid down the length of one rod to the connecting ring and trickled thickly down to the next rod. While getting off, she upset the container and it emptied itself sluggishly on the ground.

"Great! What have I done to deserve this?"

She cleaned the floor and sat on the swing. Fortunately it behaved itself and the silent oscillation helped to relax her.

*I wonder what she's doing now. There's no sound from her. Maybe she's crying into her pillow. Should I go up and see? If I do that she'll get the upper hand. I will never be able to exercise any control on her. High time she realised that she cannot have her way always. Poor girl, I was too harsh on her. She's just a baby after all, only going to be seven years. I was such a handful myself at that age. I remember how my mother used to despair of my antics and anger. I shouldn't have over-reacted. Maybe I was tired and took it out on her. But then, it is stupid to go out in this heat. What if she gets a sunstroke? It is possible. People do die with too much exposure to the sun.*

Arguments and counter arguments swirled in her mind. Finally, she rested her head on the chain despite the oil that coated it and tried to keep her mind blank. A small sound startled her. She sat up and listened. What was that? A cat? In the kitchen? That wasn't possible since she always kept the door closed. She got up and checked anyway. The door was shut. The milk she had set for curd was safe in the middle of water in a basin, keeping ants away. She went to the foot of the stairs and listened.

*Just my imagination.*

Kamala went back to the swing, picking up the newspaper on her way. After a few minutes of scanning the headlines, the print blurred and she yawned widely, not bothering to cover her mouth.

A noise stopped her yawn mid-way. This time it was louder. She cocked her ear. It was coming from upstairs.

*Good God, what has that girl done now?*

Kamala threw the paper down and rushed up the steps.

***

# 6

Kamala lifted the pleats of the sari to give greater freedom to her feet and rushed up the narrow steps. Approaching the landing she stumbled and stubbed a toe, chipping off the nail. Even that did not slow her though it did make her hold the railing as she ran.

"Take one step at a time and you won't fall," she had always cautioned Maya. "The minute or two you gain by skipping a step may cost you a leg or an arm."

At that moment, however, even the second it took to push open the door of the girls' room made her impatient.

There was no one around, not even Amrita who usually sat near the door. At the furthest corners were two beds. The foot end of Amrita's bed faced the door. Maya's lay across the room forming a 7 with her study table since she didn't want her sister to go near her books. Kamala heard a small sound, not louder than a mouse's squeak. She went round Maya's bed and gasped.

Amrita was lying on the ground in the little gap between the bed and the table. The chair was upturned, shrinking the space further. Maya was sitting on her sister's stomach. Her hands whizzed and flew through the air, hitting Amrita with agonising accuracy since her fists though small were vicious and her target so soft and big. Amrita was too busy protecting herself with a natural instinct and couldn't fight back. She had covered her face with both arms and was crying feebly every time Maya made contact, sometimes on her arms, sometimes on her chest, sometimes on her shoulders, anywhere at all.

Kamala yanked her younger daughter off.

"What are you doing?" she shouted.

Maya did not reply. Kamala tightened her grip on the girl's arm to prevent her from lunging at her sister. Amrita was still curled on the ground and whimpering.

Kamala caught Maya by her shoulders and shook her.

"Have you lost your senses? Why are you beating your sister?"

"She started it. I was lying quietly on the bed. She came to me and touched my hair, my face. I warned her not to do it, that I'm not in a good mood. I warned her so many times to leave me alone. She wouldn't listen..."

"So you had to thrash her like this? Haven't I told you over and over that you should treat her with greater kindness and understanding? When are you going to learn?"

"She's fooling you. There's nothing wrong with her. She is acting mad so that she can stay at home the whole day and not go to school."

"Enough, Maya, enough! If ever you raise your hand against your sister again..."

"That's it. Take her side. You always support her. You don't care what happens to me. Nobody likes me in this house. I'll run away and then you'll realise..."

"You will sit quietly in this chair and not budge till I tell you, understand?"

Kamala set the chair back on its legs, lifted the girl and seated her with a thump. She then went to Amrita and sat cross-legged beside her in that little space.

"Ammu, my little darling, look at me. Did she hurt you? Don't be angry with her. She's just a naughty girl. I have scolded her. She won't do it again. Look at me. Let me see your face..." Kamala's voice was soothing and persuasive.

Amrita got up slowly and sat on her haunches, arms around her knees, making herself as small as possible. Her fair skin was blotched a dull purple and pink though it was not broken. She was shivering but her forehead was beaded with sweat. Seeing her like this made Kamala want to cry in sorrow, in desperation. She had never raised her hand at her older daughter. Something had always held her back even during moments of extreme frustration when Amrita did not show any improvement after hours of parroting that made her throat feel like sandpaper. And now to think that Maya could have… Her heart beat faster and a rushing sound filled her ears.

Kamala wanted to turn her wrath on Maya. She hugged her hapless daughter instead, in a tight squeeze as if to quell both her own anger and the trembling in the little girl's body. She took a deep breath and held it till her chest ached. She didn't want to antagonise Maya but neither could she let her get away with it.

*How do I tackle her? Fighting between siblings is common, I know. I have myself acted the peacemaker when my brothers quarrelled with one another. It wouldn't be so bad if Ammu had been normal. Then I would expect her to defend herself but now? If I keep quiet Maya might attack her sister again and again. How on earth do I make her understand?*

She finally glared at Maya to which the girl responded by tightening her lips and frowning back at her mother.

*I shouldn't keep these two together again! There is no guarantee about Maya. What if she grows up hating her sister? I had hoped that she would take over from us some day. What will happen to Ammu? Oh God, isn't there a way out of this?*

She had to find a solution herself since Raghu had told her in definite terms that Amrita and Maya were no longer his concern.

She got the answer in her faithful Revabehn.

"If that is the case, then I will stay till evening. Anything to ensure that the little one doesn't come to any harm from that terrorist sister of hers. I will have to give up a couple of houses. Perhaps my eldest daughter, Daksha can work in those places. The girl already has a great deal to do at home," said Revabehn. "I'm training her as much as possible before her wedding or else her in-laws will blame my upbringing for her inexperience."

"I'll pay you like I did before. You needn't suffer any cut in your salary because of us. Really, Revabehn, Maya is giving me more trouble than her sister."

"I have told you - beating is the only way to cure children like her. A few good slaps and she'll be another person altogether."

"I don't want to use force. She's a small girl after all. When she grows up she'll understand."

"That's what you think. Mind you, whatever happens here, I'll still leave by 6.30. If I don't go home to sleep, God knows what the children will be up to. The boys will play the whole evening and return home only when it's too dark and their bellies growl. The girls too might get ideas. This *TV, kivi*, teaches them all the wrong things."

"Why did you buy a TV then?"

"Otherwise they'll spend all the time at the neighbours. It's better that they sit in their own house and watch the *film-vilm*."

"Your husband doesn't say anything?"

"Where is he home to see what his brats are up to? He comes and goes like a dog through an open door. If he does return at night, he is so sozzled it's a miracle he does not come under the wheels of a car or a bus. By the time he reaches home, the children are fast asleep. I don't wait for him either. Those days are gone when I grew anxious if he was even slightly late or opened my legs so readily to his prodding. My blood has been cold for a long time and as for him..." she snorted dismissively. "He can only lift it with his hand."

Kamala hid her smile. As long as Revabehn would look after Amrita, she wasn't going to criticise the maid's language.

*Just as well that it's Ammu who is with her all the time and not Maya. At least Ammu won't mimic the woman.*

When Maya returned from school in the evening Kamala shed one personality and donned another. With Amrita, Kamala had to be patient, reassuring, gentle, and teach her everything over and over whether it was threading a bead, writing an alphabet or combing her hair. She talked all the time, trying to evoke some response in the girl but Amrita remained silent, occasionally attentive but mostly not understanding her mother's persistence. Maya was restless, impatient and demanded Kamala's constant attention and indulgence.

"Amma, catch the ball ... oh no, you dropped it again. Let's play seven tiles. I'll teach you."

Maya piled seven flat stones in a ring on the ground and drew a line at a short distance from the ring.

"You mustn't step out of this line when you throw the ball. Aim at the tiles, topple them and run away. The players on the other side will scatter the stones within the ring. One of them will stand guard while the others throw … You're not paying any attention! I don't want to play with you any more."

She scattered the stones with a kick and walked back to the house.

"Maya … hey, Maya… don't get angry," Kamala shouted, running after her daughter. "I was listening to you. I was only adjusting my sari. I was certainly listening to you," she pleaded.

Maya stopped and looked searchingly at her mother. Kamala nodded vigorously to convince her daughter.

"O...kay," said Maya "I'll give you one more chance, only because you're my mother. What would you like to play next?"

"How about this … this… seven stones?"

"Seven tiles. It needs more than two players."

"How about asking Revabehn and your sister to join us? See, she's looking at us through the window."

"Let her. That's all she's good for. Revabehn is too old. She becomes breathless after two minutes. We won't include either of them. We won't play seven tiles at all. Any other game?"

"I don't think we should play any of these running and catching games. People will laugh at me. I can see the heads of some of our neighbours…"

"How does it matter? I'm not asking them to play."

"Why don't you? I mean, why don't you find out if their children will?"

"Forget it! That Rajesh Patel next door is in my class. He's the one who told everybody that Amrita is m… not normal. And that 'styli' Seema thinks no end of herself because she's the monitor of her class. There's no one else of my age around here."

"Shall I ask appa to take you to the club more often?"

"Such a bore! Those old people keep talking all the time. The children are busy reading comics in the library, watching TV or swimming. They don't even look at me."

"Swimming is very good," Kamala said enthusiastically. "You could also learn how to…"

"No need! The pool is deep and dirty and somebody is always shouting 'frog… frog…'"

"That's okay. Frogs also need a place to live in."

"But I don't want to share the frog's house. Moreover, the water's very deep."

"Say that! You are scared of the water. That doesn't matter. You will outgrow your fear."

"Me, scared? What are you talking about? I'm not scared of anything or anybody!"

"Good, that's how I want my little girl to be… fearless like Bhim and Arjun. You can read about them in the club library. It will also improve your English. You didn't do too well in your last school tests. The teacher has written in your diary that you need to pay greater attention to your work. Maybe we should stop playing now and go to your books. It's getting dark. Appa will come home any minute and he won't like to see us outside the house so late."

"There, another evening wasted! Why does time seem to go so slowly in school and so quickly at home?"

"That's because you don't take as much interest in your studies as in playing..." Kamala threw an arm around the little girl's shoulder and guided her inside.

"Don't start your lecture," said Maya, shrugging off her mother's arm. "I hear enough of it in school. I'll study on my own. You go to your dear daughter. I know very well that's why you are in such a hurry to enter the house."

She strode away, every step reflecting the tautness of her temper.

Kamala sighed. It seemed as impossible to break through Maya's barrier of anger and revolt as it was to reach through the fog that clouded her older daughter's mind. She sat on the swing and rested her forehead on her hands wrapped around the iron chain.

*What if I had married someone else? Would I still have given birth to Amrita? Who can change my destiny? Anyone other than Raghu may have walked out on us. There's nothing wrong with him. I'm simply not capable of understanding him. That's all. If I were to spend less time with the girls...*

"I'm leaving now," said Revabehn entering the room. "My children will be wondering what happened to me."

"Yes, go. What's Maya doing?"

"She is with her books but she doesn't seem to be in a good mood. More like a tetchy little black ant, the biting variety that draws blood. Keep baby away from her."

"You still call her that when you know she's older than Maya?" laughed Kamala.

"She'll always remain my baby. You can have that other one."

"Don't be so harsh on her," said Kamala trying to allay the old woman's prejudice. "It is not easy for anyone to accept such a sibling. Her friends make fun of her in school, that's why she's so grouchy."

"You'd better go up to them before something untoward happens."

Kamala taught Maya while trying to keep Amrita engaged in some task so that she would not sit blankly in her corner. Every so often she went to the terrace and looked down to see if Raghu was coming so that she could open the gate for him. He hated having to sit in the car with the engine idling while she opened the gate and the garage door. He washed and changed while she made his coffee. He drank it reading the newspaper and left for his club and she returned to her daughters. It was easier when he went on tour. She didn't have to wait for him in the evening. After sending Maya to school she could concentrate on teaching Amrita. At ten, she had the mental age of a two-year-old, still dependent on her mother to do everything for her.

"Maybe your progress would've been better in a school. The

teachers may have taught you something but what to do? That headmistress… what a fuss she created that you wouldn't 'fit' in with the rest. With so many children in every class like a herd of sheep no one would have noticed you. As for the other school… the less said the better! Special School… they called it. How was it 'special'? In their fees, charging so much more than a normal school. Why doesn't the government do anything about this? There should be at least one good school for children like you in every town. This one was supposed to be managed by a charity trust. They were neither charitable nor trustworthy. Misleading everyone with sweet words, eating up the parents' money and molesting the children. Such a scandal when one of their students became pregnant. What torture for those poor parents! How will I shield you from the outside world? There are only animals out there, no humans. Is your father concerned about any of this? He is happily travelling to different parts of the country or going to his club as if he doesn't have a single care in his mind. If I tell him anything, he says I am over-reacting, throwing a tantrum, acting childishly. You are not 'his problem' as if I'm solely responsible for giving birth to you."

Through the long monologue she massaged oil on Amrita's body and bathed her.

"Here, pour the water over yourself … don't splash!"

She did not move out of the way quickly enough and water fell on her.

"See what you've done, you naughty girl. Let's dry you now,"

Kamala flung a towel over the girl's head and dried her briskly while Amrita threw her wet arms around her mother's stomach for support. Kamala did not try to stop her. Even though her sari was hitched to her knees and the *pallu* tucked in firmly at the waist, Amrita's aim had been good and she needed to change anyway. She led her out of the bathroom and dressed her.

"Now sit in this chair till I come. No tricks," she warned, hoping that at least this time her daughter would disobey her.

"If it had been your sister...oh, I can't think of what she would have been up to! You are such a good girl. If only that Headmistress..."

Kamala was teaching her daughter to draw. She had been doing this for the past several months and had at last succeeded in getting Amrita to hold the pencil between her fingers and not in the fist. She covered the girl's hand with hers and guided it over the paper, making straight lines and circles. When she removed her hand the pencil remained where she had left it.

"Ammu, push the pencil forward, harder. It has to make an impression like this." Once again she enveloped her daughter's hand in hers.

"How long will you do this, *behn*?" Revabehn asked her.

"I'm sure if I persist she will learn to write her name one day."

"Then what? I can't and I'm earning enough to support my family."

"I'm teaching her to be like her sister," Kamala replied confidently.

"Her sister," Revabehn waved her hand dismissively. "Don't talk about her!"

"Oh, what did she do now?"

"When I went to pick her up from school today, her teacher was waiting to tell me that Maya hasn't been doing her ... what was the word? Home ...home ... yes, homework. That woman, her teacher, complained to me that Maya wasn't doing her homework. As if I am the one teaching her. Why is the school paying her a salary if she can't make a child study?"

"I hope you didn't tell her this?"

"Don't worry. I only replied that I would pass on her complaint to you."

Kamala began to teach Maya with renewed enthusiasm, not letting her play and keeping her bound to her books.

"Ma, I learn in school the whole day and you are making me study some more at home. This is too much!"

"I believe your teachers are angry with you for not doing your homework. What if they get so angry that they throw you out of the school? You can play during the holidays," Kamala ignored the scowl on Maya's face and quickly marked the questions in the textbook that she wanted her to learn.

"I have some work downstairs. Do your work quietly and don't trouble your sister," she warned.

"And you," she went to Amrita, "here is your drawing book. Practise these circles till I come. Don't go near her."

Revabehn had taken leave for a month for the wedding of her eldest daughter. She had arranged for a substitute maid but Kamala preferred to do the chores herself.

*I shouldn't be such a perfectionist. So what if the woman didn't sweep below the chairs and cupboards? What's a little dust? Okay, I could overlook that but the way she washed the vessels? If I have to do them once again, I might as well do them all myself. Good riddance! I should tell Revabehn not to send her here again. Of course, it'll be best if she doesn't take any more leave. She will. Her daughter will become pregnant within a year, I'm sure.*

Dust and dry leaves rose in the air as Kamala swept the front yard. She used the coarse broom made from the spine of coconut fronds for the rough cemented front of the house. Normally she wouldn't have bothered about the yard but Raghu was returning that day from a long tour and she didn't want him to complain as soon as he arrived. The two tall Ashoka trees that stood on either side of the house were shedding their long, yellowing leaves and they lay below the straight trunk like giant caterpillars stunned and twisted in a final spasm. Maya and the wind scattered them all over the yard. Kamala never tried to check her daughter. She could stop one but not the other. That's what she told Revabehn when the maid complained about the leaves everywhere.

"How long will she do this? Another six months? She's changing already. Her shouting and screaming are considerably less. Let her be. We shouldn't scold her for everything," was her constant refrain.

Remembering her own words made her smile as she began to wash the vessels in the kitchen sink.

*Who would have ever believed that 'Argument Kamala' would one day preach tolerance and patience?*

That was the nickname her brothers had given her when she had been only too ready to start an argument with them, her parents, neighbours or anyone at all who dared to disagree with her. She would go on and on till her adversaries conceded defeat. She entered teens and quietened suddenly, not rising even to the bait that her brothers threw to test her patience.

Where did that fire and spirit vanish… and when? I never realised how much I've changed.

She looked at her reflection in the gleaming stainless steel plate that she had just washed.

*It is not only my temper that has changed but also my face. How my jowls sag like an old woman's. Oh well, I am a mother of two children after all. In any case, I've never been a beauty at any time.*

She pacified herself.

*I should conserve water. The tank will get empty at this rate and he won't have water to bathe. I wonder if his flight is on time. He should come now. What are the girls doing? I've almost forgotten about them in all this work.*

She went to the foot of the steps and listened. It was quiet.

She turned to resume her work, then decided to go up and check on her daughters anyway.

*Oh, my feet are killing me. I wonder how Revabehn does all the work in so many houses. I find it difficult to do it in mine. And to think that she is much older than me! But then, she sweeps as if she's scared of hurting the ground and the clothes look like rags. I don't dare to complain to her though. Not when she's so good to Amrita. She may change her mind about Maya when that girl quietens down like I did…*

She opened the door quietly. Maya was at her table. Amrita sat with her face sunk between her raised knees, rocking from side to side. Little bits of paper fluttered all around her in the light breeze of the fan. Kamala bent down and tapped Amrita on her shoulder.

"What's the matter? Why are you crying? Did she beat you?" she asked.

"I didn't touch her," Maya replied emphatically.

"Then what's wrong with her? Who tore her drawing book?"

At the steel in her mother's voice Maya looked down and busied herself with her books. Kamala stood behind her.

*Patience… patience… remember you were just priding yourself on having outgrown your anger.*

"Look at me," she insisted. "Who tore her book? She or you?"

Maya got up, throwing her books on the table. "It's not fair that she spends the whole day drawing and I have to do sums and English and Hindi and Science and Social Studies. It's simply not fair! I go to school and suffer and she has a nice time at home with you. She..."

"Stop it. I've told you a hundred times why she doesn't go to school and even then you can't understand? When will you grow up and learn to sympathise with her? You think only about yourself, you selfish girl."

Despite herself, Kamala's right hand rose threateningly.

"Go on, beat me. That's all you know. You don't understand my problems. All the time it is 'Amrita, Ammu, that poor girl....' You don't care for me at all."

"Your problems?"

"What's the point? You'll pretend to listen to me and then give me a long lecture about your darling daughter. I don't want to talk to you any more."

She ran out of the room and banged the door shut before Kamala could stop her but not before she saw the sudden eruption of tears in her daughter's eyes that the girl brushed away as she ran.

"Fine, one has stopped crying and the other has begun..."

"Appa ... appa..." she heard Maya shout downstairs.

She quickly closed the door, leaving Amrita inside and went down to open the gate for her husband.

***

# 7

Maya was at that age when she was easily provoked. She quietened her inflamed mind by using her sister as her punching bag. At nine, she was also wise enough to wait for the right time, when her mother was too busy with her chores to check on her daughters.

Sometimes Kamala was alerted by a noise or sheer instinct made her rush upstairs but more often, she only noticed the bruises when she bathed Amrita.

"Why do you take this nonsense from her? Beat her when she raises her hand. Like this... like this..." Kamala slapped her own cheeks till they burned.

The terrified girl crouched against the wall of the bathroom and covered her face.

"It's all right, Ammu, I was only showing you what to do when she misbehaves with you."

"I knew it. I knew you were fond of her and you hate me," Maya stood outside, arms akimbo and legs apart like a wrestler.

"Then why do you beat your sister? You know she has a problem. You should be treating her better," Kamala shouted back.

"You know only to blame me for everything. Why did you give birth to her? I would've been so much happier on my own."

"How can you be so cruel? She's just a little girl like you."

"Hey, I am not a little girl."

"Then don't behave like one. I'm tired of your tantrums. You trouble your sister. You trouble me. You don't study..."

"As if you're perfect," Maya retorted, stepping out of her mother's reach.

Kamala glanced at Amrita and controlled herself. The girl was chewing her lower lip and looking nervously from one to the other, dangerously close to tears.

"Go on, say it," Maya continued. "Say that I should be kind to your darling daughter. I won't. I don't like her. I don't want her."

"If you don't stop ill-treating your sister, I will tell your father..." Kamala threatened, looking over Amrita's head as she dried her hair.

"Tell him. He doesn't like her himself."

Kamala paused and turned towards her younger daughter. Without realising what she was doing, her hands tightened over Amrita's head making her wince.

"What do you mean?" she asked.

"You think I don't know anything but you are wrong. I know very well that appa hates her and, what's more, he hates you too."

"Rubbish."

"Don't think you can fool me. How often I have seen you pretend to read but actually you'd be crying and appa will not even look at you."

"What nonsense," Kamala tried to dismiss it off but her words flaked nervously. Her hands quivered as she dressed Amrita. It was nothing compared to the chaos within her. She had tried to keep her differences with Raghu away from Maya but it looked as if she had only been fooling herself all along. She glanced through her lashes at the girl waiting triumphantly for her to respond.

"Okay smarty, what more do you think you know?" she asked finally.

"Why should I tell you?"

"Fine," Kamala shrugged. "Keep your crazy ideas to yourself, I don't care. But let me tell you one thing and you'd better get this into your head. Next time I see you picking on your sister

I'll make sure that you don't ever do it again."

Her threat worked for two days.

It was Friday evening. Normally Maya would rush home to make every second of the weekend count. Even as she entered the house, she would pull off her shoes and throw them to a side. Her school bag would fly to another corner. She would quickly splash water on her face, gobble her food and run out. Kamala always wondered at the girl's haste, since she had no friends to play with. She sat alone on the gate most of the time and watched the deserted road. Sometimes she stood on the bottom rung and swung the gate to and fro. At other times she piled pebbles on the parapet wall and threw them, one after the other as if to see how far they fell. With unfailing regularity she raised her head and hooted with the not so distant whistle of the train, the 6.15 Express and 7 o'clock goods train. After that she came home as per her father's order.

That day, however, she stomped directly to her room. Kamala heard the school bag hit the ground over her head. She tensed at once but before she could speculate on what could have upset her, Maya came down and gulped her milk.

"I am not hungry," she said, wiping the milk moustache on the shoulder of her uniform and going out.

Kamala watched her silently.

*Am I losing the maternal instinct? I know something is troubling her. Why am I not trying to find out what it is? She'll snap my head off if I ask. Let her work it out on her own.*

Despite her resolution she went to the front yard and began to water the few surviving plants. The sun was firing one last burst before fading for the day. Normally she would have waited for it to go down completely before venturing into the garden. If Maya was aware of her mother's presence, she did not show it. She continued to sit on the wall, intently studying the patches of moss that had dried to a greenish black. She scraped little bits with her nails and flicked them into the air.

"When is appa returning from his tour?" she asked, at last.

"In another couple of days."

Kamala waited for Maya to say something more but the girl kept quiet.

"Is something wrong?"

"No."

"Okay."

"Can't you leave me alone? I came here to be by myself and you had to follow me."

"I came to water the plants," Kamala protested.

"Don't think you can fool me," she said, jumping off the wall and going back to the house.

Kamala did not dare to follow her inside. She continued to water the plants though her ears were cocked for the slightest sound from either girl. Sure enough, within five minutes she heard a muffled noise. She dropped the hose and rushed into the house, up the stairs.

Amrita was bunched like a ball but that didn't prevent her sister from kicking her. Through narrowed eyes Maya made sure that her aim was on target.

"Take that … that… and that…." she hissed, not realising that Kamala was rushing to her daughter's rescue.

"What are you doing?" Kamala pulled Maya away.

"I don't have to tell you."

Kamala felt as if somebody had clamped a rough hand over her throat. She spun the girl around to face her. She had never before felt such anger. Not in her younger days when her brothers teased her mercilessly; not at Raghu's indifference; not even when she caught Maya tormenting her sister as she felt now. It was as if the dam had burst and she could no longer restrain herself. She only knew that something had snapped inside and given her freedom – at last. She did not hear Maya's pleas. She did not see Amrita sit up and inch backwards till the wall stopped her, her eyes wide in fear. Kamala was only conscious of the fact that Maya was close to her, close enough to be punished for all her slights and stubbornness. She tightened her grip on the girl's arm and hit her, not bothering where her blows fell. She only stopped when she became aware of the throb in her hand and Maya's scream penetrated the veil that had blinded her. She released her with the suddenness of catching a rod and realising that it is red-hot.

Maya ran from the room but Kamala couldn't move. She leaned against the wall, weak with the ferocity of her anger. Yet, she forced herself to go to the window and see if Maya would run out of the house as she had threatened to do so often. There was no sign of the girl. Some of their neighbours were clearly curious about the commotion. They were talking among themselves and gesticulating towards the window.

She drew the curtain and slumped to the ground, completely drained in mind and body. She did not know for how long she sat there but Amrita was the first to recover. She slowly went to her mother and touched her shoulder hesitantly, not more than brushing her with the fingertips but it was enough to arouse Kamala.

She pulled Amrita towards her. Her breathing was still laboured but she could talk.

"I don't know what came over me. Did I frighten you, Ammu? I am so sorry. Now I must make peace with your sister and that's not going to be easy. Come, she must be downstairs."

She led her daughter down the steps, switching on the lights as she went till the house took on a festive look but Maya was nowhere to be found. She took a torch and went to the front yard. She peered among the trees and the shrubs, clutching the torch with both hands but that still didn't steady the patch of yellow light. Knowing her younger daughter's fondness for climbing trees, she shone the torch on the topmost branches. The black ibis that had made their home in the Ashoka tree protested at the intrusion. Maya had not disturbed their privacy and they were alone with their fledglings. The greenish yellow flowers of the mango trees promised a good crop but the girl was not hiding among them. A line of sweat beaded her face. She wiped it with the *pallu* of her sari. Once again her breathing was becoming erratic. Once again she could only blame Maya for this. Kamala forced herself to stay calm. Amrita was clinging to her and darting nervous looks everywhere. She had never come out at this time of the night and Kamala knew that everything must seem more menacing in the dark and so close by than when viewed from the window upstairs. However, she didn't want her daughter to stay alone inside the house even for a minute when she did not know where Maya had gone or how long it would take to get her back. She stood in the middle of the yard wondering what to do next.

"If I..." her voice seemed louder in the dark but it helped to comfort Amrita so she continued. "If I call the neighbours, they'll gossip more than be of actual help. What if they tell the whole locality about it? They could even tell Raghu! No, that won't do. Thank God, he's not in town. He'll tear me apart if he thinks that our neighbours were laughing at us. Could that girl have gone to Revabehn? What if she...?"

Suddenly she spied a small dark form outside the gate. The torchlight picked out Maya trying to hide in a shallow ditch. Kamala ran, dragging Amrita along. Her relief at locating her daughter was greater than her anger. She threw open the gate, reached into the ditch and grabbed Maya. She then stalked into the house holding on to her errant daughter while, on the other side, Amrita was finding it difficult to keep up with her mother's pace.

***

Kamala was caught in an impasse with Maya. If she showed her anger once again, the girl was likely to cause greater harm to her sister or to herself. Worse, Raghu might find out and blame her for it. She ground her teeth and held back the words that threatened to spurt out. Maya had found a chink in Kamala's armour though she took care to provoke her only when her father was away. In his presence she couldn't be better behaved. They were at this cat-and-mouse stage when Raghu's mother decided to visit them.

He went to the railway station to receive her while Kamala paused every so often in her work to listen for the car. At the least suspicion she ran to the front door and peered out. It was more than 12 years since she had met the old woman, not after Amrita's birth, and now the guilt of having avoided her for so long manifested itself dully in the pit of her stomach.

*But how could I have met her with such a child? What if she blames me? I wonder if she's come to stay with us forever or she'll leave after a few days.*

Kamala went to the gate and looked up the road. Maya watched curiously from her perch on the wall.

"You'd better go in and study. Appa will get angry if he sees you wasting your time," she warned her daughter.

"He'll shout at you too, for standing here."

"Don't be cheeky. I just wanted to see if he has come with your paati."

"I'll look out for them," offered Maya.

"Okay, since you're not doing anything useful anyway."

"Hey, I was only trying to help. You can open the gate yourself," Maya turned her head away. "I heard a whistle. It might have been paati's train. You stand here and wait for them."

"Don't get angry when they're about to come. It's not nice to greet somebody with a grouchy face."

Even as she was talking, the car stopped outside. Maya jumped down the wall and pushed the gates wide open. Raghu's mother got out, holding the top of the car for support with one hand, the other clutching a cloth bag. Kamala took it from the wrinkled hand with blue veins that criss-crossed in a throbbing maze.

"*Namaskaram*, amma. How are you? How was the journey? It has been a very long time since we met. You know our problem. It wasn't possible for me to visit you. I'm so glad you could come. I hope you'll be able to stay with us from now on. This is Maya. Amrita is inside. Please come. I'll bring your things in."

Her words were drowning in the trundle of wagons on the rail track.

"That's the 7 o'clock goods train. It always makes this racket when it is empty," Kamala shouted.

The old woman responded with a smile, shifted her hand from the top of the car to Maya's shoulder and walked slowly inside. The old woman and the girl were almost of the same height. Kamala remembered her mother-in-law as a reasonably tall woman but age had shrunk her and bent her back slightly, making her look like an old sparrow searching the ground for food.

*She hasn't lost that glint in her eyes though. Such sharp eyes! I had feared her tongue would be equally sharp but maybe I didn't spend enough time with her to feel its edge. I wonder if she's mellowed. Imagine spending so many years alone! How would I feel if Maya were to leave me one day and not bother about me at all? Come to think of it, she does resemble her grandmother a bit.*

Both had the same determination in their eyes, obstinate set of the chin and a certain assurance about them. Maya, however, had a definite lilt in her step whereas the older woman's walk showed the weight of age and experience.

Raghu began spending the evenings at home with his mother. They sat together on the swing while he told her about his work and his colleagues. She listened with an occasional nod or grunt but did not offer any comment. The moment Kamala finished supervising Maya's homework and came down, the old woman went upstairs to her granddaughters. Kamala followed her a couple of days out of curiosity but stood outside the door, hesitant to enter and give Maya an opportunity to snub her. The snatches of conversation she overheard did not reveal her daughter's disposition but Kamala did not want to tempt Maya's mercurial temper in front of the old woman.

"Paati, do you know how to read?" Kamala heard Maya ask her grandmother. "Did you ever go to school?"

"Only for two years but yes, I can read," the old woman replied.

"You are so lucky. I wish I could stop studying. Appa won't permit me to leave school."

"Of course not! My days were different. Girls either did not go to school at all or else they dropped out like me."

"Why? Didn't they want to study? Don't!" Maya caught the comb her grandmother was running through her hair. "It hurts."

"Okay, take off your hand. I can't help it. Look at the state of your hair. What were you saying?"

"About girls in your generation... whether they went to school."

"Some of them did. Others couldn't go against the wish of their parents."

"So you stayed at home like Amrita?"

Paati stopped combing and looked at her older granddaughter sitting quietly in her corner.

"I don't see you playing with your sister?"

"She's boring. Tell me, what did you do at home the whole day?"

"A lot of things ... stitching, cooking, cleaning the house, etc."

"You didn't have maids those days?"

"You ask too many questions. I did it to help my mother. Why don't you also do some work for your mother? That will make her happy."

"She has Revabehn. In any case, she's doesn't go to office so she has lots of time. She can get Amrita to help her if she wants. Are you through? I want to go out and play."

Maya ran out of the room. The old woman carefully rubbed her hand on the floor in widening circles to gather the fallen hair and rolled them into a small ball. She looked up and smiled at Kamala who took it as an invitation to enter the room.

"It is good you keep her hair short. When she is old enough to groom herself she can let it grow."

"But she's not happy about it," Kamala replied. "You should see the fuss she creates to get her hair cut. She wants long hair that she can tie into two plaits. She was the one who had wanted to get it cut but now she's changed her mind and her father supports her."

"What do men know of these things? Ignore him and do what you think is best."

Kamala would get used to her mother-in-law springing such surprises on her, like the time she gave her coffee in the traditional stainless steel tumbler.

"Do you mind pouring this into a china cup? I have always wanted to sip the coffee at least once in my life."

Kamala couldn't help smiling at the twinkle in the other woman's eyes but Raghu spluttered and spilt his coffee.

"What are you saying, amma? How often have you scolded me for letting the tumbler touch my lips? Unclean, non-Brahmin... what all you used to say!"

His mother smiled.

"In that house you don't do such things," she replied. "The ghosts of your ancestors would have been horrified. But this one doesn't have any past. You can start afresh, make your own practices, customs. I had always wanted to break some of them but didn't have the courage to do it, not in the house that had once belonged to your great grandfather, bestowed upon him by the Maharaja, no less."

"I never knew you would have such double standards too. I thought at least you were different from other women."

"We have as many standards as you men have, perhaps less. All sons think their mothers are unique. You are no different. What do you say, Kamala?" she asked.

Kamala would not take sides in a mother-son conflict. She had known even as a child that these foes could become friends at any moment and then she would have to fight a lonely battle against their united force.

"You weren't so quiet when you got married. Is anything wrong? Is Raghu ill-treating you?"

Before she could reply Raghu burst out.

"Why should I do such a thing? Even if I wanted to, I don't have the time. I've cut down my tours for your sake, amma, otherwise I'm out of town for nearly three weeks a month."

"That explains it. She's got too used to staying alone. When you retire and spend the rest of your life with your family you will both find it difficult to adjust to each other."

"Did she complain to you already? You women…"

"She didn't say anything. Can't I see for myself?"

It made Kamala feel as if a camera was following her around, recording her every move. She tried to appear cheerful but Raghu was the better actor. He became the loving father, coming home directly from office, bringing sweets sometimes and even trying to teach Maya her lessons. His efforts were too late. She failed to clear her exam, the only one in her class to repeat the year. While his mother watched, Raghu dropped his mask of cordiality and slapped his daughter.

"Look at this! Just look at these marks – in 30s and 40s! What were you doing in the class? Dreaming?"

"She is just a young girl…" his mother protested.

"Amma, don't interfere. Please. She thinks I don't know anything about what's happening at home. She's getting uncontrollable and her mother just doesn't bother to correct her. Do you people expect me to stay at home and manage your affairs as well? Isn't it enough that I slog day and night for you? What more do you want?"

His glance shot across the room to include Kamala.

"I work like a slave and what do I get in return…this? Get your mother to sign your card. You can also tell her to pay the fees from now on."

Maya's tears dripped on her feet but did not move Raghu. His mother was still bound by his injunction and Kamala stood watching her little family.

"Why are you standing like a statue? Go to your room. Go and do something," he shouted, sending Maya scuttling for cover.

She paused at the first step and looked up the stairs, then changed her mind and went into the back yard. It bore signs of Kamala's attempt to grow a kitchen garden despite the fierce sun that had hardened the ground. She walked around the yard once and returned to sit on the doorstep drooping like a limp plant herself. Kamala sat beside her.

"I don't want to talk to you … or to anybody."

"Oh, I'm not planning to sit here for too long. Did I tell you that your uncle, my youngest brother failed once in school?"

"Hmm…"

"He was so upset. He cried and cried till the tip of his nose turned red. He was very fair, not like me. Not like you either. You know how to take things in your stride."

"But appa says he won't send me to school…"

"He didn't mean it. When he calms down he'll feel very sorry about what he said."

"What if he doesn't?"

"He can't keep you at home. All children must go to school, that's the law."

"Amrita doesn't. Revabehn's don't. They stay at home, they go to work or play the whole day."

"They are different. They don't listen to their mother or father. They are naughty but you are not. I want you to study well, get a good job like appa and earn a lot of money."

"My friends played with me all the time and now they have passed and I have failed..." Maya bit her lips.

Kamala put her hand over the girl's shoulders.

"You'll forget them in no time. Make the most of your vacation, study well and you'll be 1st in your class."

"They... they...will..." the words dissolved in more tears. Maya gave up pretending to be composed. Revabehn came towards them but Kamala waved her away.

"I can't make out what you are saying," she said, bending towards her daughter.

"My friends will make fun of me. So will the other children."

"They'll stop it after a while."

"But I won't be able to bear it even for a moment!" she wailed.

"Shall I meet your teachers and talk to them?"

"No!" Maya screamed. "You won't meet anyone. You won't talk to anyone."

"Okay, okay, relax..."

"I have a better idea," said her grandmother standing behind them.

Kamala got up immediately.

"My idea is this…" paati squeezed herself on the step beside Maya. Kamala shifted to a lower step.

"Why don't you come away with me?" paati asked. "To our village? You can study in the local school. You'll like it there. Lots of trees, other children, fresh air…."

Maya's eyes widened with mounting excitement.

"Ooh… can I?" Her face fell immediately. "But appa won't let me. He's very angry with me."

"I'll tell him, don't worry," assured the old woman.

Maya brightened once again.

"Are there many children there? Will they play with me or will they make fun of me like those in school?"

"Why should anybody tease you?" asked paati.

"Because of Amrita. They say I'm also mad like her."

"They are the ones who are mad if that's what they think. Anyway, don't bother about them. No one will talk like this in the village."

"Your son will get furious if he knows that you want to go back," Kamala said, before her daughter could burst out in her excitement.

"I came only because I wanted to see you and the girls. I had told him so often to bring you over but he never did. Therefore I decided to visit you at least once before it's too late."

"But it's not fair to burden you with Maya…"

"I'm not a 'burden'. If paati thinks it's fine with her, what's your problem?"

Kamala tried to ignore Maya but her voice was no match for her daughter's high pitch.

"You and appa are the ones who think I'm a burden. Appa's not too bad. You've never liked me…"

"Now look here, Maya. If you want to come with me, you'd better learn how to behave and talk to elders. I will not tolerate this kind of behaviour."

Maya was silenced immediately and the old woman turned to Kamala once again.

"I'll tackle him. It's not as if I'm leaving in a day or two. I'll write to my neighbour to arrange for her admission in the school. He's the headmaster so there shouldn't be any problem. As for you, Maya, if you don't study well … I can be a lot more severe than your father. Now go and play before it becomes too dark."

The girl nodded happily and skipped away.

"Don't worry about her. She'll be all right. Don't think that you are imposing her on me. I'm the one who suggested this and I know very well what I am doing. I have enough people there to help me."

"What will her father say to this?" Kamala's face reflected her worry.

"I told you, I'll tackle him. Now, you listen to me," said the old woman capturing her attention.

"I'm taking her with me so that you can devote your time and attention on Ammu. She needs you more than Maya does."

Kamala's eyes glistened. She did not dare to look up at her mother-in-law.

"And now about Raghu. I can see that all's not well between you and him. You will have to look after Ammu till the very end. You can't do it on your own. Make peace with him before it's too late."

Kamala was grateful for the deepening twilight that swept past them, casting a shadow on her face as it entered the house. Behind her, Raghu was also sitting in the dark, too angry to switch on the light.

"You two are still here? How long will you talk? What's so interesting?" Maya asked, running towards them.

"We were only waiting for you, child," paati said, getting up stiffly.

Before Kamala could reach out to help her, the old woman had entered the house.

***

# 8

I haven't had a good night's sleep for the last three days. Not since Kamala auntie began telling me about her family. Even now, in my restlessness I crept about downstairs. There she was, on the couch in the living room, emitting little whistles and snorts in her sleep. How can she drop off like this? Doesn't the past weigh her down? It's certainly shattering me, all of me, inside and out. The only positive outcome of her narration is that my own problem is losing its bite. What's so terrible about illegitimacy? There are greater issues at stake here. In my self-absorption I had overlooked them.

If Kittu's brothers and their wives hadn't walked out so soon after his wedding would things have been different for amma? Wouldn't she have become frustrated and warped like Kamala auntie when they have so many things in common between them? Both were in a sham of a marriage, with incompatible spouses yet neither of them wanted to break up the relationship. Their men were alike too. Neither Raghu nor Kittu could face reality. Kittu simply escaped into his younger days when money had not been important, when he could lose himself in his poetry, music and dance without anyone hauling him back into the real world. The escapist that he was, the high point of his life was when he acted as Prof. Higgins in *My Fair Lady*. The curtain had fallen that evening with the audience giving him a standing ovation. Unfortunately this was in his last year at college and he never got another opportunity to don greasepaint or stand in the wings and wait for his cue. He had told me this a hundred times, reinforcing his narration with a photograph. His face stylishly slanted was framed by a halo of studio light. The calmness in his eyes belied his age; he must have been in his late teens then. Even as a child I knew it was a calmness that was innate to him. To look older he had sported a thin Clark Gable moustache and round rimmed glasses. His brilliantined hair parted in the middle was slick and smooth. His black coat and light coloured shirt were typical of a monochrome print. Indeed, he saw the world only in these two colours.

Raghu, it seemed, had a third colour on his palette – grey. This helped him cope with the bleakness in his life. When amma was lost to him, he had married on the rebound and regretted it. To give him credit, he didn't desert his wife. Only traced his old love and went to her. Of course, amma did say that he had visited her only once. Should I believe her? I don't remember seeing him in our house. In fact, nobody ever visited us, other than Sundar's and my friends. Kittu didn't have any. Amma said she didn't want any. Why? Because she couldn't forget Raghu? After all, a woman's first love is also supposed to be her last. Where did that leave Kittu? Did amma stay with him only because Raghu wouldn't abandon his wife? Then she had been a better actor than Raghu. How often had I seen little scenes of affection between Kittu and amma! Their love for each other and for us, Sundar and me, was the bulwark in my childhood. I had known nothing could happen to me as long as I had amma and Kittu with me. Maybe that was why Maya was so difficult. Because Raghu and Kamala auntie were strangers living under the same roof.

"Was Maya happier after she went to her grandmother's?" I asked Kamala auntie the next morning while she was doing her household chores. She wouldn't let me help her. So I hovered around, following her from one room to another while she swept, hopping onto the nearest piece of furniture every time her broom swished near my feet.

"I don't know. She didn't tell me anything about her stay there," she replied.

"Oh! How were things between you and your husband? Surely they must have improved when Maya left with her grandmother?"

Kamala auntie filled a stained plastic bucket with water, added a few drops of cleaning liquid and carried it to the front room.

She dipped the mopping cloth into the bucket, squeezed out the excess water and began to clean the floor. I wondered if she heard my question. Her forehead was creased and she looked thoughtful. I waited. She finished mopping, rinsed the cloth and put it to dry, washed her hands and sat down beside me.

"It no longer mattered whether Maya was with us or not," said Kamala auntie with a resigned half-smile.

"You mean nothing changed? Nothing at all?" I asked.

"It was too late for anything to change," she said. "I didn't know that when he asked me to go with him to his boss's house. That was the first time in years that he was asking me to go with him anywhere. I was thrilled. I took it as a good omen, that our relationship would improve with this outing."

"So, this is Mrs. Raghavan," boomed Mr. Mehta, towering over Kamala. "You kept her under wraps all this time, didn't you, Raghu? You know, Madam," he turned to Kamala. "If I hadn't threatened your husband with a transfer to Timbuctoo he wouldn't have brought you over today either. You owe me something for this but don't worry. I'm a man of my word but I shall not insist the same of the lady. I must say Raghu is very lucky to have such an understanding wife. You could teach my little woman something."

"On the contrary, I'm the one who has a lot to teach her. My first lesson will be on how to stand up for your rights." Mrs. Mehta matched her husband vocally, if not in height.

The others started walking towards them, smiling and ready to take part in the conversation. Kamala felt the door of her cage closing slowly.

"It is not that I didn't want to bring her along," Raghu replied. "But something or the other always cropped up and she had to stay behind. Moreover, she's not too keen on attending parties."

Mrs. Mehta looked shocked.

"But it's good to meet others, exchange ideas with them. Very good 'timepass'," she said, shaking a stubby finger at Kamala. Her gold bangles caught the slanting light from a window and threw countless yellow specks on the wall. She spoke with her body as well. Her ample frame wriggled, sending her heavy breasts into a wild wobble.

Kamala hid her smile and looked away. Her eyes landed on the softness of Mrs. Mehta's sagging arm, on the coin sized vaccination mark that had not faded despite the many years. She sensed an expectant pause in the conversation and brought her attention back to her hostess. Too late. Some reply was needed at this point but she had not heard the question! Raghu came to her rescue.

"She keeps herself very busy..."

"Oh, I didn't know you were employed. Where are you working?"

"No, no, she's not employed. She's only a housewife," Raghu explained hastily.

"Ah, that's what I thought," said Mrs. Mehta. "But Raghu, I could pick up a fight with you for saying 'only a housewife'. I shall wait till we are alone. It's not good to lose face in front of your wife. Kamala, don't let him trample over you. You should join our kitty group and learn how to stand up for yourself. Almost all the wives of Gujtronics are members. We meet once a month in the house of one of the members, in turn. We don't pile on one person all the time. It is very impartially done, by drawing chits and..."

"Hey! No kitty talk at least here or should I say catty talk?" her husband protested laughing. "Isn't it enough that you keep telling us about your last meeting till it's time for the next one?"

"These men!" his wife retorted. "They don't want to hear anything of what we do. They think we meet only to gossip. When we talk, it is gossip but when they do the same, it is 'sharing information'. How hypocritical can you get? What do you think, Kamala?"

Kamala played safe by nodding her head.

"You are a very quiet person, aren't you? After just a couple of meetings, I promise you will not be able to stop talking," assured Mrs. Mehta.

"Now, don't you spoil her," her husband intervened. "Let there be at least one woman in the entire world who keeps her trap shut. Ma'am, you have my blessings. Continue the way you are. I envy Raghu. 'A silent wife is a gift of the Lord,' says the Good Book. Just think of my plight – my little woman is the founder of this kitty group and doesn't miss a single meeting. Morning till night she goes yak, yak… or rather, miaow, miaow…Come, Madame Cat, let's greet the other guests."

He led his wife away and the circle round them broke up. Kamala stole a look at Raghu. His disapproval hit her in waves. She knew he wanted her to talk smartly, smile confidently and pretend that she was used to such parties. She looked around hesitantly at the few who still stood near them in twos and threes. Attention was no longer on her. Soon she was standing alone, watching the guests, most of whom were adults though there were also a few children. She wondered how Revabehn was managing Amrita.

*Of course, anyone can look after her. How lively these children are … just like Maya. I do hope she's not giving her grandmother a difficult time.*

A sudden jolt on her back startled her into the present. She turned around. A small boy knelt behind her looking at his upturned plate and scattered food. Water from a Styrofoam cup flowed towards her feet. She took a quick step behind, holding her sari out of the way. A clearing formed around them as if by magic. The boy stared up at her with large frightened eyes.

She smiled at him. "It's all right. Here, I'll help you."

Kamala bent to pick up the plate even as the boy's mother hurried towards them.

"I'm so sorry! Rahul, how many times have I told you not to

run around with your plate? I should have left you at home with your naughty sister."

Rahul's eyes filled at the barrage of rebukes. Kamala wanted to comfort him. She was rusty and self-conscious. Maya had never liked anyone hugging her while Ammu did not respond to any gesture of affection. She watched the woman pick up the plate and hustle the boy away. They were soon lost in the crowd surrounding the buffet tables.

"Can't you even make an attempt to talk to somebody or help yourself to the food? Do you expect to be served or what? Standing like a boulder in the middle of an eddy…" Raghu's lips stretched in a reluctant smile while he growled in an undertone.

Before she could think of a response, he ordered her to follow him and led her to the buffet counters.

Kamala didn't know where to start. Not only were the dishes many but they were totally different from the south Indian cuisine that she was used to. She turned around to Raghu for help but he had joined others at the far end of the room.

"What do I do now?" she muttered.

"Can I help?" asked a bright voice from behind her.

Kamala looked into a vaguely familiar face.

"I'm Rahul's mother, remember? That boy who bumped into you and almost spoilt your sari?"

"Of course. He was just excited by the crowd..."

"You're too kind," she said, handing Kamala a plate. "He's one of those hyperactive brats, always on the move. Just see, I'd warned him to stay close to me and he's vanished again. I'll know soon enough where he is when I hear a plate crash, so I've decided to enjoy myself. After all, that's what his father has been doing ever since we came here."

Kamala held the plate in front of her like a shield, dazed by the other woman's rapid-fire talk.

"Stop me if you think I'm going on and on. Tell me, would you like any help?"

"I was just wondering if the food was vegetarian. I don't eat..."

"All these are pure vegetarian, authentic Gujarati. We cannot match your *madrasi idli* and *dosa* but we are not too bad either. Here, this is *dhokla*, somewhat like your *idli*. This is *kandvi*. Have some *patra wadi* and this..." Rahul's mother rattled the names while heaping both their plates. They sounded as exotic as the dishes themselves and Kamala gave up trying to remember them. It was enough for her that she need not be concerned about their ingredients.

*Maya would have liked this food.*

"Everything all right?" asked her new friend.

Kamala nodded.

Rahul's mother was younger than her, slimmer and fairer. She wore a dark blue *salwar kameez* and long silver earrings that danced merrily. Her fingers drew designs in the air with or without food, since she talked as much and as quickly as she ate.

"Are you coming here for the first time?" she asked.

"Yes, you?"

"I'm a regular. I only have to get the invitation and vroom…."

She came closer to Kamala and whispered, "You know something? Most of the people are here only for the fantastic food. I wouldn't be surprised if they had starved the whole day. That's what I'd have done myself if I didn't have to cook for my two children and diet-conscious hubby. Honestly, if it weren't for the food I wouldn't come either. Mind you, food's only my second passion. Give me money, oodles of it, and let me loose in the market … ah, nothing like it! You know what they say 'Shop till you drop?' That's for me."

She continued before Kamala could reply.

"That's also the only time when I satisfy myself with a quick bite, otherwise I tuck in heartily. My only prayer is that I should be able to eat like this to the end of my life without having to worry about BP or sugar or of course, bulging in the wrong places."

"You don't have to worry about that now," Kamala commented. "Your fondness for food certainly doesn't show on you."

"That's my family trait. Lean on both sides. 'Half-starved' my husband calls us. Who cares? At least we can eat, not like his people. The moment they see food, they bloat! You're not bad either. Healthy, not fat."

Kamala smiled.

"You have kids?" asked Rahul's mother and once again did not wait for a reply. "How our life changes then, eh? The best period of a woman's life is before she gets married. After that it is a never-ending trial of adjustment. First with your husband and then with your children. You can forget about yourself till it's time for them to leave the nest and you're alone with the old man once more. By then, who'll have the strength to do anything interesting? Are you on a diet or something? You're nibbling your food."

Kamala couldn't decide whether she liked the oily sweetness, so different from the sour pungency of her cuisine.

*There's always curd rice at home. I wonder if Raghu likes this food. He must be used to it since he attends so many parties.*

"This is *Shrikhand*, our speciality. No Gujarati feast is complete without it. Here, have some," said Rahul's mother, heaping a dollop on Kamala's plate before she could protest.

Kamala licked the tip of her spoon. The sweet-sour dish tickled her taste buds and saliva gushed in her mouth.

"I knew you would like it," the young woman said triumphantly. "This is my favourite too. It's not difficult to make at home but who'll bother? I prefer to buy it from Dhanshakbhai or Yogeshbhai on M.G. Road. Nothing much to it really – just curd, sugar, *elaichi* and lots of arm power. The last, I can't spare. Rahul is not my only child, you know. I have a daughter, Revathi. She's younger to him by nearly two years and worse than he is. I leave her with the *ayah* most of the time. My son is naughty but Revathi makes an angel of him. Just look at him! Rahul, come here…"

Seeing his mother rush towards him, the little boy took flight. He pushed his way through the legs of guests to the centre of a large crowd.

Kamala smiled to herself. *He knows she can't do anything to him when others are around. He reminds me of Maya, the same exuberance, the same vitality. It's got to do with that age of innocence, I suppose.*

The rush around the tables had thinned considerably. The serving bowls and platters with drying lines of food on their sides looked like tired soldiers, eager to retire. It was getting late but where was Raghu? Even as she looked around, he came beside her.

"Ready to leave? You must be. After all, you have hardly spoken to anyone. At least have the courtesy to thank our hosts. I don't want them to think that my wife lacks manners as well."

With every step she took behind him, the heaviness in her stomach increased. She geared herself for an onslaught of accusations. Yet, curiously, she was also looking forward to it, as a challenge to her endurance.

*However provocative he is, I'm not going to retaliate.*

Raghu manoeuvred the car out of the compound, smiling and waving to others as they went past. Kamala's smile was pasted on her face and she remembered to wipe it off as soon as they were out of sight.

She looked at him from the corner of her eye. His face could have been carved of marble, so pale and stern did he look under the fleeting bluish-white lights on the road. Soon, they came to the long straight stretch leading to their house. She wondered if he was going to say anything at all. That would be a let down.

*Now he won't have much time to…*

"Have you swallowed your tongue?" he asked, startling her. "Nothing to say about the evening? What will you have to say, anyway? You did the dumb act so well! What must everyone think of you? That woman whom you did talk to, do you know her name?"

'Know' – that's what the young woman used so frequently while talking to her but she did not tell Kamala who she was nor gave her an opportunity to ask.

Raghu snorted. "Just as I thought! You didn't find out. She is Mrs. Jain, the wife of one of our leading distributors. A dynamic woman. Typical of her to realise that you were a wallflower and make you feel at ease. You could learn a great deal from a person like her."

*To shop?*

"Her husband is good only at his work. He's quite a dud otherwise. In fact, sometimes I wonder whether she helps him out. How else could he bag so many orders? He stammers even while talking to us. How can he do so well with total strangers? But his wife… what a woman!"

Kamala realised that he was talking more to himself than to

her and kept quiet. A little twinge of something pricked her.

"They have two children. Like us. Very smart kids. Like the mother."

Raghu glanced quickly at Kamala but she kept her eyes fixed on the road. They were approaching the house. In another five minutes they would be lost in its confines, within the walls of their minds.

"Do you realise we could have kept Maya with us? The other girl I can understand but Maya? She could have been a different girl. It's all in the upbringing. If only you'd been able to bring her up properly, taught her some decent behaviour, instead of letting her grow up like a *junglee*."

The twinge became a stab.

"Am I the only one responsible for her 'upbringing'? What makes you think I didn't do my best?" Kamala didn't want to shout but that was how the words came out.

"Don't be hysterical. It's night. People will wonder what's happening," Raghu warned.

"I don't care what anyone thinks. Come on, answer me... how can you accuse me of being indifferent to our children? Remember those days when you blamed me for spending too much time with Amrita?"

Kamala could now control the decibel but not quite her breathing. It caused the words to collide and tumble, in their haste to be heard. She didn't want to carry the battle into the house, where Revabehn would be an interested spectator.

"What did you achieve in all this time? The girl's exactly the same as before. A school might have been able to do something..."

"Ha, don't we know that! What happened at that special school to which we had sent her? Almost at once we heard about the goings-on there and had to take her out. God knows what would have happened if she had continued there any longer."

"There must be another school that's better run."

"Why don't you find out?"

"That's not my job."

"Then I'll have to start a school myself..."

"You? You can't manage your own child. Worse, you only know how to spoil a normal child. If Maya is with my mother today, you are to be blamed."

"I never wanted her to go. She would have settled down with time..."

"Nonsense. You don't want to admit that you failed with her just as you failed with the other one. I suppose you are happy now."

He screeched to a halt outside the gate. Kamala got out of the car quickly. She didn't want to spend another minute with him in the enclosed space. Raghu parked the car and went into the house while she closed the gate and followed him slowly inside.

Despite her anger, she had to admit that Raghu was right about one thing. She had failed with Amrita. She no longer liked to spend time with her as she had done in the past.

*She's just the same as before ... then I must have changed. What's the point in trying to teach her anything? My early attempts have all failed completely. Those were when she was still a baby and could have been moulded but now she has crossed 12. I can't work miracles. It's up to the Almighty to do what He wills. After all, we are only His pawns. I can only rue my fate and look after her till I die. After that....?*

Kamala sat on the swing, forcing her mind not to think any further. Revabehn and Amrita came from the back of the house and stood outside the window.

"Here," said the maid, handing Amrita a broom. "I don't want a single leaf flying around."

She then sat on the doorstep and took out her little packet of tobacco. She thrust a wad into her mouth. Kamala winced. She had told Revabehn so many times to give up tobacco but the woman did not heed her. Neither would she keep Amrita within the house.

*Why can't she keep the girl out of sight of strangers, especially in the evening when it is time for people to return to their homes? And how many times am I to tell her not to pass on her work to Amrita?*

"Revabehn..." she called. "At this rate, I'll have to pay her, not you!"

"Not a bad idea. I can retire at last."

"How can you talk of retirement? You know I need you."

"So do my children but am I with them? I am here all the time, with this little one. Not that I'm complaining but for how long? I'm not growing any younger and my bones ache so badly at the end of the day."

Kamala changed the topic quickly. "Did you drink the tea I had kept for you?" she asked. "It must have gone cold by now. Go, I will look after her till you return."

The maid stood up slowly, her hand supporting her back. "*Bitiya*, finish this place before I come, okay?"

Amrita waited till the woman entered the house. She then threw the broom down and followed her inside.

"What's it, Ammu? You are not feeling well? Here, let me see..." Kamala felt her daughter's forehead. It was sticky with sweat. Amrita sat beside her on the swing.

"No fever. You are all right. Go. Finish sweeping. Look, the wind is scattering the leaves all over the place. If you are given some task you must finish it or else, Revabehn will get angry with you."

Amrita kicked the ground with her feet and the swing jerked back and forth.

"Not so fast. I feel queasy," Kamala protested, but Amrita swung even faster, her hair flying with the breeze.

Kamala shot her feet out and they dragged on the ground as she tried to bring the swing to a standstill. Since she was sitting at one end, the wooden plank swayed madly for a while before coming to a stop.

She turned to her daughter. "I told you not to do it, didn't I? What's the matter with you? Can't you understand a simple instruction?"

Amrita stared at the floor and tried to push the swing once again. Her mother's feet were anchored to the ground and she could only sway her side of the plank.

"You obstinate girl! I told you not to do it!" Kamala slapped Amrita sharply across the cheek just as Revabehn entered the room.

"What's the matter, *behn*? What did she do?" she asked, hugging the girl to her chest.

"Such disobedience! I told her not to push the swing so fast and she won't listen..."

"She's not quite herself today. Something's wrong with her."

"Rubbish. It is all your doing. If you didn't indulge her so much she wouldn't have tried to act smart with me."

"Okay, okay, blame me for everything. After all, I'm the one who's always with her."

Kamala calmed down quickly.

"Take her upstairs. Enough of her roaming around the house."

Revabehn hustled the girl upstairs, clucking and tut-tutting all the way.

***

# 9

At that early hour Kamala was not conscious of the telephone ringing. The 'tring… tring…' forced its way into her sleep and blended with her dream.

*The milkman's cycle bell sounds just like a telephone. No, that's the ice-candy man. Amma, I want ice-candy. Please, amma.*

'Tring…'

*She licked the pink coloured ice stick in quick strokes before the heat could do its bit. It was a narrow finish. Long streaks of pink ran down her blouse.*

'Tring…'

*It was her youngest brother Sridhar. He had just learnt cycling and was showing off. She jumped out of the way even as he rang the bell stridently and laughed at her annoyance.*

'Tring…'

"Hello?"

Sridhar became Raghu and Kamala's sleep was immediately disturbed. Her eyes refused to open, however, and she continued to lie in bed, listening. He was either talking nonsense or in some foreign language, she decided sleepily. It was tempting to shut her eyes once again and dream of her cherished brother rather than awake to the reality of a hostile husband. She forced herself to lift her head and look at him. Through the chink of her eyes she saw his back turned to her.

*Who on earth is calling him at this time?*

The clouds of sleep lifted at once and Raghu's gibberish unscrambled into distinct everyday words.

"How is she now? Okay, I'll reach as soon as I can. I'll leave today morning. No…no, I will come."

He replaced the telephone on its stand. By then she was standing behind him.

"Who was that?" she asked.

"Amma is serious. I must go to her."

"Shall I come with you?"

"How can you? Who will look after Amrita?"

"Revabehn…"

"There's no time to fetch her. I must leave as soon as I can. I'll take the morning flight to Bombay and then go from there somehow."

Raghu looked distractedly at the clock.

"I should get the ticket first. What time will the airlines office open? I'll ring them up now. Maybe they have a round-the-clock counter. I must be on the earliest flight. Money… I'll have to stop at the ATM. I hope she's all right…"

Kamala had no words to comfort him. She watched quietly as he packed his bag hurriedly and left the house.

He did not call her after reaching home. She hung around the telephone the whole day taking calls from his office. The second day drew to a close as well without any news from him. That evening she telephoned and learnt from a neighbour that Raghu's mother had passed away soon after his arrival. Maya was so shattered by her grandmother's demise that she had confined herself to her room. Raghu brought her home a fortnight later.

It had been three years since Maya had left home. She was nearly 13 years old, still a skinny, flat child all arms and legs topped by a large head. Only her eyes had changed. They used to flit restlessly earlier but now there was a depth in them that made her seem older than her years. Kamala bustled around Raghu and Maya, changing expressions like a chameleon, at once condoling with him and welcoming Maya back home. She tried not to show her happiness too much but couldn't help thinking that the house would now come to life with the return of her younger daughter. She wanted to hug her, flood her with questions, make her favourite dishes, treat her like a star but the little girl who had romped all over the house, scattered her things everywhere, talked and argued constantly had gone. In her place was a composed young lady who entered the house without any fanfare as if she had left it just that morning.

Raghu offered to help Maya carry her bag upstairs. She preferred to do it herself. They stood silently as she lifted the large suitcase off the ground with both hands and thrust a knee forward to rest it on a step. Step by slow step she took her bag upstairs. As if the curtain had fallen at the end of the show, Kamala went to the kitchen. Raghu hesitated, then followed her. Standing by the door he watched her keep a saucepan on the stove. She had not noticed him following her and was so startled when he spoke that she dropped the gas lighter.

"Maya is still upset about what happened," he said. "Leave her alone for some time but keep an eye on her as well. She did not speak more than a couple of sentences to me on our way back. Those were only about her sister. I hope she'll adjust well with us. After all, she's been staying with amma for a long time. The neighbours were all praise of her. It seems amma had been bedridden for more than a year and Maya had looked after her better than anyone else could have. She had taken her to the doctor, got medicines, and managed the house and her studies as well. She would not let anyone tell me about amma's ill health. It was only when they realised that nothing more could be done for her that they decided to call me. I wouldn't have believed any of this if the doctor himself hadn't praised Maya so much. He said that if it hadn't been for her, amma would have gone long ago."

Kamala stood like a statue, the gas lighter still at her feet. She bent down to pick it. Raghu talking to her so normally was as astounding as what he had to say about Maya.

"Don't pester her for anything," he continued. "We'll give her time to settle down and then send her back to school. She has not done too well this year ... not that I'm blaming her for it. She was busy tending to her grandmother but we must think about her future now."

He left the kitchen but Kamala was still rooted with the lighter in her hand.

*'We'... he had used the word 'we'!*

She turned around joyously and began to boil the milk, the tiny word reverberating in her mind like a boy newly learned to whistle. Her excitement lasted for a week. It was not very difficult to 'leave Maya alone' since most of the time she confined herself to her room upstairs with her sister, coming down only at meal times to take food for both of them. On the first day Raghu asked her to join him but she refused. She did not attempt to talk to her parents though she had a lot to say to Revabehn.

"*Kem cho*, Revabehn? You look so frail. You have become so old!"

"You have grown too, *bitiya*. You are no longer that little brat who made my life so miserable," the maid retaliated. Her wide smile exposed the dark gums and bits of teeth that had survived the tobacco.

"Yes, how I used to trouble you. But that's because I was very young at that time and did not know better," Maya protested with an embarrassed laugh.

"*Arrey chokri*, at every stage people trouble others for one reason or the other. You harassed us with your pranks when you were young. You are not much older now. God knows what you will be up to. When you grow some more you will trouble your parents to marry a rich, handsome young man. Then you will shift your attention to that poor fellow and later to your children and then their children…"

"Is that what you do now? Trouble your little grandchildren?"

"Little? They are old enough to have children of their own. Shanti, the one who looked after you as a baby has three children. Her husband is no good though. Most of the time he is drunk. Just the other day…"

Kamala put an end to the maid's recital. "Are you going to spend the whole morning boring her like this or are you going to do some work as well? There will be a big pile of clothes to wash, *Sa'ab's* and…"

"Revabehn, I'll wash my clothes myself," Maya interjected.

"You don't think I will wash them well or what?" the old woman's face crumpled into deep wrinkles.

"No, no! It's just that I've got used to it. Paati used to insist that I take care of my things myself. At first I protested about this and on some days I just left them in the bathroom but when I saw her washing my clothes along with hers I began to do it myself."

Revabehn and Kamala did not look at each other. This was the girl who used to leave her clothes in a wet heap on the bathroom floor?

"*Chalo*, at least you have learnt something good. What else did your grandmother teach you?"

"Lots more than you or anyone else could have taught me."

"Good, you can teach some of those lessons to your sister."

"Of course! Now that I've come back I'll take over. You've been very patient with her all these years and now it's my turn."

"*Chalo,* I can die in peace."

"Don't talk of dying. I need your help for some time at least."

"Your mother can help you…"

"Not like you will be able to. Stay alive till I get used to the things here,"

"*Arrey bitiya*, life and death…" Revabehn began, but Kamala turned away abruptly and went inside.

If Maya sensed her mother's displeasure she did not show it. She chatted with the maid for a while longer before going upstairs.

Kamala could hear this conversation since it took place just outside the door but not when Maya talked to her sister in their room upstairs. She itched to find out what she had to tell Amrita. Sometimes she stood at the foot of the staircase and tried to listen as she had done in the past. At first her heart pounded and made it difficult to hear any other sound. She climbed up a couple of steps and stopped. That was close enough to hear Maya's steady drone and Amrita's occasional chuckle and far enough to make a quick exit if anyone came that way. Even from these snatches she realised that Maya may not have changed physically but she certainly had towards her sister.

"Amazing! I never thought Maya would change so much and just look at her. Did you ever think the girl would quieten down like this?" she asked the maid, under the cover of running water and clanging vessels.

"The old woman had nothing else to do in the village."

"You can be vicious. Let's give her credit. She has changed Maya beyond recognition. Much more than I could and how much I tried."

"It is still too early to say anything. You know how my husband vanishes occasionally? Whenever he returns just as suddenly, this is how he behaves, a picture of concern and good behaviour. He becomes a perfect man and father. After a few days, it is back to the drinking, beating and bad mouthing. Sometimes I wish he would just go away and never come back!" Revabehn plonked an iron frying pan on the kitchen ledge.

*Any other metal would have cracked under the impact. I'd better distract her.*

"Did you eat anything in the morning? Here, have something first before you begin your work," Kamala said.

Revabehn hadn't finished though. She waved the food aside and thrust tobacco in her mouth instead.

"Mark my words," she champed her warning. "She may seem to have improved her ways but it won't last long. I only hope she doesn't start behaving as she used to. She's bigger now than my *bitiya* and I don't want my baby to get hurt."

Revabehn was wrong. Kamala could not decide if Maya was only trying to make up to Amrita for the way she used to ill-treat her or because she genuinely loved her sister. Whatever the reason there was no denying that she took custody of Amrita from the day she arrived. She relieved both Revabehn and Kamala of their responsibilities. The maid, who used to spend almost the whole day with the girl, now had the time to massage the varicose veins in her legs and tell Kamala about what was happening in the neighbourhood. Her domestic chores had reduced to a minimum since Amrita did the rest under Maya's supervision. Neither girl entered Kamala's domain, the kitchen. It was here that she had once worried and cried over Raghu's indifference and now she could marvel at the change in her daughter and ponder about their relationship. However, towards Maya she felt only anger, not the helpless dependence that she felt with Raghu.

*What does she think of herself? Am I not her mother? How can she treat me as if... as if I don't exist? Where would she be without me?*

Her questions merged with images of Maya's younger days and Kamala's anger often changed to remorse only to swing back again.

*If she hadn't gone away from me I would have been able to explain things to her. A daughter is supposed to be her mother's friend. God knows I need one. Why doesn't she understand my plight? She has inherited Raghu's indifference. Why else would she behave like this? I've done her no harm. Thank God, she's considerate to her sister though.*

She could criticise or justify Maya's attitude but the wound within her continued to fester. One day she followed Maya upstairs and opened the door that the girl had closed behind her.

"I want to talk to you."

Maya looked at her mother indifferently and went to stand beside her sister.

"Are you listening?" Kamala asked.

"I'm not deaf."

"What's the matter with you? Why are you behaving like this? As if you hate me? Did your paati say..."

"Don't involve paati in this! I'm not a child to be told anything by anyone. You think I don't know why you drove me away from the house? It's because you hate me, you hate both of us," she threw a hand protectively around her sister. "You don't want to have anything to do with us. That's why you sent me away and you've neglected her. Now that I'm back, I'll take care of her myself."

"What rubbish are you saying? Who told you that I drove you away? Don't you remember your paati wanting to take you with her?"

"I remember very well. My failing in school was only an excuse for you. You must have cried to paati and that's why she took me away. She had come to stay with us in her old age. You forced her to leave. She would have spent her last days all alone if I had not been with her."

"Then you must also recall how you used to trouble your sister…"

Maya raised her hand and stopped Kamala from speaking any further.

"I have not forgotten that either. I did it out of ignorance, foolishly trying to imitate the way you and appa behave towards her. Now I know better and I will ensure that no harm ever falls on her again as long as I am with her. I don't have anything else to tell you and I don't want to hear any of your explanations either."

Kamala left the room.

***

# 10

From the darkness of the interior Kamala looked out into the bright colours of the shrubs and Crotons surrounding the house and conceded that Maya could cast spells on plants as well, not only on her sister. Yet, she could not see the profusion of leaves and flowers without feeling a stab of regret that had lost its edge over the years. The garden reminded her of Maya's conversation with her father when she said, "I want to learn how to handle special children."

"Don't be absurd," Raghu replied. "Your marks will get you admission in a good college. You can continue to teach her or whatever, in your spare time."

"That's not enough. Either I do a specialised course or spend more time with her."

"To do what? What you're teaching her is more than adequate. In any case, it isn't as if you're going to be with her always..."

"We will be together all the time," Maya interrupted him. "I'm not leaving her alone, ever."

Raghu's nostrils flared and his lips became thin lines. Kamala cringed, fearing the consequence of his anger.

"Look," he said, controlling himself. "I don't care if you don't want to study but no more of this foolish talk about spending all your time with your sister."

The topic of Maya learning further never arose again in that house but it continued to prick Kamala.

*She should have studied and got a degree at least. If she sets her mind to something she does it. Just look at the garden. Who would ever believe that she's doing this with no one to help her except Amrita?*

Kamala also had to admit that Maya did not waste her time though she was home the whole day. She taught Amrita and gardening was part of her sister's curriculum. They had planted a line of bushes near the house and trees along the compound wall while a kitchen garden flourished in the backyard. The trees blocked the house from the road and gave them privacy but Kamala did not like the shrubs that spread before the windows and made the place so dark. The neem and the mango trees were still young, while the old Ashoka now had a rival in the Indian cork tree that was shooting up. The waxy, long pointed leaves of the Ashoka were abundant throughout the year unlike the cork that shed its leaves in spring. Its flowers, silvery white and scented, carpeted the ground around its trunk while the slender stalked flowers of the Ashoka hid themselves in the foliage.

The shrubs were better matched with the red, orange and yellow Peacock flower and multicoloured Hibiscus, rapidly blocking Kamala's view of the girls as they watered the plants or plucked the drying flowers. She would have preferred the plants to be trimmed so that she could see Amrita at work and know that Maya was around too. She couldn't say anything and the trees branched and re-branched, giving her only glimpses of her daughters. Even if they were not there she seemed to see them among the plants, so much time did they spend in their garden.

Occasionally, Kamala's imagination soared and she saw the trees as men and women surrounding her girls. The bushes and little plants were children. The trees tried to reach Maya and Amrita with their long arms while the children laughed and made faces at them from the flowers and buds. The girls stood in the middle, not seeing the faces, not hearing the voices. Kamala wanted to cry out to them, to make them aware of the danger that lay in the crowd of human faces with plant limbs thronging around them.

*Maya will think I'm intruding into their world. They could be twins the way they cling to each other. I can understand Ammu's behaviour. There was a time when she would not let me move an inch without her. Then she switched to Revabehn and now to Maya. How mistaken you were about her, Revabehn. You thought she was not to be trusted with Amrita but she takes greater care of her sister than I ever did, or you. It has been ten years since she returned home. Ten years since she has been Amrita's guardian, not letting a shadow fall on her, not even mine.*

***

It was then that my brother Sundar came to stay with them.

"Sundar is a handsome young man. Has he taken after his father or mother?" asked Kamala auntie.

"Both, I suppose. And I don't look like either of them. Kittu was handsome in his own way, like the hero in a romantic tragedy. Frail, intense, lover of all good things in life, like my mother. Amma is still very beautiful. Didn't your husband say anything about her?" I asked deliberately.

"No," she replied for the first time, looking confidently into my eye. "After the first and my only confrontation with him I never asked him anything about his friends. If I couldn't satisfy him I must let him seek gratification elsewhere. As long as I know he'll come back to me at the end of the day I have no complaints. Oh! How can I say such things to an unmarried young girl like you?" she slapped her forehead.

"Auntie, you don't know what girls talk about these days!" I laughed. "What you said was nothing."

"Even then. It was stupid of me to talk so openly like this. What would your parents have thought of me?"

"Nothing," I assured her. "You were telling me about Sundar," I reminded her.

"Yes, Sundar. He was such a contrast to your uncle. Raghu is tall but Sundar is taller. The difference could not be more than half an inch but given his youth and vigour, he seemed to loom over Raghu. There was a magnetism about him that worried me," said Kamala auntie.

"Why did you ask him to stay with us?" she had muttered to Raghu when he returned to the drawing room after showing Sundar his room.

"He's a young man. Did you forget that we have grown up girls in the house? And you have given him the room next to theirs," she added.

"Don't be stupid. He won't be a problem. He will be like a brother to our girls. Not only that, he will be of great help to all of us, just wait and see."

For the next two months when Sundar stayed with them, the house was filled with his talk and laughter. Raghu listened with the indulgence of a fond parent. Kamala admired the glibness of the young man, but Maya remained stony as if she was only waiting to run away to her sister.

"She is not happy about me staying here, I think. Perhaps I should move out," Sundar remarked, when she left the room as soon as he entered.

"Forget about her. She is moody," said Raghu. "Tell me, how do you like being here? Are you comfortable?"

"Of course. If nothing else, no one bugs me here. At home..." he shuddered.

"Go on," Raghu goaded him.

"That brat sister of mine!"

"Oh, you have a sister? I didn't know that. Is she as old as Maya?" he asked.

"She is younger. Dad has spoilt her so thoroughly that she is next to impossible. Mind you, she's very smart, excels in everything, whether it is studies or sports or other activities. She does not know the meaning of moderation but goes overboard in anything she does. Mom keeps telling her to slow down, that she'll burn herself out but who is to listen? Certainly not my dear sister," Sundar laughed.

"Well, she seems to be a very positive person," said Raghu.

"Positive? Of course, she is positive. She only makes me seem negative. Everybody says, 'Look at her - a winner all the way and look at you.' Is it my fault that I was just an average student?"

Kamala felt sorry for the young man living in the shadow of someone apparently so superior. She used to take pride in Raghu's good looks until things turned sour between them. Now she felt that if she had not been so ordinary looking perhaps he wouldn't have been so disinterested in her. Words surged in her mind and she chose them with care.

"Does she look like you?" she asked.

Sundar perked up. "Ah! There we are different. You would

never think we are siblings. She is…" he stopped abruptly, looked at Kamala and continued, "Appearances don't matter, do they? The character of the person is more important to me and my sister is a gem at heart, a real gem."

"Good," said Raghu and abruptly changed the topic. "How is your job? No problems, I hope?"

Kamala wondered if he was trying to keep her from the conversation. If that was his intention, he wasn't going to succeed always. Raghu had been promoted as General Manager and was on tour more often than before. His absences only meant that she had greater freedom to talk to Sundar or, as she did most of the time, listen to him. He always seemed to have something or the other to tell her. Sometimes it was about his new job, but more often he talked about his friends and their affairs.

"It's amazing how short-sighted these people are. Their only goals are to get a job, marry and settle down. Don't they want to find out what more they can get out of life?"

"Well, what do you want?" asked Kamala.

"Lots of things. I want to travel, make money, live like a king. No money pinching drudgery for me. I want my salary in dollars or pounds, not Indian rupees. My wife will not have any wants. I'll treat her like a Queen, the Queen of my heart."

Kamala smiled. "All men say that at first. They forget their promises when the charm of marriage wears off."

"No auntie, I'll be different because I have seen my mother suffer. Dad is full of ideals and good intentions but he has not been able to give her the kind of life she wants."

"You think you know what she wants?"

"Sure. We are very close, my mother and I. Gauri and dad make the other team. I don't understand his philosophy, if he has one that is, and he thinks I'm good-for-nothing. He won't say anything directly but just looks at me through his glasses as if I am the bane in his life. I would've been able to take his verbal lashing but not those pained looks. If it hadn't been for mom I would've run away long ago."

"Shush! Imagine talking of running away as if you are a coward. You are a smart young man. What can't you achieve if you really want to?" Kamala rebuked.

"Exactly! That's just what I told dad. And he said, 'Then do it. I have never stopped you from conquering the moon.' But I need that little push to help me take off. Only money matters in these circumstances, not words. And that he doesn't have."

"So, what are you going to do?"

"Nothing much immediately. I can't. I'll bide my time and when my chance comes I'll grab it with both hands. No one will be able to stop me then. I will wave a thick wad of notes in his face and ask, 'Now what do you think of me?'"

Kamala collected the dishes from the table and went to the kitchen, while he followed her.

"You didn't say anything?"

"Well, ambition is fine and I am glad you are concerned about your mother. I hope your dreams come true, though I wouldn't like to be in your father's shoes when you wave those notes!" She was still laughing when Maya entered.

"Ah… Maya the mirage! You know auntie, you have named your daughter very appropriately. Maya is really illusion, now here and now not here," he said, tears of laughter streaming down his eyes as well.

Maya tightened her lips and served lunch on two plates.

"Why didn't you join us?" he asked.

"I prefer my sister's company." She walked out of the room.

Sundar slumped against the wall in a dramatic show of injured pride.

"Don't take her seriously," said Kamala. "She doesn't talk readily to strangers."

"Strangers? You call me a stranger, auntie? I've been here for so long and she continues to treat me like an obnoxious weed in her precious garden," he complained.

Kamala felt like patting his shoulder to comfort him. The next day as soon as he left the house she went to the backyard. Maya had hitched her *salwar* to the calf and was strewing coriander seeds in straight lines. Amrita was working in another plot, twining the slender tendrils of a creeper along a stick. Neither of them noticed their mother till she cleared her throat loudly. Maya looked up at once and just as quickly continued with her work.

"Maya, I want to talk to you."

"Hmm…"

"Stop your work for a minute."

Maya looked up once again and paused, flicking mud from her fingers.

"Why are you curt with that boy? He was so upset yesterday, at the way you insulted him. What's eating you?"

"I don't care if he is upset or happy."

"That's not the way to treat a guest."

"I don't want to learn how to treat a guest like him."

"What's wrong with him? He is friendly, nice…"

"You don't have to say anything more. I can see that you two get along very well." Maya resumed her work.

Kamala stood transfixed. What on earth did the girl mean by this? She had only treated Sundar with the affection due to someone old enough to be her son. What was Maya hinting at? She looked at her daughter's bent head, seemingly absorbed in her work now that her time for her mother was over, except that their little exchange left Kamala perturbed. She walked away slowly, her mind playing back her conversations with Sundar to find any lapse or misbehaviour. None as far as she knew.

*I'm just over-reacting to her foolish remark. She doesn't know what she's talking about. How easy it is to spill words but I must be more careful. I don't want Raghu to think…*

"Hello auntie! Why are you sitting in the dark?"

Sundar switched on the light while Kamala got up hurriedly.

"I rarely see you relaxing. You seem so busy always."

Kamala smiled.

"What's the hot topic?" asked Raghu, taking her by surprise.

"I didn't hear the car…"

"We came together. I had been to his office and yes, Sundar, I didn't tell you what your boss Shah has to say about your work … okay, okay, I won't keep you in suspense. He thinks you have potential but you need to be systematic and organised. I have assured him that you will learn the ropes soon."

"That I will!" Sundar exclaimed fervently. "Did he say anything about raising my salary?"

"It is too soon to expect an increase. You concentrate on doing a sincere job and keeping him happy. In any case, why are you so eager for a raise? Are you sending money home?"

Sundar hesitated momentarily before replying.

"Good. Your mother … your parents will be very happy. I will talk to Shah about raising your pay the next time I meet him. He is a good chap and will understand your problem."

However, within a week Sundar came to Raghu to help him get another job.

"It is not as easy as you think. You shouldn't have quit so suddenly."

"What can I do, Uncle? They were making me slog like a donkey. The salary they promised was no compensation for so much work."

"Well, I'll see what I can do," said Raghu.

Sundar could now entertain Kamala the whole day with his jokes and glib talk. However, she was conscious of Maya's disapproval and did not contribute to the conversation. He didn't need any cues, just somebody's physical presence while he held forth. One day she realised that he no longer talked about his parents.

"Oh, they are fine," he said. "At least mom and Gauri are. I believe dad isn't too well."

"What happened to him?"

"Well, he has always been ailing with something or the other and mom gets into a flap trying to find the money for his treatment."

"Don't you want to visit him?"

"Not really. In fact, he might feel worse after seeing me. I told you, he's always felt that I would never make good and now I am beginning to wonder if he could be right after all. I can't even hold on to a job long enough to prove myself to dad."

He played listlessly with his food and Kamala was sorry that she had raised the topic at all.

"Don't worry, your time will come."

"But when?"

"Who can answer that? There's no point in worrying. Uncle will get you another job. Maybe that will be the right one for you," Kamala consoled him.

***

# 11

"Sundar left as suddenly as he had come when you telephoned about your father's demise," said Kamala auntie. "I was sorry that he couldn't stay longer to realise his dreams. By the time he came back, some four months later, Maya's wedding was fixed with Ganesh. I never thought it would happen so quickly. A few families had refused to even consider an alliance with us because of Amrita. Others demanded a dowry way beyond our means. If we gave them the roof above our heads what will we do in our old age when he's no longer capable of earning? And what about planning for Amrita? Even then I might have been tempted, but Raghu was adamant."

"'Would a house, a few acres of land, so many sovereigns of gold and silver vessels change the fact that Maya's sister is not normal?" he asked.' He had a point. So we waited."

Her story was proceeding too fast. I needed clarifications.

"But what was Maya's reaction to this? To your decision to get her married?" I asked.

"Of course she protested. Uncle had to convince her. Those days were hell! She went with her sister to the ashram ground the whole day. You have been indoors with me all the time, so you won't know anything about this ground next door. You can see it from the corner of the window from your room."

"Oh yes!" I said, switching my mind from Maya to my room upstairs. The first time I opened the shutters of the two windows I had noticed that one of them looked out on the road beyond the front yard and the other gave a glimpse of what looked like a field. A field? I didn't ask Sundar about it since he had been in no mood for small talk.

"I did notice that place. What's it?" I asked Kamala auntie.

"It belongs to a group of Swaminarayan devotees. Most of them are rich Patels with a foreign connection. With their generous donation, the sect has bought that large ground and set up the ashram. It is good agricultural land and they are using it very well. Sometimes they sell the excess milk and vegetables to outsiders. It is so fresh that it gets sold out immediately. I've never been able to buy anything even once."

"What did Maya and her sister do there?" I asked, bringing her back to her narration.

"Who knows?" Kamala auntie shrugged. "I only knew they went there all the time. Will she let me ask her anything? I kept a close watch on her. She had clearly lost interest in the garden and the plants began to wither. On some days she wouldn't even take their meals to her room. She began to lose weight and looked wan. I knew something was troubling her seriously but she wasn't going to tell me about it. Even today, Gauri, she doesn't want to talk to me," she said, not bothering to hide her tears.

Kamala auntie may have begun her narration by using me as a confidante but now she couldn't stop till she had purged the rancour, the heartbreak and the anguish from her system. Perhaps then, I hoped, she may find peace.

"Daughters cling to their mothers when they leave their maternal home," she continued. "But Maya was happy to see the last of me. She probably did not realise that she was also leaving behind her father and her beloved sister. The only time she spoke to me was after the wedding, to say that the maid had left and there was no one to look after Amrita. She also started saying something about your brother but I was in a hurry to attend to the guests. I told her not to worry, that I would take care of her sister."

Her ravaged face grew smaller. I almost reached out to comfort her but she composed herself with admirable strength.

"Gauri, I shall always regret this one lapse on my part – that I did not listen to her that day. I did not let her finish whatever she had wanted to tell me. I didn't find out what was troubling her so badly... If I had, perhaps my Amrita would have been alive today."

Her face crumpled once again. I tried to distract her.

"How did you get to know about Ganesh?"

"Through your brother," she said, cheering up. "Yes, it was Sundar who told us about Ganesh, the cousin of a colleague in his office, the one in which he had worked for a short while before he resigned and went home. I'll always remain grateful to him for getting a groom for Maya. He said the boy's parents were particular only about the girl. They wanted a widow or a divorcee or someone whose family couldn't afford the dowry and other expenses. When I heard this I thought there must be something wrong with them or with the boy. Nowadays, the intention is to drain the last drop of blood from the girl's family. To avoid any legal wrangle they may conceal their demands under other names but they cannot hide their fangs or sheath their claws for long. Ganesh's parents, however, took pride in being different. They did not even ask for Maya's horoscope. Again I wondered whether the boy was not quite normal and that was why they did not make any demand, but he's perfectly all right. Of average looks and height but very well qualified. He's an engineer in a large company. The only thing he asked was an opportunity to talk to Maya privately. I was aghast, but uncle gave him permission. We sat in the next room apparently intent in our talk but I was listening for any sound from her. It was the first time she was meeting a stranger, a man, all alone. I didn't know what she would tell him. I didn't want her to blabber something and make the boy reject her. Fortunately, things turned out well and we had the wedding soon after."

Her face reflected her mood and shone with the cheeriness of the sun after a cloudburst.

"It was the first joyous occasion in our house and your uncle did not stint at all. We invited almost everyone we know. Of course, they were mostly his friends. We got Maya a superb trousseau, no less than eight heavy Kanchipuram silk saris, gold and silver jewellery and vessels. And of course, gifts for the groom and his people. His parents were shocked at the lavishness of it all. Uncle finally told them that Maya's was the only wedding in our family so he would like to do it in style. Ganesh's father kept quiet but I could see he was not happy about the expense. His wife was more reasonable. She kept fingering the saris and telling others to admire this and that."

"And Maya?" I asked.

"What will she have to say? Throughout the ceremony she sat with a grumpy face. Every so often she looked at her wristwatch as if she was bored or she watched the people who had come for the ceremony. I had to remind her not to look around so shamelessly. She hadn't wanted a grand function but uncle and I just ignored her and did as we wished."

"What about Amrita? How did she respond to the crowd and the noise?" I asked, squashing a mosquito on my forearm and looking closely at the blob of blood with the flattened insect. The impact of my blow had even separated the thin legs from the body.

Kamala auntie got up to close the windows. She believed that mosquitoes entered the house at sunset so she sealed all the windows and doors early to keep them out. Despite her precaution they still made it impossible for us to sit without hitting ourselves on the cheeks, arms and legs. To make matters worse I was wearing a brown dress and dark colours seem to attract more mosquitoes than otherwise.

"Coffee?" she asked.

I pulled her by the hand and made her sit down.

"I don't want anything except to listen to you. There isn't much time left. He'll return in a few hours and then you won't be able to talk freely with me. So, tell me, how did Amrita react to the wedding?" I asked.

Her face clouded and she paused as if seeking the right words. "He did not want her to attend the wedding," she said at last in a low voice. "He said she might get upset since she was not used to seeing so many people."

"Oh, the wedding was held here?" I looked around. The rooms were not large and there wasn't too much space outside the house either.

"At a *choultry*, not far from here."

"Was someone with her?" I asked.

"Of course! We were not going to just lock her up in the house on her own. At Maya's insistence we had got a maid to look after Amrita. Hansabehn began working a month earlier so that Maya could train her. She didn't seem to think highly of the woman but neither did she complain about her. Just as well, since we'd got her with a great deal of difficulty. No one was prepared to look after a child like Amrita. Actually, there was no need to get anyone because I would have easily looked after her myself. I had done it till Revabehn and then Maya took over. Who else will do it but the mother? But I didn't protest when she wanted to hire a maid. Maya wouldn't have listened to me."

"What happened then?"

"Well, the wedding took place. Everything went off without a hitch. The guests were full of praise for the food, the arrangements, everything. Maya was flooded with gifts though nothing brought a smile to her face. We didn't have a reception in the evening since the groom's party wanted to leave that night itself. Uncle had tried to get them to postpone their departure by a couple of days but they were adamant and we didn't want to antagonise them in any way. They seemed very nice but we couldn't take any chances."

"How's Maya? Happy… I hope?" I asked and a smile spread to auntie's eyes.

"Very happy. Of course, she hasn't told me anything directly but uncle rings her up once in a while. She doesn't ask for me. She doesn't know that I hang around the telephone every time her father talks to her," Kamala auntie's voice fell and the light withdrew from her eyes.

For the second time in my life I was seeing the face of defeat. The first had been during Kittu's stay in the hospital, his last.

He had spent his last days watching the waves rise and fall from the window of his room. The breeze would fling the curtain inside and he would try to catch it. He couldn't since the fabric was not long enough to flutter within his faltering reach. He didn't mind losing but I felt bad. I offered to close the window and keep the teasing breeze out. He wouldn't hear of it.

"How will I admire the waves then?" he asked. "Just see the contrast between us. Life is ebbing from me and there is no way I can surge forward with new vigour. And look at the waves ... they recede but do they give up? No! They come back with greater force. There's a lot to learn from those waves, child. They teach you not to give up. Withdraw, if you must but don't surrender. Come back with more strength. This is the secret of success, I now realise."

The look on his face constricted my throat. We sat without speaking, Kittu and I, till a nurse came in importantly and rebuked me for letting 'the patient' lie in the dark. She switched on the light. We could no longer see the waves in the gathering gloam but the sound of the incessant swell, heaving and falling continued into the night lulling Kittu to sleep while I watched him. The next morning he died.

It is only in movies that nature reflects the mood of the actors. I went to the beach with my heart breaking into a million pieces but the day was bright and the water a sparkling blue. At a distance some fishermen were plying their boats. The crows that had winged to me so eagerly, hopped with every step I took. They couldn't seem to accept that I had nothing to give them. I removed my sandals just above the line of the water. I was about to let the waves wash over my feet when I remembered that I would have to return to the hospital and take charge of Kittu's body. I couldn't do that with sand sticking to my legs. The larger grains may fall off but the fine black particles would give me away. I walked along the water's edge keeping an eye on the scalloping foam and moving out of its way when it came too close to me.

Kamala auntie and I were playing a similar game, of skirting the issue and moving away every time it reared its head. I could not let her parry with me any longer. I was leaving the next day.

"How did Amrita die?" I asked.

***

Maya left her parental home on the night of her wedding with Ganesh and his family. She stayed with Amrita till it was time for her to depart. Kamala had expected her daughter to protest or create a scene that she didn't want to leave Amrita behind, but Maya had been quite composed. However, as she got into the car, her eyes filled and she kept her head down, not responding to her parents' last minute instructions. When the car started moving, she turned to the window and looked up, towards what was her room. Seeing the deep sorrow on her face made Kamala forget the many years of differences between them. Her grief at her daughter leaving her parental home caused a sudden blankness of vision but she thought Maya kept looking behind, even while the car was moving away.

Kamala and Raghu re-entered the house. It had always been a very silent place even when Maya was there but now it seemed as if with her leaving, the silence had become deeper. The furniture in every room had been pushed towards the wall to give more space in the middle and yet, the impression she got was one of clutter and disorder. Flowers were scattered everywhere. Most of them were red rose petals and jasmine that had fallen from the women's hair and some, intertwined with bits of gold thread, came from the garlands that Maya and Ganesh had worn. The garlands themselves, their purpose served, had been discarded and hung, one from the top of a door and the other on a nail in the wall.

Kamala picked up the plates with the remains of betel leaves, arecanut and lime that the guests had eaten after their dinner. There was a lot of clearing to do but she found even lifting an arm required immense will power and effort. Nevertheless, she forced herself to roll up the durries and reed mats and stacked them along the wall. Raghu walked restlessly up and down, coming in Kamala's way as she cleared the room. Finally, when she entered with a broom he said, "Leave it. The maid's coming tomorrow, let her do it. Go and lie down. It's late."

With her body screaming for rest, it was tempting to obey him but she hesitated.

"What about Amrita?" she asked.

"What about her?" returned Raghu.

"Shouldn't I see what she's doing?"

"Sleeping obviously. What else will she do at this time of the night? Maya told me specifically that she has explained everything to her. You can take over from tomorrow. Let her sleep now. Ah, Sundar … you are back. You didn't wait for the train to leave?"

"Ganesh and his father insisted that I should not stay, that you and auntie would be upset about Maya leaving. I told them that you'll be all right but they wouldn't hear of it. They said there were enough men in their group and they would manage their luggage so I came back."

"What did Maya say?" Kamala couldn't help asking.

"Nothing. She was too busy crying and the other women were trying to console her. Imagine, she was so cool while leaving and once she reached the railway station, she broke down. I felt sorry for her. It's difficult for girls, isn't it? Leaving their parents' home and starting afresh in another house?"

"All girls go through this phase and they adjust very well. Just wait and see. Maya will soon forget about us and will not want to leave her husband's side even for a day," Raghu laughed and Sundar joined him but Kamala's mind had become a vacuum.

She gave in to her fatigue and went to bed while the men talked some more.

She woke up hearing a sudden loud noise. Her body ached as if it had passed through a mill. Slowly the noises began to make sense. It was Sundar talking in a low voice that cracked and picked up and cracked again. Kamala wondered if they had not gone to sleep at all the previous night, for it was now morning. It was still dark but rapidly becoming bright outside. She knew she would have to get up but her limbs felt heavy and lethargic.

*What's with that fellow? Why is he up so soon and whom is he talking to? Obviously Raghu. Who else is there?*

Another male voice joined Sundar's, a strange authoritative one, loud, persistent, questioning to which Raghu mumbled a reply. That stirred Kamala into wakefulness. Was he ill? Why did he sound troubled? She got up hurriedly and went to the front room. She had heard only three voices but the room seemed full of men, all strangers except for a couple of familiar faces from the neighbourhood. There were more people in the front yard, peeping in. As one they turned to look at her when she entered. Her heart seemed to stop beating and she stood still.

"What's it? What happened?" she asked.

Both Raghu and Sundar rushed to her side. Her husband caught her arm and turned her round but she couldn't leave without knowing what was wrong. She brushed him aside impatiently and looked at the policeman.

"I know something has happened. Accident? Is Maya all right?" her voice shook and she blanched.

Raghu threw his hand over her shoulder. Kamala could see that he was forcing himself to talk.

"Maya's all right," he said. "Nothing has happened to her train. She's perfectly all right…"

"Then why are all these people here?"

He looked at Sundar helplessly but the young man whose talk had woken up Kamala would not meet his eyes.

"Amrita … it's Amrita…" Raghu said at last while Kamala looked blankly at him.

"What are you saying about Amrita? She's upstairs in her room."

"No, Kamala. She's not there. She…" he stumbled for words.

Kamala knew something was terribly wrong.

"What is it? Tell me," she insisted.

"Amrita met with an accident," Raghu said and paused.

No one else spoke. Kamala couldn't take her eyes off him as tears ran down his cheeks.

"She came under the wheels of a train … no one knows when, maybe early today, perhaps last night. I…"

Kamala stared at her husband.

*Amrita was upstairs. She was there always unless Maya took her out and Maya had left with her husband.*

She turned and ran up the stairs, Raghu and Sundar behind

her. The policeman and a couple of strangers followed them more sedately.

She pushed open the door of the girls' room.

It was empty.

Kamala pushed open the bathroom door.

It was empty.

"Where has she gone? She was here. She must be here somewhere. She never goes out on her own…" Kamala was talking, partly to herself, partly to Raghu, who kept close to her.

"You have to believe me, Kamala. She's not here. She's gone. Sundar went to the station and … identified … her. I don't know how it could have happened," Raghu was still tripping over the words.

"Mr. Raghavan, there's nothing strange about it," the policeman took over. "Your younger daughter got married recently…yesterday, in fact. The older girl must have been upset about this. I'm told she was not stable mentally. The picture is very clear. She must have been unhappy about her sister leaving or because she herself was still unmarried. Either way, the feeling was strong enough for her to commit suicide. As to when exactly it happened we'll be able to say only after an autopsy. Such things are not uncommon. All the time somebody or the other is giving work to the police. The peak is after the announcement of school, college results. Students behave as if failure in their exam is a verdict, a warrant to take their lives. Girls get into trouble, feel ashamed to tell the parents so…poof! Men in debt, love gone sour, drinking problem, mother-in-law harassment, dowry snarls… you name it, there's an excuse to jump off a bridge, pop in a handful of pills or come below the wheels of a train."

The policeman took a deep breath. He was not through yet but Sundar got the unspoken message in the official's harangue. He took the policeman downstairs, paid him for his trouble and sent him away. The worthy left and, in a charitable gesture to the bereaved family, he dispersed the spectators with loud reprimands and sharp orders to move on.

***

# 12

"See that plant?" asked Kamala auntie, pointing to a tall evergreen bottle-brush behind us in the garden with drooping branches that ended in clusters of red flowers.

"When I was a child my mother told me a folk tale about how it came into existence. It seems that long ago there was a young woman who was ill-treated by her mother-in-law. Nobody would believe her since the old woman appeared so gentle and sweet while talking to her in the presence of others. Having no one to confide in, she bottled up her grievances and sorrows within herself. One day a bird dropped a little seed near the woman. She planted it at a distance from the house and watered it everyday. It began to grow. She made it her confidant and told the sapling all her troubles. Hearing the young woman's hardships the tree, instead of sending its branches straight up into the sky, drooped to the earth with the weight of her secrets. With every incident, every sad ordeal it shed tears of blood. That's why the flowers are red and why the tree looks sad and droopy. I feel just like the young woman in this tale but you are no bottle-brush. You are more like a pipal or a banyan. I know I can rely on you. You will not be able to solve my problems but at least I could unburden myself to you. Whom will I talk to after you have gone?" she asked, holding the hose at arm's length and spraying precious water in an arc.

The evening sun changed the droplets into splinters of glass that fell on the leaves and became tiny dark smudges. I looked at her. It was flattering to think that my company had changed her over the last few days. Her shoulders no longer sagged and there was a sense of serenity about her that reminded me so much of Kittu.

Within a couple of hours Raghu returned from his tour and she became warped and introverted once again.

"So… how have you been?" he asked and answered himself. "Terribly bored, I'm sure. I'm truly sorry I couldn't spend any time with you. Of course, we can talk the whole day tomorrow. What else can one do in a train? I'll be travelling by train after ages. I usually take a flight. You don't know how privileged you are, young woman!"

I gave him the smallest smile possible and glanced at Kamala auntie. She signalled to me with her eyes. I mumbled some excuse and went to the kitchen.

"Do me one last favour, please..." her eyes pleaded with mine.

"What's it?" I asked as softly as she spoke.

"Maya's husband was working in Madras when they got married but within a month, he was transferred to Bombay. Talk to her on my behalf. Tomorrow, before you go back to your mother...will you?"

"But she doesn't know me at all!" I protested.

"Raghu would have told her about you. He telephones often and visits her every time he is there on work or is passing through. Her anger is only towards me and not her father, it seems. Tell her that I now have all the time for her, will you? Please."

Raghu was enthusiastic about this change in my plan.

"That's a great idea. You'll be Maya's first guest after her wedding. You must stay with her for a couple of days and see how much housekeeping she has learnt. You'll easily get your onward ticket from there. But yes, don't forget to ring up your mother and tell her. We don't want her to worry."

Kamala auntie did not accompany us to the railway station. I thought she might not even see me off from the front door but she surprised me by coming out of the house and to my side as I sat in the autorickshaw. Her smile made the corners of her mouth droop. The driver pulled the starting handle and the engine fired immediately with such a loud noise that it would have been difficult to hear anything if she had wanted to talk to me. She didn't but I did. I put my head out of the vehicle and she automatically bent towards me.

"I'll be back. Think of me as the daughter who will return to you one day," I said.

The racket was such that I was not sure if she heard me but when I turned around to wave to her, she was wiping her eyes with the end of her sari *pallu*.

***

The general compartments were overflowing. The air-conditioned chair car was full too but at least we could sit comfortably without having to share our seat with others. I sat near the window while Raghu sat next to me. Just then an old Parsi gentleman came up and said, "I think your daughter has taken my seat."

Raghu looked at the *bawa*'s ticket and told him that his number was further down.

"You know what that gentleman thought?" he asked. "That you are my daughter."

*Cue, Gauri, your cue!*

I smiled back at him, a vague, tentative one just enough to keep our relationship alive. After all that Kamala auntie had told me, did I want to open the Pandora's box and cause her greater distress? That too when she had managed to convince herself that Raghu would never desert her? Perhaps amma had been right in keeping the truth to herself.

We slowed down at Baroda station. It didn't seem possible that there could be room for any more passengers. However, despite the men clinging from the outside by a toehold, the crowd on the platform ran with the train while it ground to a shrieking, jerky stop. When it left five minutes later, the platform was deserted. The Gujarat Express had swallowed everybody into its innards.

Raghu hailed a passing vendor and bought two cups of tea. I misjudged the sturdiness of the thin plastic cup and held it a little too tight pushing the tea to the brim.

"Steady. Something to eat?" he asked.

"No, thanks. Kamala auntie has packed our lunch and some snacks as well. I don't think we should buy anything."

He finished the tepid beverage in one gulp and crushed the plastic cup. I did the same. In a third class compartment, the next step would be to toss the used cups out of the window but we were in an air-conditioned coach with sealed windows. Fortunately, the vendor went past again and relieved us of our dilemma, grimacing at how we had crushed the cups beyond the point of reuse.

"When are you visiting us next, Gauri? I promise I'll not vanish like I did this time. Just let me know in advance though," Raghu said dabbing his lips with his kerchief.

"I'm not sure I want to leave my mother alone..."

"Quite right. You must certainly not leave her alone at this time of bereavement when Sundar is also so far away. It'll be good for you too. There's nothing like being with one's mother, especially foı a girl. I didn't have the good fortune to know my father. He died when I was very young. My mother was everything to me but there are certain things a boy can only tell his father. I used to imagine what kind of a person he would have been, his appearance, interests, his hobbies. He played cricket, helped me with my studies, shared jokes – in my mind," he sighed.

"For a long time I told him everything, the trouble my mother was having with her brothers, the hunger, the beating, the sense of being crushed under others' feet... I even hated him sometimes for leaving us to suffer like this. I must have been about 10 years old when I vowed to study very hard, make lots of money and give amma all the comforts in the world. I would be the boss of my house and nobody would question anything I do. Unfortunately, the better I did in school, the worse it became at home. My marks showed my cousins in a bad light and they didn't like it.

"Good days and bad days both move on. Soon I was working and studying at the same time. I entered college. I doubled my efforts to come out into the sun quickly but now time wouldn' move fast enough! It was Nandini...yes, Gauri, your mother who stood by me in this most difficult phase of my life. Other than my mother, she was the only support I had. If it hadn't been for them I don't think I'd have survived the hurt, the insults and most of all, the helplessness of poverty."

He took a deep breath and let it out slowly.

I turned to the window towards the flashing trees, electric posts, huts, loud speakers, roadside shrines and other signs of civilisation.

"Gauri, look at me. I want to assure myself that I've not disturbed you. I didn't mean to upset you with my story. I know it's difficult to believe what a tough time I had in my younger days."

I turned a solemn face to him and he was satisfied.

"I took up the first job I got," he said. "Even though the salary was nothing to boast about. To tell you the truth, it was barely enough to support me and I had to leave my mother behind, at the mercy of her brothers. I didn't want to but I wanted to start earning as soon as possible. It was not easy to get a job even in those days and many of my seniors were unemployed. I refused to join them. My mother and teachers in college were disappointed with my decision. They had expected me to appear for the Civil Services exam and become a district collector. My uncles and aunts laughed at me for joining a small firm in a clerical position and some of my friends who had secured better jobs than me severed our ties. I was not bothered by their jibes for I knew what I was doing. I had faith in my ability and determination to make good whatever the world might think. And I did. I've made more money and travelled extensively than anyone from those days," Raghu sat up straight with a contented look.

"What about my mother? Was she one of those who remained faithful to you?" I had to ask, though I knew the answer.

He looked at me sharply.

"She has remained a very good friend to this day. The proof is you and your brother. She has entrusted both of you to me. She knows she can take that liberty with me."

*Touché. You are a smart man!*

"I think she got married before you?"

"I had responsibilities that I couldn't ignore. My mother, for one. I wanted to ensure that she was comfortable at least in the last leg of her life before I settled down."

"Oh? But I thought you got married almost soon after my mother?" I could be persistent.

"Well yes, I met Kamala and decided to marry her before I could lose her to someone else."

"Quite right. She's one in a thousand."

I meant it. No other woman would have been able to take so much shit from anyone.

"I've had my share of friends and parties and a good life. When I think of what I have gone through perhaps I deserve more but I'll not be greedy."

He folded his arms across his chest and lapsed into silence.

I turned to the window once again. The huts and trees by the side of the railway track were a blur unlike those further beyond, which lingered within the frame of the window for a long time.

Not a bird rested on the electric wire that ran with the train. It must be very hot outside. Sitting in the buffered air-conditioned coach I only felt the rhythmic roll of the wheels hurtling on smooth rails.

"How did you meet my mother?" I asked, startling him from his reverie.

"Oh, didn't she ever tell you? I must meet her and find out if she remembers that day as well as I do."

"She did tell me once, long ago, that you had met in college and that you had been good friends."

*Forgive me, God, for my little lies. They've not been said to harm anyone.*

His face brightened.

"She did? What else did she say?"

"Oh nothing much, except that one doesn't always get such friends."

*And that is certainly a universal truth.*

"She's right about that. Of course, her judgement has always been impeccable. I don't think she's ever taken a wrong step in her life."

I could have corrected him but I restrained myself. Having set him on the track, I let the horse gallop.

"Well, I joined first year of post-graduation when she was in her second year BA. I was 22 and she must have been about 19 or 20 then, a stunning beauty. Boys joined our college, the

Government Arts and Science, just because she was studying there. Those were the days when people were scandalised to see a girl and boy talk to one another and yet, Nandini and I were good friends. I have to thank my seniors for this," he laughed, looking at once so relaxed and handsome.

"I was in the gawky state of only height and no matching weight. Every other day it seemed as if amma had to let out the hem of my trousers. That tell-tale crease around my ankle made me more self-conscious. I couldn't slink and hide in a crowd since I stood at least a head taller than most of the students. Naturally, I became a favourite target for ragging. The names I earned! 'Rope', 'daddy-long-legs', 'grasshopper', 'praying mantis'," Raghu laughed again.

He certainly did not qualify for those names any longer. Age had added weight to his frame and he took care to maintain the balance.

"Well, one day a group of seniors caught hold of me just when the lunch recess bell had rung. I was not particularly disturbed or worried given the number of times I'd already been asked to do some stupid task or the other. I stood straight and looked at them without blinking an eyelid."

"They gathered around me, all seven or eight of them, some so puny I could have pushed them down with one hand. They ensured that I remembered my inferior status as fresher."

"'You, hero, what's your name?' asked one.'"

"'Right, Mr. Raghavan, do you have a Seetha in your life?' asked another.'"

"'Pardon me but I'm here to study,' I said, before I could control myself."

"The boys moved in closer like predators round the kill. The one who had asked the question poked me in the chest with a finger, 'Right, Mr. Einstein, the next Nobel is yours.'"

"The others burst into laughter attracting even more spectators. I was soon surrounded by several rows of students, all seniors. This was going to be serious. Ragging was all right but at this scale? I was the bull's-eye. I didn't like it one bit. My stomach dissolved into a mass of butterflies, dragonflies, cockroaches and every other insect you can think of – all striving to get out."

"Boss, to which planet are you going to banish this Einstein avatar?' asked someone."

"Suggestions flew fast and thick but 'Boss' didn't need any. He raised his hand and silenced everybody. 'Now you, young man,' he said. 'This is what you have to do if you don't want to be ragged any more. Go up to a girl, kneel at her feet with a rose in your hand and propose to her.'"

"Laughter hit me from all sides."

"'No tricks mind you. We'll be around to ensure you do what you are supposed to do. If she slaps you, it's back to more ragging, let me tell you,' he warned."

"Which girl would stand this ignominy, I wondered but the decision was made for me."

"Someone shouted, 'At least tell him the name of the girl.'"

"'No, I have a better idea,' interjected another. 'We'll take him to 'her' and let him find out her name after proposing to her.'"

"That dashed my plan to approach one of my classmates. Of course, my tormentor would approve this suggestion. He beckoned with a forefinger for me to follow him and we began to walk while the others fell behind us passing comments and collecting even more people along to watch the fun. We went to various places in search of this girl whose name I had to find out. She was nowhere to be found, not in her class, not in the canteen, not on the steps of the auditorium, nowhere. I hoped that we did not meet her at all so that I could wriggle out of this fix. Just then someone came running to us and said that he had seen 'her' entering college. Immediately I was propelled towards the gate and as one, everyone followed. The professors may have thought we were marching out of college, so purposefully did we walk. We stopped abruptly. I received my instruction.

"'See that girl walking towards us? Yes, the fair one in the blue sari? She's the one.'"

"And I was left all alone. The girl was walking steadily towards me but her head was down as if she was deep in thought. I felt sorry for her, like I would sympathise with a sacrificial goat. Yes, I was going to do as I was asked. I didn't have an option really, since this large crowd was waiting to attack me if I failed and I didn't want to think what they would ask next of me. It was best to face known danger than worry about the unknown, I thought."

"She was still walking towards me oblivious of her surroundings, the waiting crowd, me at the forefront. There was no way I could help her."

"The rose! They had forgotten the rose I was supposed to give her! Before I could turn around, a clammy hand thrust a soft something into mine. I didn't need to see what it was. I had my eyes fixed on the girl who had almost reached me. She was still lost in thought. Indeed, she seemed completely unaware of the palpable excitement that surrounded us, the waves of barely subdued buzz behind me, my heart beat now so loud like a sledge-hammer on my eardrum. The insects in my stomach had fused into one mass that sank with every little step I took. Even then our confrontation seemed far too soon."

"We were in each other's paths. She looked up at last, at the obstacle I made, side-stepped and went past. I couldn't let her get away, not if I wanted to save my skin."

"'Miss!' I called. "My voice seemed heavy, strange but it worked. She looked over her shoulder and kept walking."

"'Wait, please, I've something to tell you.'"

"I poured my heart in that request and she paused momentarily. I talked quickly, keeping my voice low so that no one but she could hear me. Her curiosity was aroused and she turned around fully. Now, she couldn't see the crowd that was waiting for my downfall."

"'Miss, you must believe me. I am a fresher and those fellows behind you are ragging me. They want me to give you this flower and … and…' the words wouldn't come out."

"'And?' she asked. Her eyes were twinkling in such marked contrast to the composure with which she walked just now that I could only gape at her."

"'What are you supposed to do?' she emphasised every word to make it register in me."

"'Oh, I'm supposed to propose to you.' My ears burned and now I couldn't look at her."

"'Not again! They have tried this silly stunt at least five times this year. I should teach them a lesson they'll not forget in a hurry. You're supposed to kneel before me, right? Well then, go ahead and do it. Don't be nervous. Think of this as just a game.'"

"I ran a dry tongue over my chapped lips. The rose looked more pathetic than I felt. Its yellow petals were spotted brown, crumpled and it drooped limply. Thank God this was just a charade, I thought. No girl would ever accept a fellow's hand over such a flower."

"I went down on one knee in front of her. Behind her was the sea of faces bathed in wide smiles. I thought I noticed a couple of older faces, probably of professors who had joined to watch the fun. If the girl had shown the slightest reluctance I'd have turned right round and fled, the threat of more ragging be damned, but the girl whose name I still did not know gave me confidence to go through this torture."

"'Miss, will you marry me?' I croaked as softly as I could, not daring to lift my eyes to hers."

"'Look up at me!' she ordered, though she also kept her voice down. 'And ask once again. Loudly this time.'"

"I did. Don't ask me how I got the courage to do it but I did it. I spoke louder this time. Loud and clear for those fellows to hear. A burst of laughter hit my ears. It was smothered just as quickly as the crowd and I waited for the girl to respond."

"She took the flower gently from my hand as if it had bloomed just then, kissed it lightly and gave me her other hand. I couldn't believe it. I didn't dare to take her hand in mine but touched it with my fingertips and stood up hastily."

"'Shall we go?' she asked, laying her hand on my arm and walking, forcing me to match her pace. We went past the crowd of popping eyes and open mouths. I was weak with relief but, for the first time, a little bubble of mirth rose in me. We walked sedately till we turned the corner and then she hurriedly removed her hand."

"'Bye,' she said, before leaving for her class."

"I was in a daze. The boys came running behind me and, from the babble of voices, I realised how lucky I had been. She, Nandini, had slapped all her earlier 'suitors' and no one let them forget that slap ever. I was the hero who had won the lady's hand. I went to class hearing only the violins in the air, not the compliments, not seeing the jealous looks from her many fans."

Raghu smiled at me and I returned to earth with a thud.

*Amma, behaving like this? Who would ever have thought it possible?*

"What happened when you met her the next time?" I gulped and managed to ask.

"I did not meet her for a few days, though you bet I was on the lookout for her," he said, smiling. "Then we bumped into each other in the library. It was a very dark place, full of old books and musty smells, not the right place to meet anyone though many couples made it their rendezvous. Of course, I didn't know she would be there and she wouldn't have expected me either. In fact, I don't think she even recognised me at first though I certainly did. She looked puzzled when I smiled at her and when she realised who I was, she responded with a half-smile not like the dazzler she had given me last time... It must sound all mushy and silly to you, eh?"

"Oh no, I am enjoying every bit of it. I wish I'd known this earlier. How I would have ragged her!" I said.

"That's why she never told you. Some things are best left unsaid," he smiled.

"But having started, you'd better finish it. I must hear the rest of the story," I insisted.

"There's nothing more to say. After that day we met accidentally a few times, realised that our wavelengths were the same and became friends. We began to meet by prior appointment and not by chance. One day while talking generally we found out that we were related to each other. Her father was a cousin of my mother's, several times removed. Of course, we didn't bother to tell anyone how distant a relationship ours was but word got around that we were cousins. It helped to silence the mouths of the gossips and my presence kept her admirers at bay… and how many she had! It didn't curb their enthusiasm completely though. They tried to give her letters, flowers, followed her everywhere, sighed as she walked past… She felt stifled with this attention. They showered her with love and me? I was the butt of their hatred!" he laughed.

"They called us 'Beauty and the Beast'. I quite enjoyed their jealousy. Let me tell you though Gauri, that your mother frightened away all the girls from me. I couldn't find a single one who was willing to talk to me other than her. And no one could have said that I was not good looking. Well, she was finishing her graduation and would soon leave college. I tried to convince her to join for Masters but her parents wouldn't let her. Even before her exams were over they fixed her alliance with your father. I don't think they asked her what she wanted. Anyway, something cropped up and I couldn't attend her wedding. Someone told me later that Nandini and her husband had shifted to his ancestral home. Of course, everyone ragged me about her 'ditching' me. I didn't bother to explain that just because we were good friends we need not be shackled to each other forever. I got a job, met your Kamala auntie and, well, that's that."

I thought he stifled a sigh but it could just be my imagination though he was absentmindedly turning the ring on his finger over and over.

"Oh, so you never met amma after that?"

*God, forgive my deception.*

"Let me think … hmm…"

A frown corrugated his forehead.

"Well, yes," he said. "I believe I did meet her once. It was so long ago I don't even remember exactly when I visited her but it must have been before you were born. I remember that your brother had gone to school and your father wasn't home so I couldn't meet either of them. What a beautiful house she had! And how tastefully she had decorated it. I could see that she was very happy. My visit must have come as a total surprise to her. I hadn't been able to forget the wonderful days we had at college and wanted to meet her at least once. I had her address with me but couldn't quite work up the courage to call on her. You know how conservative our society is, I didn't want to cause her any embarrassment or trouble and I was really glad when it turned out well. I was happy to spend a few hours with her talking about those old times, my job and so on. I never met her after that, not once…"

He was talking to himself and his eyes looked far away. A smile softened his features but I felt my face tighten.

***

# 13

"Mr. Raghavan, I wanted to tell you… Mr. Raghavan, are you listening to me?" I asked, as he sat there with that silly little smile looking somewhere that I couldn't see.

"Mr. Raghavan!" I called as loudly as I could without attracting anybody's attention.

He looked at me at last with those large brown eyes.

"Yes. What's it, Gauri?" he asked.

"Amma hadn't wanted me to come here. She hadn't wanted me to meet you. Do you know why?" I asked, now getting his complete attention. His eyes clouded for an instant. That was more like it. Wait till he hears the rest!

"No, tell me," he said.

I stopped myself from licking my lips. "She was worried about what I would tell your family about her and you. She didn't know how your wife would react to it."

"Did you tell Kamala anything?" he asked.

"No, I didn't have the heart to. She's already under such stress. I didn't know how she'd take it, knowing that her husband is not able to forget his old love, my mother."

The words that had been making my life miserable were out into the open. Strangely though, now they didn't seem too bad. Immoral, yes, but didn't I owe my life to that transgression? Why did it take me so long to realise this?

The shock was clearly too much for Raghu. He sat with his eyes closed, left arm across his chest, the right hand covering his lower face. After hearing Kamala auntie talk so much about herself, her husband and daughters for the past week I hadn't planned to tell him at all. But he had had an easy time while his wife had suffered. She was still suffering. It was his turn to face reality.

"Are you suggesting that Nandini thinks the same of me as she did long ago?" he asked at last, looking down at his long fingers twisting and untwisting like mating worms.

"Of course not! You are a ghost from the past. You had no place in her life once she got married to Kittu. Even then you did manage to intrude once. That once was enough for a lifetime."

"Hm…"

"Do you know the consequence of that meeting?" I asked. "You just said you did not remember when you had visited her but you knew that it was when Kittu wasn't home and Sundar had gone to school. It was at a time when amma was alone at home. Did you even think for a minute the outcome of that visit of yours?"

He did not reply.

I waited.

He looked straight into my face without speaking.

"You know?" I asked, with the relish of a serial killer sticking a knife into his victim's gut and turning it.

"You?" he asked.

I sat still. It was quiet in the compartment. Even the throbbing of the wheels below my feet seemed fainter. My heart would burst if I breathed.

"I did wonder when you came over so suddenly," he said. "In your brother's case, Nandini had called to ask me if she could send him over. At that time she didn't even mention having another child. I knew about you from Sundar. When you came I was surprised to see you. Even more surprised to see my eyes on you. Do you realise that we have very similar eyes? There's only one childhood photograph of me taken by a neighbour. Those were the days when I was always running around doing chores for everybody. This neighbour lived alone and depended on me for everything, from getting his newspaper to fetching his food from the Udupi hotel. On his sixtieth birthday he got me a new shirt, made me wear it and took a photograph. I was thin and tanned those days with eyes that seemed too big for such a small face. If you see that photograph now you won't recognise me till you look at my eyes. The moment I saw you, I was reminded of that photograph. The same small build, same colour and more important, the same eyes. Large, hopeful, ready to take on the world. Nandini's are different. I haven't met Kittu but from what I've heard about him, these eyes couldn't have been his. I was fairly certain that you were my daughter. That was probably why Nandini didn't want you to come and meet me. It was so like her not to want to upset me or my family in any way. Since I wasn't sure, I didn't say anything to you. Nor to your mother, let me assure you, Gauri."

Hearing my name brought me back to my senses.

"Why not? Why didn't you tell her what you had guessed?" I was furious with him for stealing the wind from my sails.

"If she had wanted me to know, wouldn't she have told me herself? I respect her judgement. But that doesn't mean I wasn't happy to see you. You would never understand how I feel about talking frankly like this to you. Look at you, so smart, independent, self-assured at such a young age. It thrills me that my blood is running in your veins. In you, I also have a child who's normal, well-behaved, who's everything a parent would like in his young one."

"That's Kittu's work. His and amma's."

He laughed. "Maybe. But they also have a Sundar, remember?"

He had me there.

"It is all the play of Fate, Gauri. Nothing is in our hands. We are

'But helpless Pieces of the Game He plays

Upon this Chequer-board of Nights and Days.'

Is Kamala alone to be blamed for Maya's rudeness and insolence? There was a time when I did accuse my wife of incompetence in bringing up the children. But now I realise that by not sharing that responsibility with her, I was equally at fault. Maya has always been a difficult child. Perhaps she missed me and was too young to say it . Amrita may have been different if I had spent time with her instead of leaving her with her mother all the time. Kamala herself may not be so introverted if I'd shown greater love to her. These are the thoughts that haunt me when I'm travelling and have time to think. Even then, I welcome this touring, this hectic pace of life. Know why? Because I'm scared of the day when I've retired, with no work to keep me occupied and then these 'ghosts from the past' as you put it, will haunt me. I'm scared, Gauri, terribly scared."

I had prepared to battle with the Raghu I had created in my mind with the bits and pieces of information I'd obtained first from amma and then from Kamala auntie. This Raghu was a stranger. He was honest, contrite, helpless. This Raghu was a man I could like.

"You used to confide in amma. Will you do that again?" I asked.

He shook his head slowly, thoughtfully.

"No, my dear. If I run to your mother then Kamala will be left alone. I've done too much of that all these years. I don't want to turn my back on her again. I've hurt her enough. It is now my responsibility to repair at least some of the damage. This is why I make it a point to meet Maya often. So that I can gradually make her understand that her mother needs her. Kamala probably did not know how to show her affection for the girls. Maya took it as indifference. I have been openly harsh on her and her sister. The irony is that she still tolerates me but not her mother. In fact, Gauri, if you are not too angry with me may I ask you for a favour?"

"Yes, of course."

He reached for my hand and squeezed it gently.

I smiled at him.

"Tell me, what would you like me to do?" I asked.

"Try to get Maya to talk to you," he said. "Let her spill out all her anger to you. That will make it easier for me to talk to her."

"That's what Kamala auntie also told me. Well, I'll see what I can do but from what I gather, Maya's not going to be easy to tackle," I said.

***

# PART TWO

## 14

When I recall my first, and last, meeting with Maya, there was only one thing to be grateful for – that I did not let my mouth drop when she opened the door for Raghu and me.

Kamala auntie did not have many photographs of her daughters to show me other than the stray cnes of Amrita as a child and the more recent ones taken during Maya's wedding. In those, however, the garland, the jewellery, the makeup and an awkward stiffness before the camera hid her personality. As for Amrita, she would always remain a one-year old birthday girl, peeping behind her mother or sitting on a table in front of a cake surrounded by children. Nothing much to build on, so I had created my own image of the two girls from what Kamala auntie told me about them.

Amrita, I thought, would have been fair, delicately built, of moderate height and her sister's shadow. Maya would be of average height too and small build but she would be darker, with intelligent and watchful eyes. If Amrita was a Chow puppy, cuddly, snub nosed and helpless, then Maya would be a native Rajapalayam hound, sleek, alert and pugnacious.

Standing at the entrance of her flat I realised that I had been right only about her height and colour. Maya resembled a hound as much as I looked like a bird of paradise.

Ganesh made tea for all of us while she talked about the sightseeing she had done with him. My surprise was wearing off and I could pay greater attention to her. She spoke without a pause and she spoke in two pitches – to us in a normal voice and louder to Ganesh so that he could hear her from the kitchen. Before I could react to the ludicrousness of it, he joined us and she reduced her volume.

Maya's eyes shone brighter when they rested on her husband. For the first time I was meeting a couple so deeply in love, other than amma and Kittu, of course. With one difference: Ganesh hovered round his wife like a mother bird over its fledgling, whereas Kittu had been the one to seek refuge in amma. I shook myself mentally. Ganesh was not my concern. Maya was and she was not the person I had thought her to be. Had Kamala auntie been stringing me all along?

She had projected herself as a woman wronged, the misunderstood mother, an innocent victim. Her agony had been real, her sorrow deep and her regret genuine, I had no reason to disbelieve her. Maya, however, did not seem the villain her mother had portrayed her to be. One of the two women was hiding behind a façade. I had to find out who it was or accept that I was the biggest fool ever.

Hearing my name brought me back to the present.

"Gauri, is this your first trip to Bombay?" asked Ganesh.

"Yes."

"Don't you want to do any sightseeing?" asked Raghu. "Maya seems to have enjoyed herself."

"I certainly did but do you have the time to take her around? I thought you've come here on office work? Ganesh won't be able to. He's terribly busy these days and comes home very late. I'm still new to the place so that leaves you," Maya told her father.

"Oh, I can't. I've to catch the afternoon flight for Lucknow tomorrow. Before that I have a couple of meetings to attend. Gauri, I'll get the office peon to book your ticket for 9th night. Today is the 6th. That'll give you three full days to go around."

Ganesh and Maya looked at each other. I solved their dilemma.

"No problem. I'd love to spend the time with Maya at home. I'd heard so much about her from Kamala auntie."

Maya looked sharply at me.

Aha, the fish was biting.

***

Ganesh and Raghu left home together after breakfast. Maya went to the balcony to see them off from her vantage point and I followed her.

The balcony. It was too royal a name for the minuscule rectangular projection in the wall but this was Maya's most favourite place in the whole house, not that she had much to choose from. She lived in a two-room flat on the fourth floor of an old building that had only a steep narrow staircase, no lift. The balcony was her window to the outside world. From here she could watch the boys play cricket within the narrow confines of the compound, see the regulars on their daily routine and visitors to the building or watch the unending traffic on the main road just outside the compound.

Ganesh did not let his father-in-law's presence stop him from turning around and waving to his wife before going out of the gate. Maya felt the clothes hanging on the line, found them still damp and turned them over. A crow swooped down and perched on the narrow ledge, cawing loudly.

"Meet Blackie. This is his feeding time," she said, fetching a handful of cooked rice.

No sooner had she kept it on the ledge than the crow began to eat, jabbing and scattering the soft rice in a nervous hurry.

"Let him eat in peace," she said and returned to the living room. "It's good to have someone to talk to, Gauri. I get bored sometimes."

"Your mother's bored too. You should ask your father to leave her here when he goes on tours," I suggested, helping her clear the dining table.

Maya wiped the table carefully without replying. I kept quiet like an angler waiting for the tug on the line. She must have felt my eyes.

"What did she tell you?" she asked abruptly, crushing the sponge and dripping water on the floor.

"Oh, just about how you were as a child..."

"She told you what a hateful child I was and how she wished I'd never been born?"

"Hey, relax. Her message for you was that she's missing you. She'd like you to visit her, talk to her..."

"Talk! She didn't want to listen to me when I was with her. I've nothing more to tell her," she turned to leave the room, her nostrils flaring in rage.

"Maya..." I ran behind her. "Look, Maya, I'm sorry if I have upset you. I didn't mean to. I'm only the messenger, remember?"

She patted my shoulder.

"Sorry. I shouldn't have burst out like this. You're my guest. I should treat you like one."

"No, Maya. I'd rather you think of me as your younger sister. Your mother did tell me a great deal about you and Amrita. By talking to me, a stranger, she was able to unburden herself without the fear of her words rebounding on her. They shall remain safe with me. I'll not even tell you what she told me. I don't want to sound terribly curious but you're welcome to use me the same way as your mother did to get rid of the bitterness and the resentment. You've just started your married life. Begin it as a new chapter," I said.

She slumped on a chair and I took a seat opposite hers.

After a good five minutes, she looked at me and said, "You're right. I should forget the past. I don't want to know what she said about me but I'll tell you what really happened."

***

Childhood memories never die easily. Maya found that some incidents simply refused to leave her. Like the time she found out how her sister was different from her.

Her neighbour and playmate, Rajesh stood just inside his gate and would not let her enter his compound.

"I can't play with you," he said. "You have a mad sister..."

That made her clutch the iron grill with both hands. Mad? What was that? Nobody had told her about it, not even Revabehn. What was this 'mad'? While she was mulling over it, Rajesh ran away home.

"Come back..." she shouted, but he didn't even turn around to look at her.

That was the end of their friendship. It had lasted for exactly six months, ever since he moved to the locality and looked around for somebody to play with after school.

Maya couldn't ask anyone what Rajesh had meant. She knew her mother would brush her off, so would her father. Revabehn would begin a long story that would make her forget what she had asked her in the first place. She did want to find out what was wrong with her sister. She went upstairs to their room. As usual, Amrita sat in her corner sucking a thumb and rocking on her haunches.

"Chee…how messy! Take it out."

She sat on the floor and pulled her sister's hand away from her mouth.

"Only babies do such things. You're not a baby. You're my elder sister. Wipe your mouth."

Amrita looked at her.

"You don't understand? I said wipe your mouth," Maya gestured with her hand. Her sister smiled uncertainly.

"Are you deaf? Let me do it for you," she took the hem of Amrita's skirt and wiped her mouth.

"Don't do it again. Don't put your finger in your mouth. I don't do it. Your teeth will pop out like this..."

Her gesture evoked another tentative smile.

"So, you do understand. Now, what's special about you? Let me see. Eyes, ears, nose, mouth ... you have them all," she muttered. "Now stand up," she ordered and tried to lift the other girl to her feet.

"You're heavy! You know why? You don't do anything the whole day. Just eat and sleep and rock on your bottom. I'm sure I'm stronger than you are. I play a lot, not like you."

Maya stood shoulder to shoulder with Amrita.

"You're fairer and just a little taller than me but that can't be the reason why he called you mad. Rajesh is also tall. Both of you are older, that's why. When I'm your age I'll be tall too. Maybe if I drink more milk everyday I'll also become fair. So, what's left? Your eyes ... Yes, they're small and narrow. Look at mine."

Maya widened her eyes and stared into Amrita's face. She then looked into the mirror till her nose touched the smooth surface.

"See, I told you my eyes are bigger than yours. I also like my nose better. Yours is too small, flat, almost nothing and suddenly a little upturned tip. I suppose that doesn't matter so long as you can breathe. So actually, the only difference between you and me is that you rock and suck your thumb. I don't. If I do this, will I also become mad?"

She sat down once again in front of her sister and began to rock like her. Soon both girls were moving back and forth, occasionally bumping their heads. Amrita's smile was no longer unsure. She was changing the tempo and direction to match Maya's. It had become a game that she had never played before. That was how Kamala saw her daughters when she entered the room. She stood petrified for a moment, then rushed inside and hauled Maya to her feet.

"Don't do that again ... don't you dare ... I'll kill you if I see you like that..." she screamed, till Maya managed to extricate herself and run out of the room.

She didn't know what she had done to upset her mother so badly. Whatever it was, she hadn't done it deliberately. The injustice rankled long enough to leave a scar in her memory.

After this day, however, Amrita changed slightly towards her sister. She smiled at her or even got up from her spot to stand beside her though she did not give up sucking her thumb. Maya, in her turn continued to observe her sister since she still hadn't found any difference between them. She kept a distance though since Kamala had warned her to stay away from Amrita.

Revabehn thought otherwise.

"You should spend more time with her. Only then, she'll accept you. After all, you'll have to take care of her later," she said pouring water over the girl.

"You are there to look after her." Maya closed her eyes tightly to prevent the soap from entering her eyes.

"For how long? I'll grow old. A day will come when I'll no longer be able to work then what will happen to her?"

"Why, amma's there ... oh! Will she grow old too?"

"Of course. So will you some day. You are young. You have many years to live. Not like me, an old hag."

"You're not old ... not very old... not yet," Maya clarified. "Tell me, Revabehn, why are your teeth like this? So black and some missing?'

"This is the work of the *tambacu*. I know it's very bad for the teeth. It has dissolved so many of them. I can stay without food but not without *tambacu*."

She began to undress the older girl. Maya looked at Amrita closely and shook her head. No difference at all. Amrita's body looked like hers, everywhere. She did not want to question the maid directly.

"Do you think that's why Amrita's teeth are not white like mine?" she asked instead. "But I've never seen her chew *tambacu* though."

"My little girl won't pick up bad habits. If only she'd brush her teeth properly everyday, they'll be clean. A neem stick is the best but you people use toothpaste."

Amrita's head wobbled as the maid scrubbed her scalp with her fingertips.

"Why don't you help her? Teach her to brush her teeth. Teach her all those other things you do yourself. She'll learn quickly from you rather than from me or your mother."

Maya did not have the time to teach her sister anything. Her days were already full even without a companion to play with. The pace was to become even more hectic when her father took her to school one day.

Raghu held her hand tightly and walked so fast, she had to trot. For every single step of his she had to take two. What was worse was that it didn't give her time to look around. The buildings with so many windows and doors were scattered and yet looked the same with peeling paint, dangling shutters and tiles that threatened to fall any minute. Maya would have loved to watch that happen, to see it shatter into fragments. Even as she was speeding past, she spied a rectangular iron bar hanging from the verandah of a long building.

*That's strange! What on earth would anyone use it for?*

She was to learn that it had different meanings depending on the time of the day that the peon hit it. It was the bell of doom in the morning and of freedom in the evening.

Raghu whisked her past more buildings. It was like trying to count the bogies while the train was speeding. Her father stopped only once, to ask someone for directions and off they sped again. This time along a corridor with little mounds of dry leaves, past a line of silent rooms crowded with benches and desks that seemed to stare enviously at her through the doors and windows, up a few steps till they stopped before the open doors of a big hall.

Her father left her outside while he went in. That was when she realised how loudly she was breathing. She looked around to see if others could also hear it but the only people present were all in the hall and no one seemed interested. This was how she breathed, in thick gasps, trying to catch Rajesh while playing '*chor* police'. He would insist on being the thief and she had to be the cop.

"Don't you know that the thief runs so fast that the police is never able to catch him? They show it in all movies. You are slow, you have to be the police and I'il be the *chor*."

His legs weren't as long as her father's but he could run very fast, his legs pumping up and down like a racing cyclist. After chasing Rajesh for a while, she would give up, air going in and out of her drying mouth in bursts that seemed too big for her narrow chest.

By the time her breathing became normal her father came out with a satisfied look on his face and they stood there waiting. Maya wondered if she should ask him why and decided against it. She was always full of questions that nobody answered, neither appa nor amma. They just kept piling up and troubling her. If he didn't give a reply to this one, it would join the rest.

*Something's going to happen, that's why we're waiting. I'll then get the answer myself even without asking.*

It was a little trick she played sometimes, of not letting a question finish itself. She either smothered it with a prompt answer or simply ignored it and it shrivelled and died. She could handle the innocent ones this way, those that did not demand an answer but not the other, the more persistent ones. They bothered her for a long time till she found out the answer herself or decided rather reluctantly that they probably had no solution. They remained with their little '?' even when they grew old. This time she didn't have long to wait. After a while, a man peeped out of the hall and beckoned to them. Her father sprang to him eagerly. The man didn't say anything, only gestured to a door at the end of the corridor. Maya wondered if he was dumb.

*Poor fellow... hey, wait a minute! His cheeks are puffed out like Revabehn's. His lips are red though. She said hers are not red because she eats only tambacu. Yes, his mouth is full of paan. That's why he cannot open his mouth.*

She was right. He chomped the mix of betel leaf, spices, arecanut and whatnot. He would have to spit out some of the stuff to talk to Raghu who did not look important enough for him to waste words or goo. Raghu seemed to understand the man and led her down the corridor in the direction of the pointed finger.

Maya was relieved that her father was not galloping any more. She would have loved to hear the sound of their shoes on the hushed floor but they walked quietly and the stillness was not disturbed. He knocked gently on a door and they heard a shout from within. Once again her father seemed to know what it meant before she could catch on and he went in, still holding her hand.

They were in the office of the Headmistress. The most important room in the school, she learnt later. Depending on the nature of the offence, a trip to the office could evoke enough fear to make one want to pee in one's clothes. Right then, however, she didn't know this and docilely followed her father and sat on a chair. The woman on the other side of the table was not interesting. She was just an ordinary fat woman in a bright green sari that made her look darker. Maya did not understand why her father had to cringe before her and plead so much especially when he was not used to it. At home, he usually asked for something once and amma ran to do it. And here he was, trying to please this unknown woman.

Maya gazed around the room in a wide-eyed slow motion. It seemed imposingly huge with a long table right in the middle and chairs on all sides. The headmistress sat at a smaller table with two chairs facing her. On the wall behind her was a large framed photograph of Mahatma Gandhi. Maya sat on the edge of her chair, trying to touch the floor with one foot. She was not interested in the adult talk but some words caught her attention.

"This girl's perfectly normal," her father said. "There won't be any problem at all, I can assure you. I do want at least one child to study well..."

"What do you say, girl?" the formidable lady demanded looking at Maya over her glasses poised on the tip of her nose. "Are you going to make your father happy?"

Maya smiled weakly, not knowing what it was all about. Her lack of response seemed to displease the woman in some way for she frowned at her and then glared at Raghu who hastened to reassure the headmistress once again about his daughter's mental alacrity while giving her a tight pinch on her thigh under the table. She squirmed but was too frightened to make a noise, scared now of both her father and the woman whom he was eager to impress.

"Madam, I assure you, this child is normal. Give the other one some more time. She will improve, I'm sure."

He went on and on, listening politely every time she said something and then begging and pleading once again.

*This is a superwoman! She has such power over appa!*

Maya felt a sneaking respect for the woman though she did not like her any more now than before.

She could not understand the significance of school in one's existence. After all, she hadn't missed it in all her six years and, if left alone, would have been quite all right without ever going to one. But, she remembered, all children had to go to school at some point or the other. Rajesh had said so. And he did. He still went to school. Apparently all children join a school and come out when they were much older. He had also told her about the boys and girls in his class, the crowds in the other 'sections', the teachers, the lessons, something called 'homework' which had made her think that she would have to sweep and mop in school like Revabehn did at home. He had laughed at her ignorance and said that it meant one had to read and write at home as well. That had seemed rather unfair. Surely, when one left school, one could forget about it till the next morning? Apparently that was not enough.

Rajesh had been a good guide while their friendship lasted and had briefed her well. Even then, she was not prepared for what seemed like a sea of heads when she was led to her classroom a few days later. As one, everybody turned to her when she entered the room.

She did not know where to look while the teacher muttered

under her breath about crowding and finally told her to sit somewhere. Maya sat on the third bench at the end but as soon as the bell rang and the teacher left, she had to move to the middle, where she felt like a prisoner.

This feeling of suffocation, of being trapped, never left her after that. In those early days she took it lightly. In fact, she discovered that it was good to be sandwiched like this. For one, the teachers would not wait for the child in the middle to come out and write on the board, so they almost always got one of the children in the end seats. And then, it became easier to look into a book on either side and make sure your answer was the same as your neighbours. Sometimes though, all three answers were different and left Maya confused.

On the whole, school was a reasonably happy change at first. It took her away from home for a long period and she felt important when she returned. She was almost like her father. He left home in the morning and returned only in the evening. He ordered amma around and she could do the same with her sister, except that Amrita never responded, only stared at her.

"If I looked at the teacher like you do, she'd hit me on the knuckles like this."

Maya took a long wooden ruler and smartly rapped Amrita, who clutched both hands together and looked at her fearfully.

"But I won't be afraid like you. If I don't know the answer, my friend Ramya will mutter it and I'll say it loudly. The teacher will then think that I know the answer and ask me to sit down.

Ramya cracks so many jokes it's difficult not to laugh. When the teacher's telling us something, we're supposed to sit like ... this."

Maya sat straight backed, eyes darting like a dancer's.

"Like statues. Only our eyes can move as we watch the teacher write on the board and our hands copy it in our books. We don't talk, don't even look at each other. Only Ramya has the guts to say something to the teacher. All the children in the class want to be her best friend but she has chosen me! How I wish she were my sister and not you. I would have had so much fun with her."

Ramya had also been the first to know about Amrita. Her mother had told her when she heard about their friendship.

"It doesn't matter. I won't tell anyone else about it. You can still be my best friend," she had said generously.

However, Maya's school days ceased to be fun when the other children found out about Amrita. Ram was the worst and his taunts became more hurtful as they moved to a higher class.

"Maya, does your sister beat anyone in a mad rage? Do your parents keep her locked in a room? Can I come and see her?" he asked her one afternoon during the lunch recess, his friends crowding behind him.

"She's not mad..."

"Then why doesn't she come to school?" asked one of the boys.

"She's not happy in this school."

"Oh yes, I remember how she used to cry," added Ramya.

"That was long ago, when we were young. Now we're in 3rd standard. She still doesn't go to school... why?"

"How does it matter to you?" demanded Hema, another loyalist.

"I'll tell you how it matters to him," Maya stood inches away from Ram, looked right into his eyes and continued, "Because this bully wants to tease her that's why. Do you know what happens if you tease somebody? This..." She pounced on him, grabbed him by his hair and pushed him to the ground.

She was much smaller than him and made up in fury what she lacked in strength. He was a veteran at such scrapes and Maya was clearly no match for him. The loud cheers and claps from the excited audience that was growing rapidly spurred her to give all she had behind every punch, every kick. A teacher passing by stopped and wrenched the two apart. He drove away the spectators and took the culprits to the headmistress.

Walking to the headmistress' room Maya was sure of one thing – the outcome was not going to be happy for either of them.

The teacher knocked on the wooden door that Maya remembered so well. It was not a single door but two halves, hinged in the middle of the frame leaving an almost equal space open at the top and the bottom. She remembered how the doors swung freely a few times before finally coming to a closing halt. There was no response from inside to the teacher's knock and he peeped inside.

"What's it?" growled a voice from inside sending an electric shock through the teacher who almost let the door fly from his hand. Maya and Ram shared a quick smile before remembering they were enemies. The teacher recovered and gestured to the children to wait outside the room while he went inside.

A stream of voices came out through the top and bottom of the doors that the teacher had taken the caution of closing firmly behind him.

*Will SHE remember me? How will she? There are so many children here it's not possible to know each one. Moreover, I've such an ordinary face. Nobody will remember me. She won't either.*

Maya's knees still wouldn't stop shaking.

*Is this the time, Maya? You DON'T want to go to the toilet. And stop shivering. How terrible it will be if SHE looks at your legs and sees your knees knocking against each other!*

Her worry had been unnecessary. Either the headmistress did not remember Maya or did not recognise her. Of course, Maya's right eye had changed colour after taking the brunt from a strong fist while her lower lip was cracked and swollen. Through her left eye she saw Ram clutching his stomach with one hand and rubbing the top of his head with the other. On his cheek were three deep gashes that made Maya happy about not trimming her nails regularly.

"What's all this, now?" the headmistress demanded. "Fighting?"

"Yes, ma'am. These two..." began the teacher.

She stopped him impatiently, "Let them talk."

Maya and Ram looked at each other, waiting for the other to begin.

"Go on ... have you swallowed your tongues?"

Maya flared at the woman's tone.

"He teased me..."

The teacher nudged her from the back.

"..e," she began, the word sticking to her throat and refusing to come out. The headmistress was frowning. Maya quickly cleared her throat and began again. This time her voice was louder than required.

"He was teasing me about my sister."

"What?"

"He was teasing me about my sister," she repeated.

The woman frowned and asked, "What?"

Maya wondered if she was hard of hearing. The teacher nudged her once again and she remembered the class teacher's first lesson.

"Always greet your elders when you meet them. Address your headmistress as Ma'am or Madam. When you finish what you have to say, don't forget to say Ma'am or Madam. Say thank you when you leave."

*Oh...oh!*

"Namastemadamhewasmakingfunofmeandmysistermadam

soIfoughtwithhimmadamthankyoumadam," she said.

"So you can speak. Good, now repeat what you said. Slowly," she ordered.

Maya swallowed and obeyed, much slower this time though she did want to say it as fast as before, take whatever punishment was given and get out of the room as quickly as possible.

The headmistress turned to Ram.

"I was not really making fun, Madam. I was just asking her about her sister," he mumbled.

The woman's eyebrows shot up. Thin painted arcs that curved like little shooting stars.

"Why the special interest in her sister? Is she a film star or a celestial beauty? No answer, eh? You, girl, tell me. What's so great about your sister?"

"Nothing ... Madam," Maya remembered her manners in the nick of time.

"Then?"

"She has some problem."

"Not just any problem. She's mad but she's let loose, Madam," the boy volunteered.

"Oh ...yes, I remember..." she looked over the heads of the children and spoke to someone at the door. "I'm through with these people. Do please come in and take a seat."

Maya and Ram swivelled to see two men standing at the doorway. They turned around once again to face the headmistress when she tapped impatiently on the table.

Conversation ceased while the men came inside and sat on chairs next to each other at the long table.

"I don't have time to waste on you," said the headmistress. "But let me make one thing very clear. If either of you get into any other scrap like this, then that will be it. You'll be suspended from school. Don't come to me with your parents crying that you'll behave better, etc., etc. I won't listen to any nonsense, understood?" she demanded in a low voice.

Her words hissed and sizzled like drops of water on a hot griddle, making Maya want to step backwards, away from danger. She stood still and watched the thick lips open and close over the big teeth, occasionally getting a glimpse of a gold tooth just inside the mouth which she didn't remember seeing the first time.

The two nodded. Was it possible? Could it be likely that she was not going to punish them? They looked at each other in a sudden burst of camaraderie.

"You may go," she dismissed them.

The teacher was about to open the door when she called out, "Oh, teacher ... don't forget to tell their class teachers about what happened and ask them to punish these two for disrupting the school. In addition to whatever punishment the class teacher gives, these troublemakers must write a thousand times "I will not fight in school," get it signed by their parents and show it to the class teacher. Sorry about that ... you know these childr..."

Maya did not turn around to see if the doors were shut nor did she pay attention to the headmistress' words that tapered to silence the further they went. She walked numbly. A thousand times? Just when she had thought that she wouldn't get any punishment! It was a stab in the back. One thousand times? It would take hours to write!

It didn't take as long as she had feared but she did learn her lesson even though it was too late. Ram spread the news to all his friends who passed it on to theirs and soon the whole school knew about Amrita. Now more children became curious about her. Maya heard their whispers when she went past.

Loud or soft she did not retaliate. Not in school at least. Home was another story.

***

# 15

I didn't expect Maya to describe how she tormented her sister. After all, no one would want to project a mean image of oneself. Why should she be any different?

Whatever she did, within no time Amrita became nervous even when Maya did not notice her. She would sit in her corner, legs close to her body, hands around her knees and watch Maya's every movement. That was satisfying too. Her mother tried to stop her from ill-treating her sister and failed.

*What'll she do? Slap me a few times? She's not going to tell appa about me. Revabehn's the one to watch out for. She has the eyes of an eagle.*

It was indeed the maid who first noticed Maya's black eye when she returned from school one day and asked her about it.

However, after listening through the account punctuated with hiccups, sniffles and anger, she did not say anything. The next morning Maya waited near the gate for her mother to return after meeting the headmistress. When she did, Kamala gave her a glare, followed it with a lecture and the matter ended there. Maya knew this too would be kept from her father. Some days later Revabehn took her to her house.

*House? To Revabehn's little hut?*

"I want you to meet the children in my locality," she said. "I've told them so much about you. They're eager to meet you."

That sounded good. Maya's chin went up. Oh, those poor little slum kids, they wouldn't have seen someone like her.

"Do you get angry sometimes?" asked Revabehn, holding the little girl's hand and walking briskly.

"Sometimes? Always! I always get so angry with everything and everybody."

"Excellent!"

Maya looked up sharply. Her teacher had always insisted that anger was wrong, very bad and Revabehn was praising her for it?

The old woman calmly spat out a thick mass of softened, pulverised tobacco and wiped her mouth with the back of her hand which, in turn, she wiped on her skirt. Unlike her mother who wore a sari, Revabehn wore the *chania-choli.* The skirt was wide and bounced with every step. It did not reach the ankle and so it stayed away from the mud and dirt on the road. Her blouse covered her from the neck to the waist but was open at the back, tied with a couple of strings. She would never let Maya play with the strings but pulled the *odhni* firmly around her so that the thin shawl covered her back fully.

"Excellent," she repeated before Maya could question her further.

"Did you know that anger's a very good thing? It cleans your system much better than any medicine. When someone's angry, really very, very angry, blood rushes through the body from the head to the toe and it becomes clean and red. It makes you feel energetic. You can do a lot more work. Anger will give you the extra strength. Unfortunately, I don't get very upset these days but when I was younger ... ah! You should have seen me then. My eyes would turn red. My whole body would feel so hot. I wouldn't have been surprised if wisps of smoke came out of my nose. It was the devil within me, the devil of wrath dancing with joy. I'd let him have his fun for some time but after a while I wouldn't want to be angry any more. You know how I'd drive him out? First I'd throw down all the vessels from the kitchen. Thud ... crash ... rattle...! Then I'd take a handful of *raakh* ... and begin *giso...giso ...giso*.... All that scrubbing with the ash would make the vessels shine like silver. My neighbours would look jealously at me."

"'The anger *bhooth* has caught Revabehn!' they'd say. 'Let's also give our vessels to her.'"

"As if I'm a fool to waste my rage on them, ha! All of it was reserved for my family."

"Do you think it'll work for me too?" Maya asked wistfully.

"I never knew it was a spirit in me. I thought I was ... just ... angry. Can I also drive it out by washing vessels?"

"You can but those in your house are all very clean. I do them so well though your mother's never satisfied. We'll have to find some other way to drive out the *bhooth* in you. Let me think...."

Maya watched Revabehn closely but, from her little height, she could only see the underside of the maid's jaw working steadily on a new wad of tobacco. It made her thirsty but water would have to wait. She had to learn how to exorcise the devil first.

"I'll tell you what you can do. Don't talk to anyone. Don't even look at anyone. Get out of the house and play..."

That smashed Maya's picture into smithereens. She had visualised herself in the centre of piles of vessels, some cleaned, most still greasy and dirty, smoke curling from her nostrils....

"Aw, that's so boring. Whom will I play with, anyway?"

"Don't you play in school? Don't you have any friends?"

"They won't let me take part in their game because they're afraid of becoming mad like Amrita."

"*Arrey, rey*, how stupid they are. It's good you don't mingle with such foolish children. It doesn't matter. The children in my *basti* know lots of games. They'll teach you."

Maya's initial reservation when they crowded around her vanished in no time. The difference in the quality of her frock and their clothes ceased to be important. They couldn't speak any language other than Gujarati while she could. They lived in a *basti*, in little homes that were no better than basic shelters with tin roofs and leaning walls. She forgot that her house was an independent two storeyed one of brick and concrete. What really mattered to her was their warmth, their unreserved friendliness once Revabehn told them who she was and why she had come to meet them. She wondered if they would change and start behaving like the children in her school when they would know about her sister but they remained as friendly and happy to see her as they were the first time she visited them.

She did not know for how long she would have continued to play with those children. One day a neighbour happened to see her at the *basti* and told her father. The beating she got from him ensured that she never thought of playing any game with anyone.

It was back to being lonely once again but now she found that the sight of her sister no longer angered her as it had before.

*I think the anger bhooth has decided to leave me at last. Or maybe it's because no one in school asks me any more about my sister,*' she thought more realistically.

With time to think, she began to wonder about Amrita.

*Won't it be boring for her to stay at home the whole day? I go to school, meet many children, do many things ... how can she stay like this?*

"What do you think, Revabehn? Will she ever become like me? Will she learn something?"

"Of course, why not? You remember that Munni who used to play with you? She's a big girl now. She does so much work in her house. She helps her mother a lot. Your sister can too."

"But appa won't like it if he sees her."

"He needn't know anything. She can work while he's away."

"Why don't you teach her? She can wash vessels, clean the house..."

"What'll your mother say to this? *Chalo*, let's try."

The maid gave Amrita a broom and taught her to sweep the floor with gestures and simple instructions while Maya watched. Amrita fumbled at first but over the next few days she caught on and swept the room slowly and carefully. They rewarded her with claps and smiles while she hid her face in her hands. With that, her corner opened out. Amrita no longer sat rocking endlessly but walked around with the broom even when she was not sweeping. She smiled at Maya and touched her gently sometimes. The first time she did it, Maya raised her hand to brush her sister's away but it was such a soft touch, she kept quiet. The devil of wrath hadn't quite left her though. He made his presence felt occasionally when Amrita swept the room early in the morning and disturbed Maya's sleep.

"Can't you do this later?" she would shout. "You have the whole day to sweep or mop or do whatever you want. Making so much noise, enough to waken the dead! Sit down somewhere and keep quiet."

Amrita was learning to obey her sister without a beating and she would sit patiently till she got a signal to get up from her chair. Their room had never been as clean as it was now. The floor gleamed and the windows shone. She sometimes went so far as to peep out through the window. If she saw something interesting she would pull Maya's or Revabehn's hand and bring them to the window as well. Maya was not keen on looking out but Revabehn was always ready to take a break from her chores.

"That's a *larri*. He keeps vegetables on the handcart and takes it from house to house to sell. The fellow's a crook and charges too much. Market is the best," she advised.

"See how the monkey is jumping! It can do a lot of tricks…"

"… and probably knows more than her," Maya would add if she was in a foul mood.

"That's because that fellow has taught the monkey. We haven't taught our darling girl enough!"

"Who's to be blamed for this? My parents. Don't they know that she needs to go to school? How much can we teach her?"

"Don't blame your mother. Either your sister wouldn't learn from her or she didn't find the lessons interesting. How long can anyone keep telling her the same things? It's up to you now and you refuse to spend any time with her!"

While they argued, Amrita watched the daily scene of cars, cyclists, pedestrians, animals and handcart vendors pass by. It provided her with some kind of entertainment, like a long movie with actors who changed constantly. This film had no story though, no climax and a very limited sound track. From that distance she couldn't hear the salesmen's spiel, only the sharp tring of the cycle bell of the ice or cotton candy man. These actors did nothing special except to move across her range of vision left to right or right to left. Only the very old or the very young could have watched such a monotonous show and yet, it engrossed Amrita from morning till night. Maya didn't mind leaving her to it. Those were the times when Amrita did not bother her.

One day a little boy looked up and saw her watching him and his friends. He nudged the others and as one they stood in the middle of the road to stare back at her. This was the first time someone was looking at her and it made her shy. She covered her face with both hands and looked through her fingers. Maya saw her and curiously looked out of the window. Just a few scruffy boys. She picked up a book and lay on the bed while her sister continued her new game.

"Hey!" one of the boys shouted, gesturing to Amrita to come down.

"You... come here!" shouted another.

She quickly moved to a side but couldn't resist the temptation to peep out once again. The boys were laughing and talking among themselves and looking up as Amrita played hide-and-seek. A few adults joined them and soon there was a group of people gazing at the window. Raghu returned from work just then. He glanced up to see what was attracting them just as Amrita peeped out. He rushed into the house, ran up the steps and slammed the window shut. Maya was still lying on the bed reading a book. He caught Amrita by her hair and hurled her to the ground, slapping her.

"Will you do it again? Will you do it? You ... you wretched little..." he had gone on and on, thrashing and yelling at her while Maya watched with surprise and fear. Raghu then turned to Maya and pulled her from the bed.

"Couldn't you have stopped her? Between the two of you, you'll kill me..."

"But ... I didn't do anything, appa. I was only reading a..." she protested.

He hadn't let her finish.

"I know what you did and what you didn't. Don't talk back to me," he said, slapping her as well.

He left the room at last. Maya heard the front door slam and soon the gate closed with a thud. Her tears dried but Amrita was still whimpering. It made her furious.

"Why did you make appa so angry? Don't you dare do it again," she said, kicking her sister viciously. "Because of you, I also got hit. I hate you, hate you, hate you more than anything or anyone else. How dare he punish me for your stupidity? I'll show him. I won't have my dinner tonight."

Maya woke up hungry in the middle of the night. The house was silent and dark. The darkness and her father's anger frightened her but her stomach would not let her sleep. It growled with little rumbles. She hugged a pillow but it did not suppress the noise or the pangs and both grew steadily worse. She sat on the bed wondering what to do.

*Oh, but it's simply too dark! How will I go down? Even if I do, what will I get to eat at this time?*

She decided to lie on her stomach and sleep it off. When that too failed she tried to divert her mind.

*What can I think about...? My friends? I don't have any. I only had Ramya and she too is in another section now. I miss her. She was such a good friend. From what she told me, her family seemed happy... not like mine. Her mother would cook nice things ... pulao, kofta ... I wonder how kofta looks ... how it tastes. Ramya used to say that was her favourite. She was selfish. She could have brought at least one kofta for me.*

The rumbling grew louder. Now her mouth was watering as well.

*Maybe there's some rice left.*

She sat up once again.

*It's not really so dark, Maya. It only seems like that. Let your eyes get used to it and you'll be able to see at least the shapes.*

She opened her eyes wide and looked around.

*Yes! I can see the table... the chair ... and there's the door.*

She worked up courage and stood up from her bed. She took a few steps, stumbled and fell. Amrita was sleeping where she lay on the floor and Maya had forgotten about her. She cursed her sister, kicked her and went back to bed.

Amrita never ventured near the window again.

Maya had her own worries. She was doing very badly at school and the final exam loomed threateningly. The only comfort was that her grandmother was visiting them.

"Perhaps appa won't be very angry when paati is around. What do you think, Revabehn?" asked Maya.

"If your father gets really angry I don't think he'll bother whether anyone is watching. It'll be much better for you to study and not waste time."

"But it's all so boring. Everybody laughs the moment I open my mouth in class. I hate school, I hate everyone there!"

"Learn to fend for yourself."

"Okay, okay but tell me, what'll I do if I fail?" Maya wailed.

She did fail and bore Raghu's wrath while her mother watched. The only positive outcome of her failure was that her grandmother took her away to the village, away from her parents and sister.

***

"Have you ever been to a village, Gauri?" Maya asked. "That's another kind of life altogether. My grandmother lived in a typical Brahmin *agraharam*, with two lines of houses facing each other. It's such a small village no outsider will even know about it though it is on the way to Kanya Kumari, which tourists flock to see the sun rise and set at the confluence of the Indian Ocean, Arabian Sea and the Bay of Bengal. The houses are typical, built in a straight line so that if you stand at the entrance of any one you can see through the rooms and beyond to the backyard!" she laughed.

"I still remember when I first arrived with paati … I must have been about nine years old. I was wearing a frock that was just above my knees. She hinted that it might better to change to a long skirt but I didn't like the idea of confining my legs in a swathe of cloth. We got off the bus and walked along the narrow path to the village. Even as we drew closer, the children stopped playing and stared at me. A couple of men talked to her but I could see they were curious to know who I was."

"'My granddaughter, Maya. My son's daughter,' paati announced to them and to everybody along the way who stopped us or looked at us from their verandah. I was suddenly conscious of my thin legs, the shortness of the hemline though it was till the knee, the clumsiness of my gait. I wondered if my hair was too blown by the wind, if I didn't seem too dark beside my fair grandmother."

"I know. That's how I feel when I'm with…" I began but Maya did not hear me.

"They helped us carry our bags home, opened the door, someone brought us milk, another neighbour sent a girl to clean the house, a child came with the mail, a couple of old women hurried to tell paati the local news. There was a buzz of activity around her. She introduced me to everyone till the faces and names seemed to scorch my brain. I wanted to hide myself but I had to tolerate those searching looks, the questioning and comments. Later I realised that the curiosity helped to keep the elderly occupied, bound everybody together as if they were all part of one big family. The little bickering or disagreements among them were quickly forgotten in some new excitement."

"Paati got me admitted to the only school there. It was at one end of the village while a temple stood at the other end. The temples of God and learning faced each other. Behind one line of houses was the river which served many purposes – to bathe, as a place to wash clothes, to meet and gossip, for young men to while away time by tossing stones into the water and ogling at the girls. A much smaller stream ran behind the other line, behind paati's house. It must have been a beautiful brook long ago but now the steps leading to it were worn down dangerously and the branches of trees hung above the surface of the water. Paati never let me go there. She said the trees were the home of ghosts. That made me yearn to meet at least one, to see if a ghost was really diaphanous and whether its feet did not touch the ground as my new friends assured me so confidently. I made many friends within a week of my arrival. All of them were girls. A boy wouldn't think of talking to a girl and if a girl ever committed that sin..." she shuddered.

I smiled. I wasn't going to comment if she did not want me to.

"I liked the river very much. I had not seen so much water from such close quarters. It was monsoon and the river was gushing along. Paati insisted on accompanying me. If she was too busy, I had to stay behind too. She wouldn't let me go alone or with my friends. At first I obeyed her since I didn't want to be sent back to my parents. That didn't stop me from thinking what a tyrant she was. It took me a while to realise that her restrictions were for my benefit but I learnt it, the hard way."

I raised my eyebrows in silent query. I was not going to ask too many questions and stop her from talking to me. As a child, the moment I spotted the delicate little shrub with fluffy pink flowers I rushed to touch its leaflets and watched them droop. Maya was just like this plant, retreating into herself the moment she suspected danger. This was one Mimosa pudica I wasn't going to touch in a hurry.

Fortunately, Maya wasn't waiting for me to say anything.

"She would not let me enter the water though everyone else would bathe or swim merrily," she said. "I had to sit on the bank and watch them have fun. To make it worse, she herself could swim and what a swimmer she was! She'd tie her underskirt tightly round her chest, below the armpit and walk into the river. Then her arms would cleave the water and she would thrash her feet and take off like a little fish chased by a bigger fish. Such speed at her age! I begged her to teach me but she refused."

"'I can't let you run any risk,' she said, making me so angry."

"One day I decided to learn on my own. The moment she entered, I followed. She didn't see me but the others did. They probably shouted to me but I didn't hear anything. I was simply too thrilled to be in the cool water, to feel the waves slap against me. I stood still for a while just taking it all in. My grandmother had almost reached the other bank. Before she could turn back I had to 'swim'. I quickly walked further inside. The water came up much faster than I expected. Soon I had to jump to breathe. I couldn't shout or move my arms and legs like her. Air. I wanted air and I was breathing water."

"Suddenly, a hand caught the nape of my neck and pushed me out of the water. It dragged me along. I could not see where I was going. I stumbled over the stones on the bed of the river. My panic-stricken mind couldn't accept what my feet felt. Water had entered my nose, ears, mouth, everywhere. I gulped in air deeply and coughed at the same time. Someone pummelled me on the back and I recovered slowly."

"No marks, Gauri, for guessing the identity of my saviour!" Maya laughed. "Yes, it was paati who had hauled me to safety. One or two children sniggered at me but others at the river continued to swim, bathe or wash their clothes as if drowning was an everyday affair."

"I was quaking not so much with cold as with fear. Appa's anger used to terrify me. I didn't know how angry his mother could get. She didn't say a word. No lecture, no scolding, nothing. She took a towel and dried my head vigorously. Then she caught me by the nape once again and rushed me home, to get me into dry clothes. I didn't disobey her in anything after that day, let me tell you. Some months later, she offered to teach me swimming but I refused. I'd had enough of the river. From then on I sat on the bank and watch the moods of nature and play of people. The ripples on the water, the leaves and flowers floating lazily, children catching little guppies in their towels and, above all, the expertise of my grandmother as she swam ... all these I admired from the distant safety of the bank."

"Paati taught me lots of things without making me realise that I was learning anything. I didn't even know that I was changing – in degrees. While staying with my parents I used to return home like a hurricane. Most evenings I'd be in a foul mood, ready to fight with anyone who crossed my path but at paati's, anger was furthest in my mind. I washed my feet as soon as I came from school, ate whatever she gave me, finished my homework, lit the lamp and said a few prayers. I then helped her clear up the kitchen and listened to her stories and songs as we lay on our reed mats. It was a similar pattern in the morning. I no longer complained about going to school. I didn't have the time for it really. After drawing water from the well, sweeping the floor and doing a number of little chores I'd get ready for school and wait impatiently for my friends. School was a few metres from home but we went in a group, taking as much time as we could so that we could talk."

"I wonder where they are now," Maya sighed. "I had so many

good friends there. You know, Gauri, one of the reasons why I want to be with my in-laws? So that my child, when I have one, can have the company of her grandparents, grow up with other children, have fun, study and play together. Bonding with only the parents is not enough. I want her to be loved by others in the family and love them in turn. This can happen only if she's with them all the time, not if we go there once or twice a year. What do you say, Gauri?"

Nothing. Didn't she want her child to know Kamala, the maternal grandmother? I let her carry on with her story.

"I was happy for the first time in my life," said Maya. "In a way I never thought would be possible. There was no reason for me to get angry. I made friends with children who did not laugh at me. I was doing well in school and my teachers praised me in front of the whole class. I was not made to feel responsible for anyone. It was as if my sufferings were over at last. I was wrong."

"My grandmother was already old when she visited us. I did not think of asking her why her skin was wrinkled or why the flesh of her upper arms sagged. I just accepted those as part of her. In any case, a woman who could swim so well was surely a healthy woman. But she lived only for another three years, just long enough to show me what happiness was and then she died. Appa came to do her last rites and took me back with him."

"Nothing had changed at home. Amma was as sullen as ever,

appa was hardly around and Amrita was back in her corner, sucking her thumb, arms around her knees, rocking endlessly on her haunches. I might not have left at all."

***

# 16

"Enough of this nonsense. Get up. Don't you dare do this again," Maya shouted, hauling Amrita to her feet. The suddenness of her voice made her sister cringe and hide her face.

Revabehn tried to intervene.

"What else will she do, the poor thing?"

"She's worse than before. Why have all of you left her alone like this?"

"We tried but she wouldn't learn anything. She can be more stubborn than a donkey. She wouldn't even do the usual chores always. Perhaps she missed you. Look at her now…"

Amrita was touching Maya's face with the tips of her fingers. The fear that had lurked in her eyes just moments ago had vanished. In its place was an excitement that the girl could not hide.

Maya let go of her sister's hands. She couldn't look at Amrita in the face. Her eyes fell on the dull red streaks her fingers had made just above the wrist. She wanted to rub that mark away. She wanted to say sorry. She wanted to cry. She turned to Revabehn instead.

"At least somebody is happy to see me. With paati gone, I thought I'd lost the only person who had some affection for me. Apparently my sister does, even though I've not always been nice to her."

"You can make up for that," said the maid. "Now that you're back, teach her. She might listen to you. She certainly didn't want to obey us."

Maya smiled at Amrita, making her look at the floor in embarrassment.

"You're still so shy! I'll change that too. I have to go to the school but I'll teach you as much as I learn there, okay?"

She waited for a reply.

"Come on. Say something. If you don't want to study I won't bother. Tell me what you want to do."

Once again Amrita smiled and did not reply.

"Ofo! You still won't talk? Revabehn, I know she's not dumb. Why doesn't she say anything?"

"I suppose it's because she has been alone for too long, ever since you left. Our presence did not matter to her."

"That's absurd...." Maya began and realised that Revabehn was right. They might live under one roof but Amrita had always been alone.

"I'm also to be blamed. It's true I went away with paati but when I was here I could have talked to you instead of only shouting at you," Maya said, taking Amrita's hand into hers once again and looking at her sister's face as if seeing her for the first time.

Revabehn was not convinced that Maya had truly changed towards Amrita. She kept checking on the girls till climbing the steps to reach their room became too painful. Her suspicion did not stop Maya from becoming her sister's tutor from the day she arrived till she left her parental home with her husband, years later.

"I'll teach you how to read and write," she said, taking a sheet of paper and pencil. "You can then spend your time reading books while I'm at school."

She drew a flower and asked, "What's this? You know?"

The older girl smiled hesitantly.

"Fla..ver. Say it. No ... wait. I'll show you a flower."

She ran to the front yard and looked around. It was bare except for a few drying weeds.

"This is bad. Nothing is growing here. Did amma give up gardening too?" she looked around and spied a small lantana with clusters of tiny yellow flowers.

*It'll have to do for the time being.*

She plucked a bunch and ran back.

"See ... flower. Yellow flower. Go on, say it..." she ordered but Amrita wouldn't open her mouth.

"Let's start again. From the beginning."

There was only one table and chair in their room. As the teacher, Maya sat on the chair and made Amrita sit on the floor.

"No squatting, as if you are sitting on a commode. Sit cross-legged," she said but Amrita's knees would not lie down.

"You are so fat. This will not do. You must exercise. I'll show you what we do in the PT period. Get up. Stand straight, arms down the sides. Look ahead. Watch me closely."

Maya demonstrated the first exercise of physical training she learnt in school of stretching the hands to the front, up, side and down to the count of four. Her arms moved smartly in staccato movements, swift and sure, but Amrita's flopped like a bunch of tired leaves. When she bent to touch her toes, she almost fell on her face. Her clumsiness might irritate her sister but she herself was enjoying every moment of it. It was as if she had forgotten how her sister used to beat her. This girl was a playmate, someone she had never had before. Maya, however, meant business, even though it was clear that Amrita would take a very long time to reach anywhere near her own level of competence.

"I'm not the best student but Amrita, you're worse than me!

My God, we have a lot to do," she said.

At the age of 12, she was still fired by exuberant optimism and did not think of questioning her ability to teach her sister anything at all. She took every little sign of progress as a great achievement and was eager to experiment some more. Only once did she hesitate, at the outset, when Amrita couldn't move her arms and legs in co-ordination. It was not for want of trying for she flung her arms around all the time, suppressing her laughter whenever Maya looked at her. Other lessons were much easier though boringly repetitive. Yet, she persisted, till Amrita learnt how to bathe and dress herself, comb her hair, fold clothes, make the beds and do several other sundry tasks. It was a roller-coaster ride that took several years. When Amrita learnt something quickly, Maya's mood would swing up. When the progress was not so good, she got angry, irritated or despondent. Those were the times when flashes of her old temper surfaced but they lacked the fury of the past. Even a rap on the knuckles made Amrita turn to her work, but Maya did not like the heaviness she felt when her sister looked at her with fear in her eyes.

To reduce physical distance between them she joined Amrita on the floor. They lay on their stomachs while she pointed out the pictures in a book or sat cross-legged and wrote with the book on the lap. Amrita could now sit on the floor for longer periods. She had lost some weight, her movements were better but the most important development as far as Maya was concerned was that her sister now understood everything that she told her. She was still reluctant to speak and when she did, only Maya could understand her slurred words.

One day she asked Amrita to fetch a pencil from the table. Proudly she watched her sister's prompt obedience and froze. On the back of Amrita's skirt was a big dark patch.

"Ammu ... wait. Come here. Turn around," she said getting up and inspecting the back of her sister's skirt. She looked at the mat. There was a mark there too, though much smaller than the one on the skirt. Maya touched it lightly. Her fingertips showed red. Blood?

"Did you get hurt? When? Where? Show me," she ordered.

Her hands had turned cold and she was suddenly very afraid. She made her sister lift her skirt. There was no sign of injury on the back of the thighs but the seat of her panties was stained.

"Is it paining? Did you sit on any sharp thing? No? Then where is the blood coming from? I can't see any wound. What do we do now? Should I call Revabehn? How will she help? Maybe it's nothing serious. Change your panties and dress and lie down. The bleeding may stop by itself. No more class today."

She helped Amrita change her clothes.

"Lie down. Don't get up whatever happens. I have to go to school. I'll come back in the evening. Revabehn will come in with your food. If you lie down quietly she may not suspect anything, okay?"

She found it difficult to concentrate on what the teachers

said. The classes seemed to go on forever. Finally the peon rang the bell to announce the welcome end of the long school day and Maya rushed home.

Her sister was as cheerful as when she had left her in the morning though she had changed her dress yet again. Maya tried to find out what had happened in her absence but her sister continued to smile without saying anything. She went downstairs and peeped into the kitchen. Kamala was busy cooking. Raghu would return in a couple of hours and he didn't like to be kept waiting for his dinner. In any case, ever since she returned after her grandmother's death, Maya had reduced talking to her mother to the absolute minimum. Even then, she debated whether she should ask her about Amrita, when Revabehn came along. Maya caught her by the hand and led her to their room.

"Is Ammu very ill? Is she going to die?" she asked. "Don't laugh. Tell me."

"Nothing to worry about," said the maid trying to hide her amusement. "All girls go through this. This is what makes them women. You will get it too some day and then it will soon be time to get you married and packed off. You will have kids, they will grow, the process will go on."

"What about you? You also get it?"

"I'm too old. It stopped long ago."

"So, it will stop some time."

"Yes, when you're old, when your children are grown up, then it'll stop."

"But why does it begin in the first place?"

"I told you, to make women out of girls."

"What about boys? What happens to make them men?"

"I don't know. Enough of this chatter. Go and study."

"But what does one do when it starts?" Maya persisted. She wanted to be better prepared than her sister.

"There's no need to worry about it now. I'll tell you at the right time or your mother will."

"Amma? What will she tell me? She sent me away because she's not fond of me. When I was younger I thought she preferred Amrita to me and that's why she spent all the time with her. Now I know she doesn't care for her either. Why else would she neglect her like this?"

"What are you talking about? Which mother will hate her child?"

"I knew you'll be on her side. That's why I didn't tell you anything all these days. It doesn't matter. I don't need her help with my sister."

"If you don't need your mother, you won't need me either..."

"Don't say that, Revabehn," said Maya. "I can't manage without you. At least you look after her while I'm at school."

Amrita could now say and write the alphabet without too many mistakes. She could read a few simple words and count up to 30. Her favourite activity, however, was drawing. She could fill page after page with stick figures but she was so scared of her sister that she laboriously wrote out the alphabet in capital and small letters, the few words that she had learnt and solved simple problems in arithmetic – all before Maya returned from school.

A B C D E F G H' I J K L<br>
M N O P Q R S T U V W X<br>
Y Z<br>
cat rat bat hat PEN RUN<br>
MAN FAN CAN SUN FUN VAN<br>
bag cap map JUG MUG PIG<br>
LEG egg eYE OWL ANT POT<br>
TOP CUP FOX YAK DOG TAP<br>
ZIP ZOO INK KEY Car GOd

4 + 4 = 8   5 + 3 = 8   6 + 2 = 8   7 − 3 = 4   8 − 6 = 2   6 − 2 = 4

Anyone would have laughed to see how this grown up girl wrote. Her tongue peeped out and she held the pencil with the tip of all five fingers. She scratched her head to recall the sequence of the letters or muttered the numbers while adding and subtracting but there was no one to see her except the maid who came up occasionally to check on her. Revabehn did not laugh, she only sat with the girl and admired her literacy. She could not write her name herself but she was no fool. No one could cheat her off 10 paise. She could mentally total the price of even 25 items and give Kamala an accurate account.

"What will I do after learning how to read and write?" she replied, when Maya offered to teach her. "Your mother will not be happy to see me with a book. Don't waste time on me, girl. I'm a gone case."

Age, however, did not stop Revabehn from praising Amrita's big letters that sloped down the page unless they were caught in small boxes.

"How well you have written, my *bitiya rani*! Your sister is going to be very proud of you when she returns from school. This old woman wouldn't have been able to do half as well in double the time you've taken."

Amrita flushed with happiness and brought out her drawing book. The more abstract the drawing, the greater the clarity with which Revabehn seemed to see the details.

"Is this a ... let me see ... a temple? Ah! I know. It's a house. Look at the windows, the door. How clever! Did you draw this yourself or did your sister help you? How can you draw so beautifully? I'm sure even she can't draw as well."

Amrita beamed in pleasure and lifted her skirt to hide her face in its folds.

"Maya will get angry," warned Revabehn and the girl dropped it immediately.

Lapses like these were becoming considerably less frequent and often the maid couldn't believe that this was the same girl who had once given her so much trouble. Neither could she believe that it was Maya who had effected the change, the girl who had given her even greater trouble.

It was Maya's last year in school. A good six months before her final exam she stopped teaching Amrita in order to concentrate on her books. Seeing her nervous and irritable, her sister retired to her corner. She could not understand the change but instinct made her stay away. Maya walked up and down the room trying to memorise important dates in history or formulae in science. The more she tried to remember the less they stuck to the mind. When it was time to enter the examination hall, she couldn't remember a single detail that she had slaved over. She answered the papers mechanically one after the other and then began the wait for the exam results to be announced. She didn't know which agony was worse, the tension during or after the exam. That wait too came to an end at last and she was relieved to find that she had passed with marks that surprised her. If she couldn't study what she wanted, then she was going to spend all her time with her sister, she decided.

"What can I teach her next, Revabehn?" she asked, when the maid visited them. Age and ill-health had finally caught up with her and Revabehn had quit working in their house a few months ago. She dropped by out of habit to see the girls and to gossip with Kamala.

"What can this old woman tell you? I've grown too old to even remember my name."

"Grow! Yes, I'll teach her gardening. What do you say?"

"Teach her whatever you want."

"Don't be so indifferent. After all, this concerns your favourite girl. Say that you like me more than my sister," she challenged.

"Ask me which eye I like, right or left?" Revabehn countered.

"Even though you refuse to say it I always knew you liked her more. I remember only too well that you never had a harsh word for her, it was always reserved for me."

"Listen to you talking like this, to me, the one who taught you how to speak and look at my other child, still so innocent, not like you," the old woman shook her head in mock resignation.

"Now that you've conceded that I have grown, listen to me for a change. Go and see a doctor. You don't look very good," said Maya.

"What will the doctor say? Give up *tambacu*, eat better food, take more rest. When I know what they're going to say why should I go and pay them my hard earned money?"

"Maybe they'll say something different. Who knows?" Maya argued.

"If at all they do say something different it will be 'your time is up, old woman, pack up.' I won't be sorry either. It's best to leave when I can still walk without anybody's support."

Revabehn had been prophetic. Two months later she was diagnosed as having terminal oral cancer and within a week she died.

***

# 17

Their little garden helped Maya cope with Revabehn's death. She did not tell Amrita about the maid's demise nor did the girl ever enquire.

*Will she remember me if I leave some day?*

Maya looked at her sister and wondered. Amrita had a bright red Hibiscus flower tucked behind each ear and was holding a big bunch in her hand. Even as she watched, the girl brought it close to her face and inhaled, making specks of yellow pollen stick all over her face. Maya sighed and went up to her.

"You do like gardening, don't you?" she asked, rubbing Amrita's nose and looking around.

The once barren and dry front yard bore a profusion of

flowering plants, while a kitchen garden flourished at the back of the house. At first Maya had planted at random and they shot up everywhere clashing colours of leaf and flower. She learnt from this and designed the kitchen garden well, marking out plots for different varieties of seasonal vegetable. That, she soon realised was the easier task, the more difficult one was to work according to her plan.

The soil was hard and dry and the sharp point of the pickaxe did not make a dent. She persisted and managed to nudge small clods that Amrita could break up further. Sweat dripped down her earlobe and along the jaw. From the edge of the chin, it slid down the neck between the breasts and settled at the waist where the knot of the *salwar* would not permit it to go any further. Even then the cloth stuck to her legs and made it difficult to walk. Amrita's condition was worse. Her nails chipped and she tanned quickly under the sun. Her tongue seemed to hang out even more than usual but she did not complain.

After working for a couple of hours Maya stopped to assess their progress. At first glance it looked as if they hadn't done anything at all. In spite of all that hard work she had dug up no more than a little patch of ground and Amrita was still breaking the clods sedulously. She was looking carefully at each lump in her hand, poking it with a finger and picking out even small stones. Maya laughed to see her sister looking like a roasting crab clinging to the ground under the burning sun. Neither girl was about to give up too easily. Finally, it was Maya who called a halt. She leaned on the pickaxe and looked at her sister still at work.

"Ammu," she called. "Let's do this early in the morning or late in the evening when the sun is not so hot. At this rate we'll get dehydrated. Stop for now, we'll continue later."

They resumed their work that evening. It was still exhausting but much easier to tackle in the dying hours of the day. Moreover, Maya had left the water running and the soil had become dark. The water had managed to do what her pickaxe couldn't – seep in and loosen the soil. With hard strokes, she quickly turned it over and, within a week, had broken the entire backyard into a neat formation of little plots each segregated by a small mud border.

The seedlings in the nursery were growing very well. Maya taught her sister how to pull out each one gently with a little ball of soil clinging to the roots and how to replant it in their patch.

"Each seedling must be planted at a certain distance from each other. Only then will they grow big and healthy so don't put them very close together. Some varieties will need support. Strew the carrot and radish seeds along the ridges. Cover them with soil. It'll be easier to take them out of the little mounds than digging them from the ground."

"It's very important to water the plants every day. Like we need to drink water, plants need it to make their food. Sprinkle some on the leaves to wash out the dust."

"Ash is good for plants. If you scatter ash around the base and on the leaves, the little black insects will stay away."

"This is the compost pit. We will put dry leaves, flowers and other waste into it. Not tin or glass. They will not change. Leaves and vegetables will rot and make good manure for the plants."

To all these instructions, Amrita nodded as if she understood everything but Maya had to tell her over and over till she learnt to do it on her own. Then they worked in tandem like a pair of trained bullocks in a field. During the mild winter, they could work at any time of the day though the sun could still burn the skin if they stayed out for too long. Nights set in sooner, giving them less time to work. Winter is also the season for the more exotic vegetables such as cauliflower, cabbage and peas and Maya took great delight in growing them. Ironically, when their garden was lush with the produce, the market was flooded with the same vegetables at ridiculously low prices. At times she wondered if the effort was worth it but more than the physical work or the resultant tomatoes, lady's finger and other vegetables, gardening was teaching Amrita a great deal, more than Maya had ever expected.

Amrita showed a deeper interest in gardening than she did in drawing or writing. It was as if she had discovered a vocation. She loved to water the vegetable patches, walk in the slush, squelch mud between her toes and poke around for earthworms. She could spend hours inspecting every individual plant, its flowers and fruits and carefully select those that were ready for plucking. Maya was inclined to dig roughly and at times cut through the potatoes and onions in her haste, but not her sister. Within a year they had a well-tended kitchen garden that ensured a steady supply of fresh vegetables for Kamala's kitchen.

It was Amrita's 23rd birthday. She did not know it but Maya did and wanted to give her sister a gift.

"I don't have any money, what do I get you? I was a fool! I should have done some course like tailoring. I would have been able to buy you something. Now look, I don't have even a coin. I don't want to ask appa. He'll ask a hundred questions. How can I earn quickly? I can't take a basket of vegetables to sell in the market, can I?"

Amrita did not hear her. She was engrossed in the yellow flowers of the lady's finger and plucking the vegetable carefully. She held the pointed tip between her fingers and cut the stem with a sharp knife like her sister had shown her. Experience had taught her that the fine hairs of the plant could hurt her fingers but she liked to pluck them more than she did the profusion of cluster beans. She also liked the brinjals with their violet flowers, smaller than those of the lady's finger but just as beautiful. They dropped off giving way to little green buds that grew into rich purple balls and hung here and there among the big green leaves.

Maya had taught her to look at the brinjals carefully for the smallest black spot that meant a worm was working its way inside. Amrita liked worms too but not inside the vegetable or on the leaves. She loved to turn a big stone over and see the thin white worms wriggle for cover from sunlight and the fat brown earthworms below the clods. Now that the planting was over, she didn't get to see many earthworms so she poked around with a small stick which sometimes broke off without yielding a single worm. She then found another stick and poked some more. She could do it when her sister was not watching, or like now, when she was busy with her thoughts.

"You poor thing!" said Maya, coming out of her reverie. "You are admiring our little garden! You don't know what a wide world it is outside. Hey, that's what I will do. I'll take you out. Show you what it's like beyond the walls of our compound."

In her excitement her voice rose and she quickly lowered it.

"Wait here. Let me see what amma is doing. If she's busy, we can go. Just a quick walk. We'll return before she realises we've gone out."

She did not pause to think or worry about the consequence of her action. For the second time in her life she gave in to her impulse. The first time was when she got into a fight with her classmate over her sister. Once again she was prepared to run a risk for her sister's sake.

Maya did not need to see what Kamala was doing. The electric mixer roared so loudly that the sound of even the doorbell or the ring of the telephone would have been drowned. Nevertheless,

Maya closed the door and the gate without making a noise. No one was around, not even the stray dog that had made its home outside the gate. Amrita hung behind her.

"It's been ages since I went out anywhere! We'll just go down the road and come back. This is the first outing for you and I don't want to exert you. But if you are a good girl and do your work well, I shall take you out more often. What do you say?" she turned to her sister.

Amrita was chewing her fingernails. Her fair skin seemed even paler with two pink spots on the cheeks. Maya knew it was not caused by the thrill of adventure. Her sister was scared.

"Ammukutti, don't be frightened. Nothing will happen. You don't have to worry about anything or anyone when I am with you. Amma is busy in the kitchen and doesn't even know where we are."

In the excitement of taking her sister for a walk, Maya did not notice her neighbour watching them and calling out to his wife to come and see 'the next door girls'. Amrita dragged her feet. She was clearly reluctant to go any further. At last, Maya gave up the struggle and brought her back to the secure familiarity of their home. They hadn't gone even to the end of the road. While her sister recovered from her experience Maya exulted that she had done something without the knowledge of her parents. She was so confident that they had not been noticed that when her father called her she thought he had bought a gift for Amrita and ran down the steps.

Raghu stood at the foot of the steps. He had nothing in his hands, not even his usual newspaper. Maya slowed down automatically but there were not many steps left and too soon she had reached him.

"What's this I hear?" he asked.

"I don't know."

"Don't act as if you are innocent. You know very well what you did today. Why? Why did you do it?"

Maya gulped. She felt blood drain from her face. She clenched both hands behind her back. At least that way he couldn't see them shaking.

"Well?"

She took a deep breath. "I took her out today. Not far, just outside the house..."

"Why? Did she ask you to?"

"No ... I felt like it ... like making today special for her..."

"What's so special about today? Did I die?"

"It ... it is her birthday..."

"Oh, yes ...yes... that does indeed call for celebration. Kamala, why didn't you cook a feast today? Don't you know it's your daughter's birthday?"

Maya kept her eyes fixed on the ground. She couldn't bring herself to look up and let him see her reaction.

"Forget about her, how old are you, may I ask?"

"Twenty-one."

"That's old, isn't it? Old enough to take decisions. Old enough to know what's good for your sister and what isn't? What are you going to do tomorrow? Take her to the beach? I forgot, there are no beaches here."

Maya flushed and took a quick breath. She let it out slowly. She was not going to show her feelings, not then.

"Let me make one thing very clear to you. So long as I'm alive and you are with me I insist that you obey me. I don't want your sister to be seen outside the house. Is that clear?"

Maya nodded. She was beyond speech.

"You may go now. And mind you, no more excursions, birthdays or any other days, got it?"

She nodded once again and went to her room. Amrita had gone to bed. She had seemed rather tired with the unaccustomed strain.

*Maybe the sun was too much for her. Poor girl! She's not used to such excitement.*

Maya looked at Amrita lying on her side, cheek resting on a palm. Sleeping or awake her mouth always remained partly open. She gently brought the lips together and smiled to herself as they opened out like a bud when she took her hand away. She went to bed but couldn't sleep. Her father's words came back to her in an echoic replay.

*Why did he have to be so harsh? Can't we have a life of our own without worrying about what he would say? Are we to become his shadows like amma? Okay, she's married to him and Amrita is like this but what about me? Don't I have any right, any freedom in this house? Am I to remain bound within like a prisoner? When will I become free from this bondage?*

She got up from the bed and went to the window. It was so dark that she couldn't even see the silhouette of the trees in their garden, their little garden that she had struggled to create.

*Everything has been one big battle. Each step, an achievement. Whether it is Ammu learning something new or I doing something on my own. I have not asked them for anything all these years. How long can I continue like this? I don't want to lead such a life any longer. I might be able to survive on my own but what about my sister? I can't leave without her.*

For the next few days Maya stayed within the compound wall. Then once she noticed Amrita standing on her toes and looking over the wall. She went quietly behind her and looked out at the sea of sunflowers in the adjoining field. Amrita was clearly amazed at the sight of so many flowers. Maya looked around. She couldn't see her mother anywhere.

"I don't care even if you see us," she muttered under her breath.

She caught her sister's hand in a firm grip and led her out through the rickety gate. A ditch and wire fencing separated their compound from the neighbouring ashram ground. As a child Maya used to sail paper boats in this ditch, sometimes with an ant for a frantic passenger. Those days she used to think of it as a river but now she saw it for what it was – a narrow ditch that she could cross easily, but which made her sister hesitate. She had to jump across a few times to encourage her and finally Amrita followed, almost slipping at the edge but Maya pulled her to safety and they went on to their next hurdle: the barbed wire fence. They walked a little way beside the fence. The wire sagged like a slack mouth at various places where people crossed and re-crossed frequently. Maya stooped and went to the other side. She then held the wire up for her sister to pass.

They were trespassing like many others, for whom this was a short cut to avoid the main road. A line of mango trees stood within the fence. At that time of the year the trees were full of dusty leaves. The only visitors were a few birds that came to rest among the thick foliage. With the onset of spring, the trees would be covered with clusters of greenish yellow flowers that would bear fruit and attract both bird and child.

The two sisters stood at the edge of the sunflower field, the huge flowers towering over them.

"These are *sooraj mukhi*," Maya said. "They are called that because they always face the sun. So, in English they are called Sunflower. Aren't they pretty? We get oil from the seeds. We won't spend too much time here. Just look around a little and then we'll return. I don't want amma to know that we have come here."

Amrita was clearly awed by the profusion of flowers. She was used only to those that they had planted and now she looked excitedly at the big leaves, the showy yellow petals and large core of dark seeds.

Despite the bravado with which she had decided to defy her father's order, Maya worried about getting caught and chastised once again. She hustled her sister and took her back the way they came. It was as if they were taking a tentative step to test the depth of the water before plunging in.

***

# 18

Maya stretched her hand to push open the gate when it suddenly swung inwards. Her heart did a little somersault. She hadn't expected her mother to come looking for them and now she could neither say a word in explanation nor pretend to be nonchalant. She instinctively tightened her grip on Amrita but she wasn't going to be the first one to break up the tableau. Finally, Kamala stood to a side and Maya walked in with her sister. She geared herself to face Raghu's anger that evening.

*It'll be worse than last time because he had forbidden me specifically. But that poor girl was looking so yearningly at the plants. She wasn't asking for the moon or the stars, only to see the flowers. What's wrong in taking her? Oh, I can only argue with myself. When I'm in his presence my lips will be sealed and my mind will become completely blank. Let's face it, I lack courage.*

*That's him...Amma is opening the gate...he's coming in...he has parked the car...he's washing his feet...the swing is creaking...he's having his coffee...she'll tell him now....*

*Maya, this is it. Be ready. He'll call now. Any time now.*

She waited. And waited. Her anxiety increased with every passing minute but, as the minutes lengthened to hours, she began to breathe, although uneasily.

*She didn't tell him? He's not likely to keep quiet if she had. Why this concern for me?*

She went downstairs, unable to bear the suspense any longer. Kamala ignored her while Raghu looked up casually and went back to his newspaper. For the last few hours tension had coiled around her in a pythonic embrace. Now, with every step Maya took towards her sister, it loosened its hold, leaving her so drained and exhausted that she couldn't even wonder at her mother's discretion.

She began to take Amrita more often to the ashram ground. They walked between banana suckers or cut across the fields chasing lapwings and babblers. The girls watched water pumped into canals slither down furrows and finally seep into the soil, out of sight. They rushed past rows of strong smelling tobacco, flicked tufts of wheat and maize at each other and admired the soft whiteness of cotton bursting from its bolls. Amrita's nose twitched like a rabbit at the medicinal smell of the eucalyptus leaves that Maya crushed for her. She felt the smoothness of the trunk after peeling off the loosened strips of dry bark. They watched the tractor groove the ground and the long legged heron and egret forage for worms in the newly turned over soil. The girls stood at the edge of the field while the sadhu-cum-farmers sowed seeds, irrigated, harvested and stocked the yield. Sometimes Maya felt bored but she didn't want to deny her sister her only happiness. One day when they heard the long drawn hoot of a train she decided to show it to Amrita. They crossed more fields, crunched neem fruit under their feet, made their way between prickly bushes and came to the railway track. Maya led Amrita up the little slope of gravel to where the metal gleamed in the sun.

"This is the line on which the train runs. Oh, it's blazing. Look further down ... see that tree? Come, let's go there. Quick."

They ran on the wooden sleepers till they came to a *gul mohar* tree. Maya's mouth was dry and Amrita was puffing with the exertion. As far as they could see there was no other human around, only a few goats grazing at a distance.

"You know, Ammu, I used to come here as a child. Stupid really, what's there to see? The fields are still there, the neem trees are as tall as I remember... what else? Nothing, only you, Ammu, you're the addition," she laughed.

"Look at these two thick metal lines. The train runs on big wheels on them. Don't touch it. It'll be hot," she warned, holding back her sister who had bent down. "You can see how smooth it is. It has to be like this or else the train will jump off the rails and people will get hurt. They could die. When a train moves on the tracks you can feel the movement way down the line. It has so much power, such great strength. People travel in boxes called compartments. You know Ammu, people sleep, eat, use the toilet – everything in the compartment. Paati took me by train. It was fun."

Amrita nodded as if she understood everything.

"Any questions?" asked Maya. "You never have any. I wonder how much you understood. Come, let's go back to the shade of the *gul mohar*. Just before summer, the tree is almost bare except for long black pods. Let's see if we can get any..." Maya looked around and found one, dry and hard.

"Here. Shake it near your ear. Do you hear the rattling? Those are seeds inside the pods."

She then picked up a flower from the ground and held it out to Amrita.

"See how beautiful the flower is. How many petals does it have? Count. One ... two ... go on, say it ... three ... four and five. Bad girl, Ammu, you didn't count with me. Okay, leave it, at least look at the flower. It has four petals of the same colour, a bright reddish-orange. The fifth is bigger. It's also lighter, see? Almost white with tiny flecks. Take it. There are so many everywhere, it looks like a carpet but look at the tree. It's still covered with flowers. That's the beauty of it. How would you like to be a bird and see it from the top? I wouldn't mind. I would fly round and round over the tree. If I were a crow I would caw loudly and call all other crows to come and see it.

Like this..." Maya ran around her sister, cawing hoarsely.

"Ammu, come, join me. You be a cuckoo. Go on, say 'coo'," she called.

Both girls were soon running in circles, one behind the other. Her arms stretched to the fullest and hands flapping, Maya circled the *gul mohar*, ran across the railway line and did figures of eight with Amrita imitating her. A sudden crack of laughter stopped her abruptly, making her sister bump into her back.

"I thought we were the only ones here!" Maya looked around. At first she didn't see anyone, only the expanse of shrubs and trees, not even birds or insects. Even the goats that had been grazing seemed to be hiding from the heat.

"Nothing. No one. Did I imagine it?" she muttered and looked around once more. A bush, not far from where they stood was shaking suspiciously.

"Hey, you. Come out," she called.

No one responded.

"Shall I come there and catch you by your ear?" she called again.

Two little boys came out looking at each other and sniggering.

"So ... what are you two doing here?" Maya asked sternly.

They nudged each other to reply and both kept quiet, staring at their bare feet with a sudden fascination.

"Well?" insisted Maya.

"Nothing..." said the taller boy at last.

"Nothing?"

"Well, our goats..."

"Where are your goats? I don't see any."

Both boys turned around together and gestured somewhere at the back. Maya did not bother to follow their direction.

"If you have come here with your goats, then you'd better be with them. Don't hang around watching us, understand? We have not come here to entertain you. We have some work...," she said in her fiercest voice.

Without waiting for her to say anything more, the boys took off like rabbits, stopping only when they came to a tree far away. They turned around to see if the girls were watching them. From the safety of distance they flapped their hands and ran around, their laughter floating towards the girls. Maya turned to her sister. At the sight of the boys Amrita had hidden behind her and was biting her fingernails.

"*Ofo*, Ammu! I told you not to be afraid. Forget those urchins. They're just having a little fun. It's getting late. Let's go. We'll come another day to see the train." She held out her hand to her sister and they walked back home.

After more such trips, Amrita grew brave enough to wave when the train rushed by even if it was only carrying goods. In fact, her enthusiasm was so high on some days that Maya had to physically hold her back from the railway track. Their outings did not make them neglect the garden. By now, it was well laid and they only had to maintain it with weeding and watering.

Amrita would have done both if Maya had let her.

"Don't be silly," she said. "We'll divide the work equally. You can decide which one you want."

Amrita immediately fixed the hose to the tap and turned it on.

"All right, then," said Maya. "I shall pull out the weeds. I'll finish it quicker than you. There's hardly any weed."

Since they were working in the kitchen garden they did not see Raghu come home with a young man. It was only a good while later, when the girls entered the house that they heard the sound of voices. Maya sent her sister upstairs while she went quietly to the drawing room and peeped inside. Raghu was talking to someone sitting beside him on the swing, but from where she stood she could see only their backs, not their faces. The stranger laughed at something her father said. The richness of his voice made Maya want to see his face. She looked at her hands and feet soiled and streaked, quickly went to their room, freshened up and came down again. There was no one in the drawing room. The swing was coming to a gradual stop. Slowly she straightened herself and looked up right into the face of a tall young man who stood not two steps from her. He looked back at her from head to toe, the smile never leaving his lips. He then raised his eyebrows and broke the spell.

She turned on her heels and ran back the way she came. Behind her she heard her father call, "Sundar…"

Raghu accommodated his guest in the spare room upstairs.

Maya kept within whenever Sundar was around and that was most of the time. He seemed to have plenty to talk about – with Raghu when he was home, with Kamala when Raghu had left for work. She wanted to find out who he was and why he was there but the embarrassment of their first meeting was still too fresh in her mind and made her curb her curiosity. However, it did not stop her heart from beating faster when his footsteps approached their door and sink when they went past without a pause. It irritated her no end that he used his room only to sleep at night.

"What kind of a man is he, so indifferent about others? This is our house, not a lodge that he can walk in and walk out whenever he wants," she complained to Amrita. "It's not as if we are invisible or so ugly that he can't even greet us. Perhaps he thinks I don't deserve a second look..."

She peered critically into the little rectangular piece of mirror on the wall.

"Too bad I can see my face only in parts but it'll have to do. Let's see. Face ... all right ... I think. My best features are probably my eyes and that's not saying much. They look sad! Am I so melancholic? I hope not. If only I could talk to someone interesting occasionally I'd be much happier."

Amrita stood behind and watched her intently. Then she turned to the wall and began to imitate her sister, patting her hair, opening her eyes wide and inspecting the sides of her nose.

"You....! I'll show you!" Maya chased Amrita and they flopped on the bed, laughing.

"So… you're in high spirits, are you? I'll make you work it off. Come, let's go to the garden," said Maya. "It's been a long time since we looked at our plants."

"Hmm… lots of weeds," she said, looking around. "Tell you what… you start from one end and I'll start from the other. We'll meet in the middle."

Soon they were sitting on their haunches and pulling out the weeds. Fortunately, Maya's preoccupation over the past few days had not affected their garden too much since they were in the middle of monsoon and the plants had sufficient water.

"Preparing for winter, are we?"

Maya looked up and slowly, like a zombie, she stood up. Her face felt hot and she wiped it, not realising that her hands were covered with bits of grass and mud.

"How come I've never met you all these days? Are you two some kind of moles?" Sundar asked, smiling at them.

Maya continued to stare at him. She did not notice her sister hiding behind her. She was only aware of the fact that here was a handsome young man talking to her and her tongue had changed to lead.

"So, Mayamrita, you won't talk to me? That's too bad. Do I look like a villain or something? Please say 'no'!"

Maya smiled at that. "Well…"

"That's better. Now I know you can speak. Let me finish your sentence… 'Well, we are busy. Don't disturb.' Isn't that what you're going to say? You don't have to. I've no intention of keeping you from your work." He walked away.

Amrita recovered first and resumed her work. Automatically, Maya followed suit but kept looking in the direction that Sundar had gone.

***

"Gauri, after those few years with my paati and Amrita, it's now that I've found happiness, with my husband," Maya said. "But there have been times when I felt so burdened by the past that I wanted to wrench it out of my mind as if it were a diseased growth. That's what I'm doing by confiding in you, relieving myself of all the heartache. However close you are to your husband there are still many things you don't want to tell him. You clam them within yourself till they threaten to burst out or seep through your body like a slow-acting poison."

I nursed the teacup in both hands and looked into the dregs, though I knew Maya's eyes were on me. Amma cleared her conscience by telling me about Raghu. Not knowing what I was letting myself into, I invited Kamala auntie to confide in me. And now Maya wanted to do the same. Why did they want to make an Atlas of me? If Maya saw the query in my eyes, she ignored it and went on.

"You are someone who strayed into our lives. It's not likely that we'll meet again. My secrets will be safe with you. Even if you were to tell somebody . . . well, I've suffered enough within myself. It will not affect me any more."

She stared into my eyes and I looked back with all the calmness I could muster but did not feel. What was she going to divulge about my brother?

"Sundar is the nightmare that I must get rid of first. I know he's your brother but I'm not going to hide anything from you."

Words surged to my lips. Words of consolation, explanation for my brother's wrongdoings whatever they were. Noncommittal sounds that she could take in any sense she wanted. I didn't have to say anything.

"Your brother was the first man I met, other than appa of course," she continued. "And he behaved as if I didn't exist. It hurt. I didn't know why. I wanted to make him conscious of me, as a person, as a woman. I found myself wearing my best clothes even though I had nowhere to go. I looked often into the mirror. If only I had taken after my father, I thought. If only I were taller, not so dark. I no longer wanted to go to the garden and get tanned. I didn't want soil under my nails. I wanted to talk and laugh loudly whenever he was around but I only had Amrita to talk to. Poor Amrita, who did not want to reply in words even when I asked her a direct question."

"She was puzzled by my behaviour. I did not know that I had changed. I shouted at her if she stood around looking blankly at me, awaiting my instruction. I didn't care when she doodled lazily in her notebook instead of writing her letters or numbers.

For the first time I deliberately kept her indoors, not taking her anywhere. She got bored and restless but I didn't feel like entertaining her any longer. All I wanted to do was to go downstairs and eavesdrop on Sundar's conversations. He had lots to tell my parents and they talked to him with an affection that I didn't know they had in them. Even that didn't hurt me as much as Sundar's continued indifference to me and my sister."

"Then one day I went for a walk alone to our usual place, next door. I wanted to get rid of my perplexing madness and the best way to do it was to tire myself physically, I decided. I must have walked several kilometres. I was sweating when I returned, sweating and breathless. Breathless because I ran most of the way back. It was the first time I was leaving Ammu alone for so long. I was terribly worried about how she must have reacted to my absence. The door of our room was ajar. I scolded myself for being careless and pushed it fully open. There was Sundar, sitting in my chair and rifling though Amrita's books while she stood near the window as if she was ready to jump out of it."

"'At last! I was about to leave,' he said. 'I thought you only knew the way from here to your garden and back. Looks like I was wrong.'"

"He was the last person I'd expected to meet and that too, when I had finally resolved that I was being foolish to hanker for attention from someone who was not bothered about me."

"'My name is Sundar,' he said. 'I suppose you know that at least. I didn't want to impose myself on you all these days but I thought it was time I met both of you. She's a very sweet girl. For the last half an hour she has been looking at me as if I'd eat her up. Look at her now! She is your shadow, isn't she?'"

"Well…." I dragged, wishing that Amrita would not hide behind me.

"'Take your time. I'm not going to speak for you like I did before. You must have thought that I was such a brute. I'm sorry. I'm not used to people avoiding me.'"

"We weren't avoiding you," I replied hastily. "It's just that my sister is very shy so…"

"'So you keep her hidden from the outside world. For how long will you do this?'"

I had never thought about it.

"'There's no virtue in hiding behind your parents or isolating yourself. You have to face the world and so will your sister.'"

"I was stung by his accusation. What did he know about all that I'd done for her? What did he know of my reasons for keeping her with me? What did he know about my parents from his interactions with them?"

"Sundar began to drop in often. The way he spoke that day, I thought he was a very serious person but I found that he was just the opposite. He cracked jokes, teased me… oh, when I think of all that he said … I could kick myself for laughing at his cracks, for enjoying his company. My only excuse is that I was naïve. I was meeting someone like him for the first time. When Ganesh pulls my leg, my mind immediately goes to something Sundar had said. I feel terrible, to think of another man even though I hate him now. Mind you, it wasn't as if I was in love with your brother or anything like that. Not at all. It was just a fascination for someone so unlike my parents. At most I would have accepted him as an elder brother. Yes, I would have accepted him as wholeheartedly as my parents did. He had been staying with us for nearly two months and fitted in as neatly as if he were a part of our family."

"Sundar appreciated my concern in my sister's welfare. 'A rare gesture,' he called it. I felt nice about it though I was only discharging my duty towards my less privileged sibling. Do parents feel virtuous or noble in bringing up their children? I wasn't doing anything different except that she was my sister, not my child. My attempt all along had been to make her independent but, in Sundar's presence, she behaved like a child, a very cranky child. She wanted my exclusive attention when he was around. She didn't want me to talk to him. She would try to cover my mouth with her hand. If I told her to sit quietly, she would sit behind me and push me with her knees or hug me from the back like a baby monkey. It was so embarrassing and so frustrating! I used to yell at her the moment he left and immediately feel sorry since she would be her normal self again. It wasn't as if she hated him. She had her dislikes but I don't think she really hated anything in her life. Even your brother, if she didn't like him at first, she learned to tolerate his presence."

"One day, she was at her worst, turning my face to her when I was trying to listen to what he was telling me. I pushed her hand away but she nuzzled against me and held me so tightly that I couldn't even breathe. I started coughing and struggled to loosen her grip. Finally he had to pull her away. Oh God, the scene she created! Crying, throwing everything down from the table, from the bed, the pillows, the sheets. He walked out of the room quickly saying that it was probably his presence that was irritating her. I knew better. She didn't want to share me with anyone."

"A few days later he peeped in. I sensed Amrita bridling and hugged her before she could throw her hands around me. It probably reassured her for I could feel her relaxing. He had brought chocolates for her. I had to take it from him and pop it in her mouth since she wouldn't stretch her hand to his. She loved sweets and let us talk for as long as the chocolates lasted."

"Naturally, our topic that day was Amrita's dependence on me. Sundar suggested that the best way to teach her was to leave her alone, for me to deliberately stay away from her."

"'Remember the first time I came to meet you and you had gone on a walk?' he asked. 'She was all right that day. That's what you should be doing, leave her alone for increasingly longer periods so that she gets used to being on her own."

"I suppose you're right but what if she gets upset? It's very difficult to bring her out of her tantrum…"

"'She's just a kid, a petulant child. Even kids cannot be permitted to have their way all the time. They must be taught some discipline. You've indulged her so much that she's taking advantage of your goodness. Teach her to be independent. It isn't as if you're going to be with her all your life.'"

"I will. I will not go anywhere without my sister," I said firmly.

"'This is what I like about you,' he said. 'That you're prepared to sacrifice your life for your sister. But shouldn't you have a life of your own? You'll be able to take care of your sister only if you are in good physical and mental health. That's what I'm asking you to ensure. Tell me, you have never felt claustrophobic? Never felt the urge to go somewhere? Talk to someone? Go on … tell me.'"

"I couldn't reply. I couldn't tell him of the times when I have envied the supreme confidence of the eagle as it draws large circles in the sky, frightening smaller birds out of its path. My favourite dream of running barefoot down a grassy slope fast, alone, with the air in my hair. My yearning to look up into the rain and feel the drops knock on my eyelids. My biggest wish to be a girl just like others, happy, unconcerned about anyone or anything."

"Sundar was right. I had to teach my sister to stay on her own. I began to leave her behind and walked among the eucalyptus trees and fields on my own. Only he knew what I was doing since I took care not to let my mother see me leave. It wasn't because I was scared that she would try to stop me or report to appa. I no longer cared about what they thought. My only concern was how my sister would react to my long absences."

"'Don't worry about her. I'll take care of her,' he said."

"I believed him."

"It was good to be by myself at last. I used that time to think about a lot of things, like what caused a communal flare-up? Why were we building temples when there were already so many? How can anyone hope for salvation with such hatred for their neighbours in their hearts? I know it sounds foolish Gauri, but those were the debates I had in my mind because I was scared to think of my future. I didn't want to think about what would happen to my sister and me when appa retired. When he died? Wouldn't I have to take care of my mother as well? How could I when I had no way of supporting myself? I tried not to think on those lines but it wasn't easy. The moment it overwhelmed me, I returned to the present, to my sister waiting for me impatiently in our room upstairs. Sometimes Sundar would be with her, trying to teach her from where I had left off. More often he would be telling her stories from movies that he had seen."

"One day I left as usual, promising him that I would make definite plans for my future. It was hopeless. I had no clue about what I was going to do with myself. I decided it might be more sensible to discuss it with him instead of grappling with it alone. I turned back and hurried home."

"He was with my sister. He was not telling her stories, not trying to teach her the alphabet. He was doing more. He was lying on her, on the bed, kissing her, running his hands over her body..."

"I stood petrified. Amrita's face was turned towards the door. She didn't know what was happening. Whatever it was, she didn't like it. She was squirming and making little noises that didn't stop him at all. But that first plaintive sound was enough to bring me back to life. I rushed into the room and pounded his back with my fists. He sat up laughing, caught my hands and pulled me close to his face."

"I wanted to shout. I wanted to scream. Till amma came up to help me."

"'This is the power of a man... that he can do what he will. You can't stop me,' he said softly."

"'Amrita, get up. Go!' I shouted."

"'Shh... we don't want your mother to come here and see what her daughters are doing, do we?'"

"Amrita..."

"'Relax. I just wanted to introduce some variety to her lessons and you had to come and spoil everything,' he complained."

"Let me go or I'll scream... even if amma thinks the worst..."

"'You're one hell of a girl. If you create a scene and bring her here, I'll be thrown out of the house but what about you? They're not going to keep quiet about this,' he said, releasing my hands."

"I felt like hurling everything in the room at him. He was

right though. I couldn't afford to act in haste. And then, I reasoned, he did say that nothing untoward had happened to her, yet."

"My walks ended that day," said Maya. "I wanted to get out of the house, more desperately than before but I wasn't going to leave my sister behind."

***

# 19

Kittu died and Sundar returned home.

"Appa was concerned," Maya said. "About how your mother would manage without her son so he told him to go back to her. In any case, Sundar had just resigned from his job and wasn't doing anything. Other than smiling at me, of course, when he was sure that my parents weren't watching."

I forced myself to speak.

"You should have told them about him," I said.

"How could I, Gauri, with his threat looming over my head? When I know how fond they were of him and how indifferent they were to my sister and me? I did the only thing I could do – keep our door firmly locked from within and not permit Amrita to move an inch from my sight. Fortunately for us, he had to leave almost immediately. Your father could not have died at a more opportune time!"

"My sister was happy to have me to herself again. At first I worried whether she'd suffer from the trauma of what she had gone through. I took her all the time to the ashram ground so that she could forget that day but she hadn't changed in any way. She was just the same as before. Perhaps she didn't know what had happened between them. But it certainly affected me. I realised for the first time how vulnerable she was, what a responsibility lay on my shoulders. Till then I'd been vague about our future. I'd only been sure that I wanted to be with her all my life. I was 23 years old and dependent on my parents. Even if I wanted to take up a job I'd have to leave her behind. I didn't want to do that. Who'd employ me anyway, when I had no skill? I felt trapped. I wanted to escape but how? Where? Whenever appa raised the topic of marriage, and he had been doing it for at least four years, I had always refused. Going by amma's experience, it meant escaping from our room upstairs and entering the kitchen in another house. Now I began to think even this was preferable if I could take my sister along."

"Without waiting for my consent appa had been tapping even the most distant contact to find a suitable boy. Suitable as in one whose family did not object to their son marrying a girl with a sister like Amrita. There were few takers. The exceptions were those who thought a bigger dowry would be reasonable compensation for my sister's condition. Thank God, appa did not give in to their greed and discrimination. Ganesh was the only one who was not bothered about Ammu, our wealth or anything material. I remember that day so vividly when appa received the letter from Ganesh's father," Maya smiled to herself. She seemed to have forgotten my presence completely.

"Maya… Kamala…come here, both of you," Raghu shouted.

Kamala came rushing from the kitchen but Maya had to run down eighteen steps. By the time she reached her father she was breathless. Raghu waved a letter triumphantly at them.

"At last, we have received a positive reply from a boy's parents," he said, beaming. "Their only concern is getting the right girl for their son, Ganesh. Everything else is secondary, writes Mr. Seetharam, the boy's father. They would like to meet Maya and want to know when it will be convenient for us."

"What details have they given about the boy?" Kamala asked.

*If they are so liberal-minded they might not mind Amrita coming with me.*

Maya suppressed the deep sigh of relief that rose from the pit of her stomach.

*I must make it very clear that I'm not leaving without her.*

Raghu read out the details about the groom, interspersing them with his comments.

"Ganesh is 28 years old. Engineer. Ah, excellent salary… Rs. 18,000 a month. Maya, you'll live like a *Rani*. Happy? I certainly am! So, where was I? Engineer … he's the youngest of five – one sister and three brothers. That's a large family. All are married. Good. One brother lives in the States, the other two and their families are living with the parents. They must have a really big house to accommodate so many people. You'll have to adjust with others in such a large family, my girl. It'll be good for you. You hardly come out of your room here. Mr. Seetharam says 'No horoscope, no dowry.' What a gentleman! Listen to what he says,

"Having a child like your daughter is no crime. Why should the younger sibling suffer because of this? We certainly have no problem in Maya marrying Ganesh. The girl is our only consideration. We would like to meet her and, of course, her parents. Kindly let me know if the 29th of this month will be convenient for you...."

"Twenty-ninth... that's a Friday. That should be fine, eh, Kamala? Good, I'll telephone him so that they can make their travel arrangements," Raghu rushed to the telephone.

"Kamala, should we..." he called out as he went and Maya was left alone in the room.

She did not get much time to brood about what would happen on the 29th since the intervening days got over so fast. Most of them were spent in listening to her father make plans with an enthusiasm that she did not expect from him. Kamala showed her happiness in spring cleaning the house and making sweets and savouries for the guests.

"Do you get that lovely smell?" Maya asked her sister. "That's cardamom. Amma must be making some sweet. Should I offer to help her? After all, she's doing everything alone, even those tasks that Revabehn used to do. Will you stay without me?"

Amrita immediately took a book from the table and gave it to her.

"Why this sudden interest in studying? You were not so keen all these days. You don't want me to go, do you? Okay, sit down and write. I'll stay with you."

Maya watched her sister as she sat writing, the tip of her tongue peeping out, her brow corrugated with the strain of trying to recall her lessons.

"Am I doing the right thing? What if this boy doesn't agree to your coming with us?"

Amrita looked up from the book and smiled at her.

"Continue writing. I was only thinking loudly," she patted her sister's head. "That shouldn't be a problem really. I'll ask them point-blank: Do you agree to Amrita coming with me after the wedding? If you don't, then this alliance is off. I will not leave without my sister," she said, the sternness in her voice and expression making Amrita drop her pencil and look at her.

Despite her resolution, Maya did not know how to broach the topic while her parents and Mr. and Mrs. Seetharam were planning so enthusiastically for the wedding. She was grappling with different options in her mind when Ganesh inadvertently came to her rescue.

"I would like to talk to Maya privately. Do you mind?" he asked Raghu.

"Sure, no problem. We have a lovely garden, Maya's creation, if you would like to go there or else you could sit in the verandah," Raghu offered.

There was total silence as both sets of parents watched Maya and Ganesh walk out of the room. Her silk sari came in the way of her feet and she seemed to walk with heavy steps though hope was beginning to swell within her. They went to the verandah and the buzz of voices broke out once again behind them.

"They have a lot to talk about, it seems," Ganesh remarked, pulling out a chair for her and sitting down on another.

Maya gave a faint smile in reply.

He looked at the plants growing in profusion.

"Your father said you are a keen gardener?"

"Hm.."

He bent towards her and spoke in a low voice.

"Maya, I wanted us to have an opportunity to talk to each other at least once before our wedding. If nothing else, I want to know if you are happy about marrying me or have your parents pressurised you in any way. I don't want that to happen. If you have anything to say, you're most welcome to do so – now."

She looked up at him, into his dark eyes that were inviting her to open up.

"I did want to ask you something about my sister," she said, hesitantly at first and then with growing confidence.

"You know about her...," she continued, her insides shrivelling with tension. "We haven't hidden anything about her from you or your parents but there is something that I have to find out..."

"Yes?" he asked.

"She can't stay without me. Not even for a moment. Is it ... will it be possible to take her along with us?"

"Well...," he paused.

She did not take her eyes off him. Now that the question had left her, she had no more fear, no more hesitation. She was prepared for any answer he gave.

"As far as I'm concerned why only your sister, even your parents are most welcome to stay with us. The problem is that ours is a large joint family. Moreover, my brother's wife is in the family way. She can't go to her parents for the confinement. My sister Parvati is also coming at about the same time for her delivery. This is why my parents are so keen on holding the wedding immediately, before the hospital rush begins."

"And then," he continued while Maya's heart sank. "We always have some relation or friend visiting us and with two babies on the way, our house will be overflowing with people. I don't think it is right to impose Amrita on them. 'Impose' is probably not the right word but you know what I mean?"

"But I'll look after her entirely on my own. I don't expect anyone else to help me," she protested.

"That's fine but you must also remember that we, you and I, need a little time to get to know each other...."

"So," she interrupted. "Are you saying that I can't take her with me?"

"Oh no! I think you should leave her with your parents for a while. In another six months or so I'll have to move to Mumbai to supervise a major project there. It'll take more than three years to complete. You can get her to stay with us then. By that time my people would have accepted her as a part of my family and not object if we take her back with us. So it's really a question of about six months. It may be less but certainly not much more than that."

"What'll I do with her till then?"

"Why, she can continue to stay here. Your mother will look after her. Maybe you can get a maid to help her out. That shouldn't be difficult."

"Are you sure about this?" she asked.

"About the six months? Yes. I can try to get it advanced but I'm not sure if it'll be possible. The paperwork is almost done, the necessary permits have been obtained but we'll still have to finalise a number of things before the project can begin."

"Oh..." Maya's thoughts were swirling in confusion.

"Anything else you would like to know?"

She shook her head. Six months did not seem a very long time, but....

"If you can stay without her for just six months then she could be with us forever."

That was tempting but she was not going to give in easily.

"Will you find out if it is somehow possible for you to get this posting earlier?"

"Not unless it's an emergency," he said.

"You can tell them that it is very important for me."

Ganesh smiled.

"What if I join you in Mumbai?" she asked.

"Tell me ... are you keen on this wedding at all?" he asked quietly.

"Oh no ... I mean, yes, of course... That is.... I have no problem in getting married. It's just that I don't want her to be alone..."

"She won't be alone. Your parents will be home, at least your mother will be even if your father goes to work. What harm can fall on your sister? Get an *ayah* to look after her," he said. "And really, it's only a matter of a few months."

If Maya hadn't got Hansabehn to look after Amrita, she would have called off the wedding. The woman was in her early thirties, a widow with no one else in her family to prevent her from looking after Amrita day and night. Maya was satisfied with the firmness with which she handled her sister.

"Ammu, I was too lenient and you took advantage of that. Let me see how you manage this woman," Maya laughed.

She laughed easily those days. Nights were not so pleasant when anxiety jolted her from sleep. The questions that she deliberately kept at bay during the day charged to the fore, assuming greater urgency in the dark.

*Will she be able to adjust to my absence? Will she remember all that I've taught her or will she lapse into that state in which I found her when I returned from paati? Will Hansabehn be able to keep her engaged all the time?*

Questions like these left her looking haggard in the morning and the circles round her eyes grew darker.

"Maya, what's the matter with you? You look dreadful these days," said Raghu.

"Nothing. Just the worry about what my sister will…"

"Will you stop thinking about her? She will be perfectly all right. You take care of yourself. I don't want the Seetharams to wonder if they had made a mistake. You'd better apply some cream or lotion to look less strained."

"Yes, appa," she replied obediently. No face cream could erase the tension that churned in her as the wedding day approached. She fired instructions to Amrita all the time.

"Even if I am not here to tell you, you must bathe everyday and wear fresh clothes."

"Keep the room clean."

"Be especially careful on 'those' days and change your napkin."

"Don't lock the bathroom door from within. It is enough if

the outer door is closed. We don't want you to get stuck inside, unable to come out."

"Ask amma if you want anything. I'm sure the new maid will be as good as Revabehn. You could also ask her for whatever you want. It'll take Hansabehn some time to understand you but she'll catch on soon enough. Try to speak as clearly as you can and as much as possible."

"If you are upset about something or you want to see me, give this postcard to Hansabehn. You don't have to write anything. I'll come as soon I get it. I'll only be in Madras, a matter of two days' travel," Maya gave her a bunch of postcards on which she had written her name and address.

"We have less than a month. I want to spend every single minute teaching you. I'm getting married on 18th January, in a few days. I'll have to leave you. I know you'll miss me but don't feel too bad. You'll soon learn to get along without me. You must. I don't know how I will manage without you..." the words strangled her throat and she gulped.

"The most important training I should give is for you to stay without me for long periods but there are so few days left, I don't want to leave you alone. What can I do except talk to you and try to make you understand? Do you follow what I'm telling you? Do you understand?"

Amrita nodded her head happily.

'Understand.' Maya knew her sister had heard this word often enough to know what it meant.

"I hope so," she said. "Anyway, tell me what you would like to do. Go to the ashram ground? Appa has given his permission, at last."

She took Amrita across the terrace to the steps leading to the back yard. Her sister had not forgotten the wire fence and carefully bent her way through to the other side even though some trespasser like them had cut a couple of wires at the bottom and pulled them back to ensure easier passage. They stood up and looked around. Further down, a woman guided two children through the fence. They ran along the narrow raised path between the fields. One was waving a red balloon while the other had a paper kite fluttering behind him. The woman followed more slowly, balancing a mud pot on her head.

The girls stood at the edge of a banana plantation. Row after row of new leaves curled into long green tubes stretched before them like soldiers waiting for a command. Amrita's eyes shone with excitement. Normally she wouldn't have waited for her sister's permission to run around but it had been a while since they had come there and she hesitated just that little bit.

Suddenly Maya felt like returning home.

"Let's go back," she said. "There are lots of interesting things happening at home."

Amrita dragged her feet and took her time to walk back the way they had come. She inched down the ditch and up to the other side, slipping a couple of times while her sister held the gate open for her.

Raghu had been awaiting Maya's return. He forgot his impatience and smiled indulgently as she stared at the assortment of jewellery boxes and silk saris.

"But why did you get so many things?" she protested. "His parents specifically said they don't want you to spend a lot of money. They didn't ask for a dowry or for any of these!"

"These are gifts for my daughter. Why should they object? I'm not giving it to their son but to my dear daughter. Don't deny me this pleasure, Maya. Yours is the only wedding we'll ever celebrate. I'm giving you the best I can afford without borrowing from anyone. I don't want anyone to think that we are dumping our daughter on the boy's family, empty-handed. You'll go with your head held high and everyone will realise that Raghu is no miser."

She carried the boxes upstairs and Amrita came eagerly to see what was in them. Maya flipped open each one and watched her sister run a finger on the smooth silk saris as gently as if they were flowers. The necklaces and studs rested in their cases, glinting against the dark blue velvet. Amrita looked at them closely but did not try to put them on.

As the wedding day approached, the number of visitors to the house increased. Amrita knew something strange was happening. It made her fidgety and start at every new noise.

"It's all right, Ammu. That's just a motorbike. You want to see it? Come here and look out through the window. Somebody has come to meet appa. Why don't you listen to what I have to tell you rather than be nervous about such small things?" she asked but for once Maya couldn't pacify her sister. "What'll you do when I leave? Who'll console you then?"

The maid was her only hope.

"Hansabehn, promise me you'll look after her like I do," she said over and over, till the maid's replies became mechanical.

"Don't say 'yes' so casually. She needs special attention. You can't handle her like any other child. Do your best. I'll come and take her away as soon as I can."

"Look *behn*, I told you not to worry about her. I'll be with her for as long as you want me to."

"Good."

"Now you can relax and look forward to the wedding."

On the evening of the formal engagement Maya dressed her sister in one of the two *salwar* suits she had insisted her father get for Amrita. It was the second best, a dark blue suit with faint silver work.

"There! You can wear the beautiful red dress for the wedding tomorrow, okay? Now sit here quietly while I get ready," she ordered.

She sat in front of the dressing table Raghu had bought her a week ago. While combing her hair she looked into the mirror at Amrita sitting behind her. The girl was finding it difficult to sit on her chair. She swayed to and fro, ran her hand over the blue glass bangles and made them tinkle. She looked down at her new dress or lifted her *salwar* to see her silver anklets one more time. Maya was resplendent in her green silk sari with gold border and emerald jewellery. Raghu came up to see her and expressed his satisfaction.

"I knew it would suit you. Come, it's time to leave for the *choultry*," he said.

Maya took Amrita's hand and gave her a wide, happy smile of assurance.

"Where is she going?" he asked, stopping at the door. "Leave her behind. We can't run any risk with her."

"What do you mean? She's coming with me. She has to," Maya insisted.

"Don't spoil everything with your obstinacy. What will we do if the guests turn their attention to her? She's not used to a crowd and you won't be able to control her. Be reasonable and leave her here. Hansabehn will take care of her. Hurry, we're getting late."

Sheer habit of obeying her father made her listen to his diktat and she left for the marriage hall shouting instructions to the maid as she went down the steps. She was caught up at once in the excitement at the beautifully decorated and lit *pandal*, the women in silks and masses of jasmine on their hair, Ganesh and his horde of relatives and friends waiting to greet her. It was not easy to remember the girl she had left behind but in the monotony of the rituals she wondered how her sister was coping with her absence. Telling herself that the maid must be keeping

Amrita engaged did not help her concentrate on the priest's prayers and her thoughts kept straying back home to the room upstairs.

*If only appa hadn't rushed me like this, I'd have been able to talk to her, make her understand what was happening. I've told her several times but I'm sure she doesn't remember anything. I hope she's not moping for me. She must think I'm cruel. Tchah, I'd wanted to prepare her specifically for this!*

"Do a *namaskar*," said the priest and brought her into the present.

*Oh, but this ceremony is going on and on. Did Hansabehn give her something to eat? Can I really trust her with my sister? I don't like the way she smiles when she looks at Ammu. What's the priest saying now?*

He was reading out the invitation to the gathering: "*Chiranjivi* Ganesh, son of *Shri* and *Shrimati* Seetharam and grandson of ... is to wed *Sowbhagyavati* Maya, daughter of *Shri* and *Shrimati* Raghavan and granddaughter of ... on Monday 18th January at 12.30 p.m. All are requested to attend the function and bless the couple."

The declaration marked the end of the evening's rites but Maya could not rush away to console her sister. She had to endure the curious eyes while Ganesh's mother introduced her to the sister, aunts, cousins, nieces and uncles who seemed to float in a haze before her. The dinner that followed the introductions was just as endless.

Finally Maya opened the door of her room and went inside. Hansabehn had told her that Amrita was sleeping. Indeed, she was fast asleep, curled on the bed, still wearing her blue dress. A few broken bangles lay on the floor along with the string of jasmine that Maya had fastened to Amrita's short hair with such difficulty. She gently brushed the hair away from her sister's face. In the faint light of the night lamp she saw patches of dried tears on Amrita's cheeks.

*She's taken badly to my absence! How will she react when I leave her tomorrow? And why is it so cold in here?*

Hansabehn had forgotten to close the windows and the winter breeze made Amrita's feet and hands cold to Maya's touch. She quickly shut the windows and covered her sister with a blanket.

Despite her tiredness she found it difficult to sleep. With her eyes getting used to the darkness, even the night lamp seemed too bright. She switched it off and lay down again. When finally she slept, it was to dream of her sister dancing with Sundar. Amrita's hair was loose and untamed, making her look possessed by a spirit. Sundar called to Maya to dance with them. She was on the other side of the glass door that wouldn't open however hard she pulled. In desperation, she began to beat on the door with both hands. That was when she realised that her mother was really knocking on the door.

"Wake up. It's time."

***

# 20

Maya sat up and rubbed her eyes. Her dream had been so vivid that she looked at the other bed to ensure that Amrita was indeed there. With the windows tightly fastened, it was dark in the room and she could barely make out the uneven hump that was her sister. The faint glimmer of the timepiece showed that it was nearly 6 o'clock. She got up and went to Amrita. The blanket had fallen to the ground and her sister lay curled with knees raised and hands across her chest. Maya covered her, throwing her own blanket as well over Amrita.

*Poor girl! Let her sleep but I must tell her where I'm going so that she doesn't react like yesterday. What if I insist that she come with me? I don't know how she'll cope with so many strangers and loud noises. What if she creates a scene like appa said? No, it's better to leave her here.*

She showered quickly in hot water. It helped to revive her spirits and she began to hum softly. It was her wedding day. Soon she would be able to take her sister with her. She dried herself while the steam rose gently from her body.

"Coffee ... *behn*, are you awake?" Hansabehn called through the door. "It is your wedding today or have you been ready since yesterday?"

"Leave it outside. I'll take it. I'm getting ready," Maya replied in a loud whisper, with an eye on her sister, but that was enough to rouse the girl.

"Good-morning, Ammu. Did we disturb you? I am sorry. You can sleep some more if you want."

She switched on the table lamp and set it beside the dressing table. It shone on her face leaving the rest of the room in darkness. Maya began to do her face while Amrita lay in bed and watched her sleepily. Slowly she began to pay greater interest to what Maya was doing. After a few minutes she sat up and watched her.

"Look, if you're not going to sleep any more you might as well get up and brush your teeth."

Amrita obediently got off the bed.

"And switch on the light."

The tube light flooded the room and Maya could now dress with greater speed. By the time Amrita came out of the bathroom she had changed into a rich mustard coloured silk sari with red border.

"How do I look?" she asked.

Amrita smiled in approval.

"Can't you say something for once? At least today? Good or nice or something?"

"Go on," she insisted. "If you like me, you'll say something. Good, nice, not good, bad… anything. It doesn't matter if you don't know the meaning."

"Nice," said Amrita shyly.

"You did it! After all these years of mumbling, one clear word," Maya hugged her sister. "Now look, I must tell you something important. It's my wedding today. I'll be gone for a longer time than yesterday. I'll lock the door so that no one can enter. Hansabehn has a key. Like yesterday she'll bring your food. I want you to eat properly. Don't waste anything and don't pine for me. I'll come back but you have to get used to being without me, understand?"

Amrita nodded.

"I don't have time to help you but here's the red dress. Even if you're not coming with me, you must still wear it. Be careful with the glass bangles. If they break, they could hurt your hands. Before you wear your new dress remember to have a bath … in warm water. Take care," Maya kissed her sister lightly on the forehead, locked the door and pinned the key to her chain. She shoved it down her blouse, out of sight. As she walked towards the steps her mother was coming up to call her.

"Hurry. It's getting late. Your father has sent word twice already."

The car approached the *choultry* and Maya heard the blare of music. It was still too early for the guests but there were a few rituals to be gone through before the main ceremony.

"You'll take care of her, won't you?" she asked hesitantly.

"Of course, don't worry," replied her mother, looking at Raghu walking up and down at the entrance of the hall.

Maya was not convinced by the reply and wondered if she should repeat her question but by then the car had come to a halt. Raghu's irritation burst in a splutter of words.

"At last! I was about to send Sundar to fetch you two. The priest is getting impatient. And that hairdresser has been waiting for ages. How can you be so late today of all the days?"

Maya stood still. Sundar?

"Hurry up now," he ordered. "Everything under control, Sundar? It was so good of you to come. I badly needed somebody to help me. Come on, you two, be quick. There! The priest is calling out for us. Sundar, you stand here to welcome the guests."

Maya did not know how her feet could carry her forward so calmly behind her parents when her heart was thumping wildly and everything round her seemed to go in circles.

Her eyes kept darting towards Sundar as he stood at the entrance of the hall sprinkling rose water on the invitees from a silver container while a girl standing beside him offered flowers.

Between visitors they talked and laughed as if they had known each other for a long time. Not once did he return Maya's look.

*What on earth is he doing here? Perhaps he's just come for the wedding.*

Maya sat with Ganesh to her left, facing the priests on the other side of the *agni*. The head priest, an elderly man with thick black hair sprouting from his ears led the chanting and signalled to Ganesh with his hand every time an offering was to be made to the fire. The smoke soon created a thick screen between the bridal couple and the guests who were rapidly filling the chairs in the hall. The prayers, the general excitement and the hum of talk among the guests could not prevent her from searching for Sundar with her eyes, to ensure that he was still around.

"Keep your head down," her mother kept muttering from behind.

It was nearing the *muhurtam* time of 12.30. Ganesh's sister Parvati led Maya to an inner room and helped her change into the traditional nine yards sari. Like a puppet she followed her instructions while Parvati manipulated what seemed like an endless stretch of wine red silk. She knotted, pleated, tucked it at the waist, got Maya to hold it down with a heel and finally flipped the ornate *pallu* over, folded, brought it across her stomach and shoved the end firmly into her side. If Maya was bewildered by this complexity she found walking out of the room a bigger ordeal. All eyes seemed to be on her as she walked stiffly to where her parents waited.

She sat on her father's lap while Ganesh stood before her. At the propitious time the priest signalled to the musicians and they played a crescendo while Ganesh tied the *mangalsutra* round her neck. Parvati knotted the yellow thread deftly twice more and Maya's status changed in a shower of flowers and turmeric-coloured rice.

*I am married. How do I make Ammu understand this? When will Sundar leave?*

Maya distractedly watched her new husband go through the routine to initiate them into the next stage of their life with the sacred fire as witness. The smoke made her eyes water. She looked away and noticed Sundar still flirting, this time with three girls, all of them laughing more than they talked. The formalities ended at last and Ganesh and Maya finally had some time to themselves.

"Happy?" asked Ganesh.

She shrugged. *Where was Sundar? Where the hell was he?*

"There you go! I'll have to take lessons in your language of half-smiles, shrugs and nods."

To this too Maya had no answer. *Would he have gone home? What can he do? I have the key. Hansabehn has the duplicate. What if she gives it to him?*

"Oh Maya, don't be so passive with me. We are married after all. We are partners now."

That got her attention.

"That's not the way my father treats mother," she said.

"He's from an older generation. If I've read him correctly he's pretty outdated in his views. You're not like your mother either so we'll start our relationship on our own terms. I want you beside me always and you can be sure of my support in whatever you do," he declared.

"In everything?"

"Absolutely."

"Did you think about what I told you?"

"About your sister? Indeed yes, quite a lot really. I've already informed my office that I should be given the Mumbai project. Work will start in another eight months."

"Eight? You had said six!"

"I know but these things don't move as quickly as we want them to. In fact, I wouldn't be surprised if it's a little longer than eight months but we'll certainly take her with us when we go to Mumbai. That's a promise."

Her shoulders sagged.

"I'm so sorry to disappoint you but believe me, I did my best to get them to start the work earlier. It was simply not possible they said. Nevertheless, I've told them that I want to shift to Mumbai at the earliest opportunity. You may think that I don't keep my word. I really did try to convince them."

Maya glanced at him quickly and looked away. She didn't know him well enough to read his expression but it did seem that he was telling the truth. What about Ammu? Her sigh came out louder than she intended.

"Are you feeling terribly tired? We have a long journey ahead. I told appa that I could stay here for a couple of days and then we could join them at Madras but he wouldn't listen. He can't postpone the reception he's arranged for us there. I'm sorry to rush you like this. I'll make up for it when we get home."

Maya smiled.

"That's better! I don't see your sister anywhere. Where is she?" he asked, looking around.

"At home."

"But why? She should have come," he protested.

"Appa wouldn't let her."

"That's terrible! I wish I'd known, I would have talked to him."

Maya shook her head. "It wouldn't have worked. He said we couldn't take a risk bringing her here. He was probably right, I don't know."

"Would you like to go home? I'm sure you want to spend the little time we have alone with your sister."

"May I?" she asked eagerly.

"Of course, why not? I'll get somebody to take you," he looked around once again.

"Will you come with me?"

"It'll be better if I stay behind, otherwise people will start wondering about our absence."

"What if somebody asks for me?"

"I'll tell them, don't worry. We'll have to leave by 9 o'clock. The train's at ten. Let's have lunch and then you can go home. It will be our first meal together after all. You'll still get to spend a few hours with your sister. You've explained to her that you'll visit her often?"

"I have. But I don't know how much of it she understood."

"Don't worry. She may manage better than you think. Let's have lunch."

The guests had fun at the expense of the newlyweds, making them feed one another and laughing at their own jokes. Ganesh rallied back but Maya was quiet, thinking that she would get over the meal sooner if she simply did whatever they asked.

"Hey, Ganesh! Your wife is wasting food. You'd better tell her to eat properly," Sundar shouted, joining the crowd from somewhere and lifting Maya's spirit.

"That's all right. Obviously she can't eat too much today."

"Why not?" asked another voice.

"She's full already – of thoughts about me."

Everybody burst into laughter while she blushed.

"Is that so, Maya? But see how much he's hogging!"

"I need the strength now that my responsibilities have increased."

The banter went on and on, making her impatient but she couldn't leave the table and walk away. Ganesh sensed her restlessness and managed to break up the crowd. He called Sundar aside and quietly arranged for him to take her home. By then it was past four.

Sundar drove the car while she sat at the back. She waited till the car crossed the gate of the hall.

"I suppose appa invited you for the wedding?" she asked.

"In a way, yes. Things didn't work out back home. Mom and Gauri were worrying all the time about money… money… money. I didn't think it wise to be there so I used your wedding as the excuse to leave and here I am, come to stay," he looked at her in the rear-view mirror and smiled.

"Stay?" she asked, licking her lips that had suddenly dried.

"Yep! Not forever, thank you. Only till I can get a good job and silence my sister once and for all. I'm sick of her cribbing about me."

"I suppose you might want to stay somewhere else…

"Oh, stop hedging. I know very well what's bugging you. I don't see why I should suffer the inconvenience of a paid accommodation just because you are worried about your precious sister. Don't worry. I'll take good care of her. In fact, I'm eagerly looking forward to spending time with her. Quality time. Without you hovering around like a mother hen. Or shall I say Guardian Angel? I can certainly teach her a lot of things … much more than you could…" he turned around in his seat and smiled at her.

She wondered for a wild moment if she should tell him to take her back to her father.

*What will I tell him? That I'm afraid this fellow will harm my sister? And how do I tell him this with so many people around? Oh God, what's to happen now?*

Sundar took the car in smoothly to the front of the house and stopped. Maya remained rooted to her seat. She did not even realise that they had reached.

"There you are, madam," he opened the door with a flourish and bowed slightly for her to step outside. She did not hear him.

"Hey! This is where you get off, remember?" he bent down and looked through the window.

"What are you thinking about? Don't worry. I'll take excellent care of your dear sister," he laughed. "Now will you please get out? I've to go back to the *choultry* however much I'd like to spend time with both of you. We don't want your in-laws to think that you and I have vanished so soon after you got married to their son, do we?" he laughed again and left.

Maya walked slowly into the house. It was quiet. Nearing the kitchen she heard Hansabehn's voice burst into sudden laughter. She paused outside the closed door and listened.

"I'm telling you there's no need to worry. No one's here, except that one upstairs," said the maid confidently.

"It's better to be safe. I thought I heard a car," a strange male voice replied.

Maya did not wait to hear more but ran up the stairs and unlocked the room. She opened the door cautiously and peeped inside. Amrita was sitting on the floor facing the wall. Her blue dress was crumpled and stained while her hair hung around her face in tangles. Maya rushed towards her sister, the jangling of her bangles and the little bells on her anklets making soft music, but Amrita did not seem to hear it. She continued to sit on her haunches, rocking gently. Her eyes were closed and she had a thumb in her mouth.

*She hasn't done this for such a long time! God, she's taking it far worse than I thought. How am I going to handle this?*

Maya touched her sister on the shoulder.

Amrita continued to rock. Maya sat down and threw her hand over the other girl but the rocking wouldn't stop.

"Amrita ... Ammu... it's me. I've come back," she said loudly and clearly.

Her words finally penetrated into her sister's consciousness and Amrita slowly opened her eyes. She saw Maya and burst into tears.

Maya held her sister tightly while the girl cried on her shoulder.

"It's all right. Shh... it's all right. I should have taken you with me. I didn't. I couldn't. Please stop crying. Please, Ammukutti. I've come back. Don't cry. I've come back to you," she pleaded, patting her all the while. The tears ceased finally.

She ran a hand down her sister's back to soothe the heaving spasms.

"Here, look at me," she said, but Amrita wouldn't lift her head from her shoulder.

Maya caught her sister's shoulders and held her away to look at her face.

"*Chee*, you are in such a state! Go and wash your face."

Amrita left her reluctantly, looking back at her as she walked to the bathroom.

The red *salwar* suit lay where Maya had left it that morning, on the table. The matching bangles strung on a red ribbon were intact on top of the dress. Next to it were two cups with dregs of coffee long dried. Even then a fly drew imaginary circles in the air over them.

"Oh my God! Did that woman give Ammu any breakfast? Lunch?"

She rushed to the top of the steps and shouted, "Hansa ... Hansabehn. Come here at once!"

The kitchen door flew open and the maid rushed out. Seeing Maya she stopped at the foot of the steps.

"Why didn't you give my sister anything to eat? I told you to take care of her. Is this how you do it? The poor girl has been starving! How can you do this to her?" she shouted.

The maid mumbled something but Maya was beyond listening to any explanation.

"Go and get something to eat immediately. Something hot. Quick!" she ordered.

Hansabehn brought the food upstairs. By then she had recovered from the shock of seeing Maya home so soon after her wedding.

"What was the hurry, *behn*? She is not a baby that she should be fed at fixed times."

"Don't talk. Don't say another word. I had entrusted her in your care and you have not done your duty..."

"There is no need to act so high and mighty about this. What 'duty – buty' are you talking about? I have not committed any crime. I was actually doing you a favour by agreeing to look after such a case. If you are not happy with my work you can get someone else."

The maid walked out of the room, banging the door behind her.

"No, wait! Let me..." shouted Maya but the woman had left.

*Oh great! First that fellow dropped a bombshell and now she! What's going to happen to Ammu now?*

Amrita was eating without lifting her head from the plate. With a little burp she kept the plate down, smiled at Maya and began to lick her fingers.

"Oh, don't do that. Go and wash your hand. Must I tell you that too?" Maya was close to tears.

Amrita dried her hand on her dress and began to play with

Maya's long plait intricately woven with little red roses.

*It's my fault. I shouldn't have agreed to the wedding. What'll happen to Amrita when I'm not around? Ganesh had said we could take her with us after six months and now he says eight. When I asked him if I could join him at Mumbai, he thought I didn't want to marry him. Sundar has come back. Who'll save my sister from him? There's no Hansabehn either to look after her. What do I do now?*

The more she thought, the more helpless she felt. She paced the room feeling that the walls were closing in on her.

*I wouldn't mind that. At least then my worries will cease.*

But the walls stood as firm as ever, giving her enough room to pace and worry. When her feet ached, she sat down. However, after only a few minutes she got up again, trailing rose petals as she walked. She did not notice Amrita stooping behind her and gathering them joyfully. Neither did she notice that it was getting dark outside.

A car entered the compound, its horn breaking into the storm in her mind. She looked out through the window. It stopped beyond her vision but she heard her father, loud and happy, calling to Sundar to bring the things inside. Maya wondered if anyone would come upstairs to check on her or her sister. No one even called from downstairs. More cars followed and more voices rose in the air. Soon she would have to go downstairs, leaving Amrita behind.

*What if I don't go? If I tell them that I'll join them a few days later? That would give me some more time. What will Ganesh think of me? Is this a problem I can resolve quickly? What can I do? Get another ayah? What's the guarantee that she'll be reliable and not turn into another Hansabehn? It would be best to send her to some institution. Why didn't I think of this before? But I thought I'd be able to take her away with me. I never thought a day would come when I would have to leave her. What can I do now? Institution? But which one? There is no time to find out which one is good and which will take her. Can I talk to appa? Will he appreciate why I'm so desperate to send Ammu away from here? What if he doesn't listen? If only I had been employed. If only I had made her capable of looking after herself. Did I fail or did she? I didn't have enough time with her. If only I had been her elder sister…*

"Come and have your dinner. It's getting late," her mother called from outside.

Maya ran to open the door but Kamala was already halfway down the steps.

"Wait here, I'll be back in a moment."

She hurriedly switched on the light and ran down the steps but could catch up with her mother only in the kitchen. The cook and his assistant were getting ready to serve dinner.

"You should have got another person to help you," said Kamala. "How can the two of you serve so many? And you, Maya, how could you rush away like this immediately after the ceremony? It was so embarrassing!"

"I couldn't help it. I want to tell you something."

Maya did not give her any time to refuse but dragged her mother to the storeroom and closed the door.

"What's all this?" Kamala asked.

"I don't want Sundar to stay in this house. He must leave immediately. Otherwise I'm not going anywhere."

"What are you talking about?"

"I can't explain everything to you now. Get him to leave the house at once."

Someone knocked on the door.

"Coming," Kamala shouted and turned to her daughter. "Have you gone crazy? Everybody's waiting for us and you're babbling some nonsense."

She tried to push open the door but Maya held on to her hand.

"You don't understand…"

The knock was more insistent.

"Just a minute." Kamala shouted again. She was trying to control her anger. "Maya, you are hysterical. It happens with some girls. It's all right. There's no need to worry."

"Hansabehn's left. She got angry because I shouted at her. She had neglected Amrita since morning…"

Kamala's face cleared. "Is that all? Don't worry. I'll take care of everything, including your sister. Whatever else is troubling you, this is not the time to talk about it. If your father doesn't see me, he's going to start yelling in front of all the guests. Believe me, everything will be all right. Don't worry about your sister," she opened the door. "Don't make everybody miss the train because of you. Wash your face and change your clothes. You look pathetic!"

She spoke the last words over her shoulder as she went out of the storeroom into the kitchen where the cooks were waiting for her instructions.

Maya freshened up and went downstairs. The guests were sitting on mats on the floor and eating from banana leaves. Ganesh and his sister Parvati were waiting for her. After an indifferent lunch, she should have been ravenous but Maya had no appetite.

"Are you such a poor eater?" asked Ganesh.

"I'm not hungry."

"It's the excitement. I remember how nervous I was on my wedding day," said Parvati.

"You nervous? I thought it was your poor husband who quaked at having to walk into the lioness' den!" he laughed.

Maya did not wait for Ganesh and Parvati to finish their meal.

"Will you excuse me, please. I have some work upstairs."

"Maya, we'll have to leave soon, in about half an hour. Shall I bring your bag down?" asked Ganesh, hurriedly getting up to wash his hands.

"My suitcase is already here. I only have a small bag left. I shall bring it down myself," she gave him a quick smile of gratitude.

He accompanied her to the foot of the steps and whispered, "You look troubled. Everything all right?"

Maya's eyes filled. She nodded her head and went up quickly. The anxiety on Amrita's face changed to relief as soon as she opened the door.

"Oh Ammukutti, if you can't stay for half an hour without me, how will you spend the next eight months alone? How can I leave without making some arrangement for you? I will die with worry, not knowing what's happening to you...Oh God, why are you doing this to me?"

The tears that had threatened to overflow at Ganesh's concern now broke their breach. She rested her head on the table and cried while Amrita plucked the flowers from her sister's bent head and added them to the little heap of petals on the floor.

"Maya, hurry up," Sundar called through the closed door. "Your father will blow a fuse if you don't come down soon."

He lowered his voice and continued, "I told you not to worry about her any more!"

His laughter grew fainter as he went down the stairs. Amrita was throwing the petals into the air and trying to catch them. She did not react to Sundar's call but it was enough to bring Maya back to the present.

"What do I do with you?" she asked, despair overwhelming her once again.

The loud laughter and medley of voices downstairs assailed her and she covered her ears to block the sound. Sitting on the bed, she swayed involuntarily without realising that she was imitating her sister. A gentle tap on the door made her conscious of the need to act without further delay. She did not want to know who had come to call her this time.

"Coming. Just a moment," she called and turned to Amrita. "Ammu, get up," she said, helping her to her feet.

She took a deep breath and spoke softly, emphasising every word.

"Ammu, Ammukutti, listen to me very carefully. I can't leave you alone in this house even for a day. I want you to do exactly as I tell you, understand?"

She was not satisfied with a nod from her sister.

"Tell me, you will obey me! Say 'yes'," she ordered.

"Yes," said Amrita, reaching for her sister's necklace that glinted under the white brightness of the tube light.

Maya caught her sister's face with both hands and forced her to look into her eyes. She tried to talk but the words wouldn't come out. She ran a hand down her throat to ease the block and spoke slowly, clearly, holding her sister's eyes with hers. She was sure of herself at last.

"You know the way to the ashram ground. Go there now. There won't be anyone around at this time. You know that, we have been there so often, even at night. Walk between the eucalyptus trees and you'll come to the railway line. Keep your head on the line and listen carefully. Close your eyes. You'll be able to hear well. Don't lift your head. Don't be afraid. Stay calm. Everything will be all right. Listen carefully. You will hear me come in the train, understand?"

Amrita nodded her head.

"You will do exactly as I have told you?" asked Maya.

Again Amrita nodded.

Maya knew she would. Her sister had never disobeyed her, not even once.

She wrapped a shawl around Amrita and guided her across the terrace. Maya led her down the steps to the backyard and opened the little gate. She gave Amrita a quick hug and sent her into the dark.

***

# PART THREE

## 21

I went home to my mother.
And Kittu.

***